PUZZLE
OF PIECES

A NOVEL BY

SALLY HILL BROUARD

◆ FriesenPress

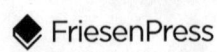

Suite 300 - 990 Fort St
Victoria, BC, V8V 3K2
Canada

www.friesenpress.com

Copyright © 2017 by Sally Hill Brouard
First Edition — 2017

All rights reserved.

No part of this publication may be reproduced in any form, or by any means, electronic or mechanical, including photocopying, recording, or any information browsing, storage, or retrieval system, without permission in writing from FriesenPress.

This is a work of fiction. Names, characters, businesses, places, events and incidents are either the products of the author's imagination or used in a fictitious manner. Any resemblance to actual persons, living or dead, or actual events is purely coincidental.

Cover design by Zachary Arnold

ISBN
978-1-4602-9319-5 (Hardcover)
978-1-4602-9320-1 (Paperback)
978-1-4602-9321-8 (eBook)

1. FICTION

Distributed to the trade by The Ingram Book Company

This book is dedicated to my husband, children and grandchildren who inspire me and to my friend, Jacqueline Barley, all of whom provided support and encouragement while I grappled with writing. To my friends who provided realistic information -- Jan Brister, Mary Merriman and Bill Bain, and to the many people of the legal community whom I have known over the years, thank you all.

PUZZLE
OF PIECES

CHAPTER ONE

Paulette McNeil had to face the fact that she was 45 years old and her life had not turned out as she expected. She was the late (and only) child of parents who were often mistaken for her grandparents. A brief marriage had ended tragically, when her young farmer husband died in an accident while trying to help a neighbour. After his death, she moved back into town from the farm. Eventually she inherited her parents' house in an older neighbourhood of Swift Current, Saskatchewan. The town and her life never seemed to change and, after a particularly cold and isolating winter, she decided that she needed to expand her horizons or go mad. Quiet whispers in dark corners of the town, that she had lost her mind, did not deter her. She sold the house, filled with a lifetime of memories, packed the possessions she could not part with into a Budget rent-a-van, and moved to Victoria, British Columbia: the 'garden city' of Canada. People told her it never snowed in Victoria. She hoped it was true.

After a shaking, shimmying, adventurous drive through the Rocky Mountains, and a ferry ride across a very choppy Georgia Strait to a place she had never been before, Paulette arrived on

July 27, 1980—a beautiful warm sunny day. She found a ground-level apartment in a safe neighbourhood near the south end of Cook Street, close to Beacon Hill Park. The living-room window revealed an extraordinary view of a myriad of colourful flowers, shrubs, and some large sprawling trees.

Settling into her new apartment didn't take long. She bought a three-room set of matching tan furniture from the bargain centre at a big furniture store. Groceries filled the cupboards. Clothes and personal items filled the closets and drawers. The place quickly felt like hers, and she loved the way the light filtered through the leaves of the Garry oak trees outside and infused the living room with shafts of gold.

People seemed friendly in Victoria. There were tourists everywhere. She bought a newspaper, and over a cup of coffee at an outdoor cafe, scanned the employment ads. Right away, one caught her eye—especially the part about 'no experience necessary.' She hurried home, called the number, and made an appointment. She had been too excited to grasp the name of the business, but she had the address of her prospective employer and an appointment for two o'clock that afternoon.

Paulette showered, curled her hair, dressed in her only dark skirt and white cotton blouse, and called a cab.

Paulette had a soft, gentle voice with excellent diction, and her perfect posture and neat appearance drew attention. She was five foot five with dark ash blonde hair that was already beginning to show the first sparks of white. She was reliable and well organized, and looked it. The job she was interviewing for was to cover a maternity leave for the position of receptionist. A deal was struck. She was to start Wednesday, August 15, 1980 as the temporary receptionist at the very prestigious law firm of McDowell Hill, Barristers and Solicitors.

Paulette picked up a bus schedule to study her morning commute. Her plan was to have a leisurely breakfast and coffee before work, at the cafe that had become her favourite in the short time she'd been in Victoria.

Earning money was not the most compelling reason for taking this job. Paulette had little working experience, and this would be a start toward re-entering the work force. Sure, she had done various jobs over the years, but never anything that she thought had made a difference. She felt out of touch with the workplace. This was going to be a good opportunity.

As it turned out, her new employer, McDowell Hill, was noted for its high political profile and meticulous work.

On her first day, introductions were made, instructions were given, and Paulette slipped quite easily into the role assigned to her. On Friday she went for lunch with the staff. She was congenial and likable; not only that, she was capable and efficient.

Paulette spent Saturday shopping for some new work clothes and Sunday at an outdoor art exhibit along Moss Street. She looked forward to work the next day.

Monday turned out to be a frightfully busy day. Exhausted, she went home, put on her dressing gown, heated a bowl of soup in the microwave, and puttered about the apartment. She fell asleep in front of the TV. Around 11:30, she woke with a pain in her neck and down her arm. Her couch was not the most comfortable. She made her way to the bathroom, flicked on the light, and stared at the strange face in the mirror. She saw puffy eyes with laugh lines starting at the corners. She saw that she had some of those horrid little lines around her lips. She wondered if anyone would ever love her again or if it was too late for that.

The next morning, Paulette dragged herself out of bed, dressed in one of her new outfits, skipped breakfast at the cafe, and caught the bus, despite feeling very sluggish. She didn't want to call in sick when she had only worked for a few days.

At the corner of Fort and Cook Streets, the bus pulled to a complete stop. Early morning commuters poured off the bus and scurried away like ants.

"Hey lady! This is your stop!" the driver shouted. There was no answer.

"This is your stop! You gettin' off or what?" the driver bellowed, in a very agitated tone, while looking in the rear-view mirror.

Paulette appeared to be reading. She was the only one left on the bus and she hadn't stirred. He didn't want to be horribly impolite. She didn't look like some snotty teenage brat just trying to antagonize him or get a free ride.

The driver shouted again, "Hey lady, this is your stop!"

There was no response. Zac pulled on the parking brake, jumped out of his seat, and strode to Paulette's seat. He put his hand on her shoulder. His arm recoiled instantly! He stumbled to the front of the bus and blurted into the two-way, "Jesus Christ! One of my passengers is dead!" Any emergency protocol training had been instantly abandoned.

"Did you hear me? One of my passengers is dead! Call the police or ambulance or somebody! Now!"

"Okay Zac. Enough with the jokes," the voice at the other end of the two-way crackled.

Zac fumbled with the microphone and stammered, "No, no honestly! She, she really is dead! Just sitting there, and now she's dead!"

The panic in his voice made the dispatcher realize this was no joke.

"Okay, Zac, okay! Hold on. I'll call the police right now. Did you check for a pulse, shallow breathing, or any vital signs at all?"

"Christ, I told you she's dead! Hurry up. Get somebody here. I'm not driving this load anywhere!"

He could hear the dispatcher in the background making the call to the police. Dispatch came back on the radio. "Where are you, Zac?"

"Corner of Fort and Cook."

"Okay, hang tight, the police are on their way."

The two-way fell silent.

Zac shut the motor off, stepped out onto the sidewalk, and reached into his pocket for a smoke. He pushed the bus door closed as two eager passengers approached. They tried to make small talk with him. He was evasive.

The police car, lights flashing and siren blaring, pulled to a stop behind the bus. A small crowd of passengers and street people gathered at the bus shelter. The officer spoke quickly to Zac and then mounted the bus stairs with Zac right behind him. The officer pushed open the door and quickly surveyed the interior of the bus before approaching Paulette's slouched form on the seat.

"Don't touch anything," he warned Zac. The officer felt Paulette's neck. "Too late for this poor soul. Can you ask your dispatcher to call the ambulance?" he asked Zac.

Zac did as he was asked, and then he and the officer stepped back out onto the sidewalk. Zac went to the group gathered at the stop and told them that another bus would be coming shortly. Some were peering in the windows of the bus, while others shouted questions. Zac and the officer ignored them. Some people appeared distressed at the thought of being late for work or their appointments, and were already complaining about the inconvenience. The police officer instructed them to move away from the bus as there had been a death. It would take some time, but another bus was on its way to resume service. The group shuffled down the sidewalk, talking amongst themselves and speculating about what might have happened.

The officer turned to Zac, "I am Officer Kevin Lewis. Are you able to make a statement at this time, Mr. ...?"

"Barnard. I'm Zachary Barnard."

Zac tried to organize his thoughts but was interrupted by the appearance of the ambulance. A few seconds later, another bus pulled in with two uniformed drivers. One was the relief driver. He approached Zac. "The dispatcher says to take a couple of days off. Call her tomorrow."

Zac felt stunned.

"Zac, give me a few minutes and I'll give you a lift home," Officer Lewis offered.

Home sounded good to Zac. He flicked his second cigarette to the sidewalk and stepped on it. How could this happen so fast? How could she die without him even knowing?

Zac stared at the sidewalk and kicked at a little pebble.

The relief driver stood by Zac. "Hell of a way to start the day."

"No kidding!" Zac replied.

Officer Lewis approached the drivers, instructed the relief driver to take the bus to the police compound. "Lock it and give the keys to the desk sergeant. The investigative team may want to see the bus later today if the death is suspicious."

He turned to Zac. "Come on, I'll drive you home now. You can compose yourself, put your thoughts together, and come down to the station at two this afternoon. I'll be there to take your statement. There's nothing to worry about, but there is a protocol for sudden deaths. There doesn't appear to be any foul play, but we need to be sure."

Zac nodded. It was starting to spit rain. He really wanted to go home. His wife would probably still be asleep, since she had worked the late shift at the hospital. He would crawl back into bed and feel her soft hair against the pillow.

At precisely 2:00 p.m., Zac presented himself to the detachment where Officer Kevin Lewis served.

"Come in Zac," Kevin called to him. "Do you want a coffee or a pop, anything?"

"No thanks."

Zac was led into a small room with a desk, given a pad of lined paper and a pen, and was instructed to write down, in detail and, in chronological order, exactly what he remembered.

Kevin had the contents of Paulette's purse strewn across his desk. There were all the usual items: lipstick, wallet, keys, a pad of bus tickets, a pair of glasses, and some loose change. The wallet contained a temporary driver's license, $47, and a few counter-cheques with Paulette's account number printed on them. No pictures. No emergency phone numbers.

He called the hospital. "Morgue please." Once his call had been directed, he asked, "Any results on that DOA brought in this morning?"

"Jack can't do anything till after three today. It'll take a few hours, and then I need to transcribe the coroner's findings. Try back about nine tomorrow morning. Off the record though, he said it looks like your regular heart attack. By the way, do you have a name and address for the deceased?"

"Yes, Paulette McNeil, Suite 4, 900 Cook Street. Looks like she just moved here. I'm going to check her place now. I'll call Jack tomorrow. Thanks."

He hung up just as Zac appeared in the doorway with the pad of paper.

"Finished?" he asked.

"Yeah, I think I got everything."

Kevin took a quick glance at the notes. "One question, did you ever see her before on your bus?"

"Not that I recall. I pretty well know all the regular commuters, but she wasn't one of them."

"All right, thanks for coming in, Zac. If I need anything more, I'll call you. Take those few days and let the shock wear off."

"Officer Lewis, please let me know what happened to her, if you can. It's not every day one of my passengers dies on board."

"No problem. But I probably won't know for sure for a while myself. Thanks for your cooperation." He placed his hand on Zac's shoulder.

Zac's wife was in the waiting room when he emerged from the office.

Kevin went back to his desk, scraped the contents of Paulette's purse into a large brown envelope, scrawled a description across the front of the envelope, tagged the purse, and shoved Paulette's keys into his pocket.

He had no trouble finding her place. He knew Victoria like the proverbial back of his hand. He had grown up and graduated from high school in Victoria, and had only left for training and his first deploy of six cold years in Edson, Alberta. He figured he was back to stay.

Kevin buzzed the manager's suite. A gruff voice snarled an answer.

"This is Officer Kevin Lewis of the Victoria Police Department. Please come to the front door," he asked.

"What is it this time?" the voice grumbled.

"Come to the door sir," Officer Lewis commanded.

A few moments later the manager appeared. He didn't look as gruff as he sounded.

"I believe you have suite number four rented to Paulette McNeil. Can you confirm that?"

"Yes," replied the manager. "She took that apartment on August 1st. Seems like a nice enough woman, quiet and well mannered," he ventured. "What's going on?"

"Paulette McNeil died this morning on her way to work."

"What?" the manager said in amazement. "I just saw her this morning as she left. She looked fine to me. What happened?"

"Nothing has been confirmed yet, but I need to see her apartment."

"Just a second and I'll get the key for you."

"I believe I have her key. Let me try it first."

"Sure. This way." The manager was now eager to comply.

Kevin stood in front of Paulette McNeil's door and knocked authoritatively.

The manager volunteered, "I think she lived alone."

Kevin tried the key and swung open the door.

"Thank you. I'll examine the apartment myself. Do you have a business card with your name and phone number, in case I need to contact you?"

"I don't have a card but my name is Al, Al Smythe. 384-1922."

Kevin quickly jotted down the information on a pocket-size notepad. "Thank you, Al," he said, and gently closed the door.

Kevin made a mental note of the details of the apartment. There was a closet on the left, a telephone stand, and an answering machine. The light blinked frantically indicating a message. The kitchen was tidy, except for a bowl and cup in the sink. The living room was orderly; the TV and stereo were off. The bed was made. No windows were open. There was a damp, crumpled towel in the laundry basket in the bathroom. Four rings of the phone interrupted his quiet observations. He heard the answering machine engage and the voice of the caller.

"Hi Paulette, this is Sandra from the office. We were wondering what happened to you today. Hope nothing is wrong. Give someone here a call as soon as you can, just to let us know what's happening. The number is 384-1357. We hope to see you tomorrow. Bye for now."

Kevin lifted the receiver and dialled the number. "McDowell Hill. This is Sandra. How may I help you?" He hung up quickly and jotted the name of the firm in his notebook.

Kevin slid open the desk drawer and found a small black address book. He slipped it into his pocket. He closed the apartment door and locked it.

On his way out, he saw Al in the foyer.

"I'm finished for now. I'll contact Ms. McNeil's next of kin and have one of them contact you. Until then, don't disturb anything. If you have any questions, call me." He handed Al his card.

The usual paperwork demanded Kevin's attention back at the office. He stopped by McDonald's for a Big Mac, large fries, and a coffee to go. He arrived at his office as the five o'clock shift was leaving. He knew them all and couldn't take a stair without greeting someone on the way down. Of course, someone commented: "Good meal there, Kev!"

He knew he would probably have regrets, but it was convenient and he was hungry. The burger and fries were edible, but the coffee was cold and too strong by the time he got to it. He checked his messages.

He pulled the packet of forms, required in triplicate, from his desk drawer to document the death of Paulette McNeil. He had her name, address, phone number, and employer. He did not have a confirmed cause of death or a next of kin. He retrieved the address book from his coat pocket and turned each page looking for information. The book contained only three phone numbers, Al Smythe, the law firm of McDowell Hill, and Helga McNeil. He looked up Helga McNeil's name in the phone book. There was an H. McNeil on Dallas Road. The numbers were the same. He decided contacting Helga could wait until tomorrow afternoon.

First thing for tomorrow morning was a visit to the prestigious law firm of McDowell Hill, Barristers and Solicitors. He only knew one lawyer at McDowell Hill, and that was Dan Moody. Kevin never liked Dan on the defence side of any arrest he'd ever made. Dan was the only lawyer in that firm who did criminal work, and he was very good. He had his own reception area within the offices of McDowell Hill, so that his criminal clients wouldn't rub shoulders with the aristocrats of Victoria, although sometimes they were one and the same.

Around ten o'clock, Kevin turned the key in the lock of his own apartment. It was not half as orderly as Paulette's apartment. He unstrapped his holster and put it on the top shelf in the closet. He pulled open the fridge and poured himself a glass of cold milk.

* * *

As soon as Kevin arrived at his office the next morning, he dialled the morgue number. "Hi Jack, any results on McNeil yet?"

"Yeah. Confirmed. Massive coronary. She never knew what happened. Great way to go if you have to," Jack chirped into the phone.

"Thanks Jack. That makes my life easier."

Kevin arrived at the offices of McDowell Hill precisely at 9:00 a.m.

"Good morning, I'm Officer Kevin Lewis," he said to the receptionist. "Do you have any partner in the office this morning that I could speak to?"

"Yes, I believe Frank Hill is here. I'll tell him you'd like to see him."

Within seconds, Frank appeared in the reception area. "Come in, Officer Lewis," he motioned and led the way to his office and closed the door. He said something vague about his office being disorganized, because the staff had to take turns relieving on reception, his own secretary included. He also offered an apology for his messy desk. He said that the firm had hired a new receptionist but she had not shown up yesterday or today and that had plunged the place into chaos.

Officer Lewis asked, "Would that be Paulette McNeil?"

"Well I don't know her name. She just started work here. Is that why you're here? Hold on a second," he activated the intercom on his telephone. "Hilary, could you come in for a moment, please?"

Hilary gave a quick knock and entered the room. Kevin immediately noticed she had a certain confidence about her.

"Hilary, what was that receptionist's name, the one we hired who hasn't shown up?"

"Paulette McNeil."

Kevin, usually stone-faced, nodded his head. Hilary asked what happened.

"Close the door and sit down, Hilary," Frank asked.

Officer Lewis began, "I am sorry to tell you that Paulette McNeil died on the bus on her way to work Tuesday morning."

Hilary and Frank stared at each other. As long as either of them had worked, nothing like that had ever happened before. After a few moments, Kevin asked if either of them could tell him anything about Paulette. Frank said that he knew nothing. Hilary said that she would consult the personnel records.

Frank glanced at his watch, offered an apology, and said that he had a meeting with the University of Victoria Law Faculty that he could not miss. He instructed Hilary to assist Officer Lewis in any way possible. He and Officer Lewis shook hands and Frank hurried to the elevator.

Hilary retrieved the personnel file and flipped it open. She scanned the two pages of notes in the file and the copy of the tax form Paulette had filled in.

"Officer Lewis, it appears we don't have a resume on file for Paulette. She telephoned the office for an interview in response to our advertisement in the local paper for a receptionist.

"Alan Arnold was in charge of interviewing and hiring. According to Alan's notes, she was the most suitable candidate and he hired her. The position was only a term to cover a maternity leave. I'll make a photocopy of his notes so you can have them. Would you like to speak to Alan?"

"Yes, I would." Kevin nodded.

"Just a moment and I'll find him for you."

Alan Arnold entered the room ahead of Hilary. He was a short round man with a crew-cut and a beet-coloured face. He did not wait for an introduction.

"What's all this about?" Alan demanded.

"I didn't have the opportunity to tell him anything yet, Officer Lewis," Hilary said, in defence of Alan's abruptness.

"Sit down, sir." Kevin instructed and tilted his head toward the first available chair. Alan sat on command. Hilary was impressed. Perhaps it was the uniform. Alan could be so damned obnoxious sometimes. He had an ego the size of Manhattan, but despite his blustery façade, he was a good lawyer. A twinge of guilt tweaked Hilary for a moment at her unkind thought.

Alan was already twitching at having to sit. Officer Lewis asked Alan to relate the details of the interview. At the end of the discussion, he was really no further ahead. Alan reiterated Frank's instructions for Officer Lewis to contact Hilary if he needed any further assistance and, in a manner inconsistent with his outward nature, said, "Officer Lewis please convey our firm's condolences to Paulette's family."

"Yes," Hilary said, "I am sure the staff would want to do something in her memory, even though we did not know her well." She handed Officer Lewis the photocopies of Paulette's interview notes.

Kevin's next stop was 1262 – 300 Dallas Road, Helga McNeil's apartment. He pressed the buzzer for Helga's top-floor apartment. What a place to live, he thought. Seaside on Dallas Road ... nice.

"Hello Bert, is that you?" a tiny voice responded.

"Madam, this is Officer Kevin Lewis of the Victoria Police Department. May I come in and speak with you for a moment, please?"

"Who?" the tremulous little voice asked.

"Officer Kevin Lewis of the police."

"Where is Bert?"

"I'm alone, Mrs. McNeil. I am a member of the police department. I want to come in and speak to you."

"I'll have to find Bert."

Finally Kevin rang the manager.

The manager appeared at the door. "Can I help you?"

"I want to see and speak with Helga McNeil."

"Please come in. Helga is very elderly and frail. She gets confused at times. Bert was her late husband, and every time she hears the phone ring or the intercom buzzer, she thinks its Bert."

The manager led the way to Helga's apartment, rapped loudly on the door, and called out to her. Kevin could hear Helga fumbling with the lock, and finally the door opened a crack. The manager told Helga it was all right to speak with the police, and so she invited Kevin in. She offered tea. Kevin thought it wouldn't hurt. She might relax and make the conversation easier. After he accepted Helga's offer, he wished he hadn't. She was so slow, what should have taken only a few minutes, was dragging on for more than an hour. Helga explained to Kevin that Bert and Paulette's grandfather were brothers. She began to digress with yet another story about Bert. Kevin tried to keep her on track. Finally she remembered that Paulette had telephoned and told her she was moving to Victoria. Paulette was to visit when she got settled, but she hadn't yet seen her. She did expect to hear from her any day, although she had never met her.

Officer Lewis took her delicate hand in his and told her very gently that Paulette had passed away quite suddenly.

"Bert will be very sorry to hear that," Helga replied.

* * *

For the next few days, other matters diverted Kevin's attention. On Thursday afternoon Kevin checked Paulette's apartment again. There were no new messages on the answering machine.

There were no clues as to the location or identity of any family other than Helga. He had a few ideas, like checking Helga's will, if she would show it to him, for beneficiaries who might be next of kin, but that would have to wait until he returned from his vacation.

He called Hilary at McDowell Hill and asked if he could see her in about an hour. She said that she would be at the office until five.

As he had promised, he phoned Zac and left a message as to Paulette's cause of death.

Hilary was with a client when Kevin arrived. He waited with a cup of that awful reception-room coffee. Just as he took his last gulp, Hilary emerged from her office.

"Tell me, Officer Lewis, what's happening regarding Paulette?" She seemed more casual this time—not quite so formal. He relayed what information he had. Hilary asked what would happen regarding Paulette's apartment and the contents, and he said that he didn't know. She asked if she should go to Paulette's apartment and gather any important documents.

Kevin agreed that, under the circumstances, Hilary could go to Paulette's apartment and do a quick inventory, dispose of perishables, and try to find information that could help him contact any other next of kin. He passed Hilary the keys to Paulette's apartment. He noticed the intricate gold band on her finger.

Her question interrupted his thoughts. "What arrangements have been made for the disposition of her body?"

"None," he replied, "until someone can positively identify her. The body is at the morgue. You can speak to Jack Jonesburg there, if you need any information."

"Thank you, Officer Lewis. I'll take care of as much as I can," Hilary offered. "I am sure the firm would want to under the circumstances."

"I'll check back with you as soon as I return from vacation. I'll be gone for two weeks. My file will be assigned to someone else in my absence. So if you need to speak to anyone about this matter while I'm away, just call the staff sergeant at the detachment."

On Monday, one week after Paulette's death, Hilary and Sandra left the office to retrieve any documents and mail that they might be able to find at Paulette's apartment—anything that might tell them who Paulette McNeil, the person, was.

The apartment was dark and lifeless. Both Hilary and Sandra moved noiselessly around, making an inventory of Paulette's belongings and pondering the frailty of life.

Hilary set Sandra to work emptying the refrigerator and the cupboards of any food. Hilary opened drawers and cupboards, and eventually found forms that Paulette had signed to transfer her bank account to Victoria, and a zippered leather folder that contained Paulette's personal papers and documents. She slipped these things into a large envelope. She could not find a will. The job didn't take as long as Hilary thought. The boxes of food were dropped at the food bank and she and Sandra returned to the office.

Hilary made her way to Frank's office. He motioned for her to come in when he saw her approach.

"Frank, I need some direction as to how to handle matters relating to Paulette's estate. Officer Lewis has not been able to find any next of kin yet, other than Helga McNeil who is very elderly and not able to handle anything. He gave me the keys to Paulette's apartment and I have found some documents, but no will. According to her bankbook, she only had $6,000 to her name. What should I do now? I feel so sorry for what happened to her: dying alone with no family or close friends around her. I don't mind continuing on with things, if that will help," she volunteered.

"Don't waste your time, Hilary. You have better things to do around here. Give everything to Elisabeth. Deborah Ruxton can take charge of the file." Frank instructed.

At five o'clock, Hilary left the envelope on her desk and packed up her files so that her desk would be somewhat organized for the next day.

CHAPTER TWO

The law firm of McDowell Hill had spawned some powerful figures over the years: two judges, a master, and an attorney general, and had generated some precedent-setting law. The firm was founded in 1918 by Alexander McDowell, and had flourished ever since. They were the best firm in Victoria. There were eight partners and two associates. Together, they were a volatile but creative group. The partnership had an interesting configuration. Each partner had a vote weighted on the basis of the length of time with the firm as a partner and his or her individual billing power. This made for an interesting shift of power from time to time, as the junior partners vied for status within the firm.

Andrew McDowell, now the senior partner, was a brilliant civil litigator. He was accessible only to politicians and those affluent enough to sway the tide of politics.

Frank Hill was the senior solicitor of the firm. He didn't like the courtroom, but he could move vast sums of money around the world, close the most complex business transactions precisely on time, and cover every detail. He was entirely devoted to his clients and their well-being.

On the administrative and support side of the law firm of McDowell Hill was Hilary Britt, Frank Hill's assistant. She got the most difficult tasks to do, but at least they were challenging. She had the respect and admiration of her fellow employees. They all looked to her for help in with dealing with difficult people, assistance with their work, and even setting their own priorities. They considered her their confidante. Hilary had an amazing ability to put people at ease, but her most valuable attribute was that she never panicked under pressure.

Then there was Elisabeth Nielsen, who had worked for many lawyers over the years and in many different areas of law. She was a well of practical knowledge and the historian of the firm. She never forgot a client and they never forgot her. She had a compassion and kindness about her. Elisabeth thought that she was beginning to lose her edge. The pressure took its toll and sometimes she would get frustrated and cranky, although she tried never to show it in the office.

In her private life, Elisabeth was also desperately lonely, not so much for people, but for intimacy: feeling loved and having someone to love in return. Sometimes the loneliness manifested itself as depression. To make up for what she perceived to be her own inadequacies, she would work long, late hours. Sometimes her productivity would be so low by the end of her day that she really didn't accomplish much. Her peers admired her dedication and devotion, but it was not always enough to sustain her.

Elisabeth had overdone it this particular week and, when she left the office after eight o'clock on Friday night, she was tired and depressed. Late that night, she looked out her bedroom window across the darkened city. She knew loneliness first hand and trying to shake it off was like trying to climb out of a deep hole that just kept getting deeper. She felt powerless. She wondered what she had ever done in life to deserve such loneliness. She could not recall a single event—no sin, no wrongdoing, no wickedness that lurked in her heart...

Why did life have to punish her like this?

Elisabeth felt alone and she was alone. She never had brothers or sisters. Her parents were dead. Her best friend had recently passed away and watching her die had been a gruelling ordeal. Her friend died too young and left far too much unfinished. She missed her desperately.

The only time Elisabeth's handful of cousins and distant relatives ever bothered with her was when everyone attended the biannual family reunion. She wondered cynically why she even bothered to attend. When they met at the reunions, they would always be happy to see her; they would say that they should get together. They would promise to call her, but when the cars rolled out of the parking lot, she would never hear from them again until the next reunion.

Oh sure, there was always the occasional wedding or funeral to keep the family together—nothing like a good funeral as an excuse for a family gathering. She imagined her own funeral. Maybe all the long-lost, distant relatives would come. Maybe they would weep and say what a fine person she had been during her lifetime. Maybe they would say how much they would miss her. But how many, five years after her death, would stop to put flowers on her grave?

All the real and imagined injuries and injustices of her past spun through her head and made her dizzy. What had she done? In desperation, she buried her head in the pale blue satin cushions of her bed as tears streamed down her face. A quiet but frantic desperation almost drowned her hope. Exhaustion eventually overtook her and she fell into a restless sleep.

Elisabeth lived in a small, modest apartment on the third floor of a brick building, exactly two blocks from where she worked. Between the walls of her apartment were housed her most valued possessions: her photographs, jewelry, needlepoints, and most of all, her deceased mother's fine fur coat. Most of her furniture was now considered antique, except for the new couch she had saved so diligently for and covered with a throw—to keep it new forever, or at least, until she died.

Nothing in her apartment was out of place. She lived a very ordered life. If Elisabeth died suddenly, no one would find any surprises among her possessions. There was nothing hidden under the mattress or behind the bookcase. There were no love letters in her jewelry box or man's bathrobe in her closet.

Suddenly a screech of tires, a loud bang, and the sound of breaking glass jarred Elisabeth from her restless sleep. At first the noise hadn't really registered in her consciousness, but then she heard yelling and commotion on the street below.

"What do you think you're doing, asshole? You just wrecked my car, you fuckin' jerk!"

She hurried to the window to see the neighbour from across the street, standing in his ski jacket, pyjamas, and slippers beside his crumpled car. He tried to wrench open the door of the car that was firmly implanted in his. His car was not in great shape, but the Toyota that struck it was not going anywhere and neither was the driver. Elisabeth could only hear deep moaning from the driver, and hoped he was not seriously injured.

"Calm down! The police are coming!" Elisabeth recognized her building manager's voice before she could actually see him. "I just called them. Let's see if we can help the driver."

"I'll help him all right," threatened the neighbour, and grabbed the handle of the Toyota again and tried to yank open the door just as the police cruiser rounded the corner. She knew the ambulance was not far behind, because she could already hear the siren. She watched curiously. The breeze from the ocean was chilly. It was still dark. She glanced at the clock. It was four in the morning.

She wondered if her idea about living close to work for convenience, close to the police station for protection, and close to the fire station, just in case of fire, was really working in her best interests. Granted, she was usually one of the first to know what was going on in town, but she spent too much time at work and one siren or another was forever waking her in the middle of the night.

The commotion caused by the accident was almost cleared away. The driver was more drunk than injured, but he was carted off in the ambulance. What was left of his car was towed away and the neighbour stomped up the sidewalk to his gaping front door. Dick, the manager, looked up at her lit window and gave her a wave. She gave him a quick wave back and slid the window closed. Even though she felt tired, she couldn't bring herself to return to bed. Instead, she wandered into the kitchen and made herself a pot of hot tea.

Nothing interesting would be on TV, so she turned the radio on softly and sat down in front of her latest needlepoint project. It was almost finished, except for the easy parts. She put her cup down, switched on the arc light, picked up her needle and worked calmly and patiently, losing track of time. It seemed only a moment before she saw the sky light up and heard the first crow caw. She put her needle down and looked toward the sunrise. It was indeed beautiful. So peaceful. She poured herself a cup of luke-warm tea and sipped it. She pulled her afghan around her shoulders and lay back on the couch. She rebuked herself for being such a snivelling fool, for feeling so sorry for herself. Really, she was lucky. There were lots worse off than she. How could she be so selfish? Sleep came again, but this time it was a rejuvenating rest. The bright sun and traffic noise woke her later in the morning, and this time she felt infinitely better.

After a leisurely bath and her favourite dusting powder, she wrapped herself in her blue velvet robe and switched on the morning talk show. They were making Eggs Benedict, but she had oatmeal, because it was good for her.

Elisabeth got out her appointment calendar to see what commitments she had made for herself for the weekend. Lately she felt forgetful. She resolved not to go to the office this weekend at all, no matter what. Saturday mornings she generally spent doing errands and shopping. In the afternoon, she would wander into the office. At night, she watched a movie, if it wasn't scary. Early Sunday mornings, she did her laundry. She had to get up for church anyway and she never missed the 11:00 a.m. service at St. Andrews United, unless she was ill. Sunday afternoon she usually spent at the office, but she had to be home by eight o'clock in order to prepare for the week ahead. Her life was very structured.

Two of her greatest joys in life were following the Toronto Maple Leafs and the New York Yankees. She tried never to miss any games on TV and, much to everyone's surprise, she knew the strategies of both games and the stats on most of the players.

On good days, Elisabeth accepted her life. On bad days, she thought her life drudgery—merely existence—but reason, based on a lack of money and self-confidence, always prevailed. Any alteration to the schedule constituted a major event that took days, or even weeks, of planning. There were times, though, when she chided herself for her lack of adventure, maybe even a lack of ambition. But she also knew that, if she ever allowed herself an indulgent or reckless moment, karma would catch up with her one way or another.

* * *

By Monday, Elisabeth was ready to go back to work. The weekend had delivered some happy moments and she had even purchased a new pantsuit that had been on sale for half price! When she arrived at work, there were already three women seated in the reception area, all eagerly awaiting an interview for the position of relief receptionist. This time Hilary was doing the interviewing.

As Elisabeth was taking off her jacket, Hilary called over to her. "I need to see you sometime today about a file I have for you. Buzz me when you have a minute, please."

"Sure," Elisabeth responded.

Just before noon, instead of buzzing, Elisabeth popped her head inside the door to Hilary's office and asked about the file. Hilary waved the file folder and motioned for Elisabeth to sit down. Once off the phone, Hilary said, "I have collected some documents and information about Paulette. Frank asked me to give you the file. Paulette had very little; probate may not even be required."

Hilary went over the details with Elisabeth, and said that she would leave it to her to brief Deborah, who would take conduct of the file. Elisabeth rolled her eyes as much as to say, Why Deborah? Hilary smiled, because she knew exactly what Elisabeth meant. Deborah was the newest associate with the firm. She was a high maintenance woman: expensive wardrobe, luxury spa visits, Harvard education, ski chalet in Vale, and a retreat in Maui. She met her husband when he was doing his MBA at Harvard. She thought he had a bright future and expensive taste. She was loud, aggressive, and not happy to be in Victoria.

If anyone could be difficult it was Deborah. Every secretary around the office knew that if you gave Deborah a letter to sign on Friday, she would pick it to death and refuse to sign. If you gave her the same letter on Monday, there would be no problem; she would read it and sign it almost every time. It was silly, but true.

"Oh, by the way Elisabeth," Hilary added, "Officer Lewis is away for a couple of weeks. Probably nothing much will happen until he gets back. He will have more access to searching for

Paulette's next of kin than we do, unless we hire a skip tracer. Just monitor the file for the time being."

By the end of the day, the new receptionist, Toby Lamb, was being introduced to everyone. She would start the next work day.

After a couple of weeks, work returned to normal around the offices of McDowell Hill.

CHAPTER THREE

The day after Labour Day, Officer Lewis telephoned Hilary for an update.

"If you have a minute, please stop by the office so we can discuss a few things," Hilary said. "I'll be here till five." That seemed to be her favourite saying lately. I'll be here till five! She was sick of hearing herself say it over and over. She really did need a vacation. Oh well, she thought. She knew that she and her family would be away over the Christmas break. Her son was playing in his first big hockey tournament. She could hold on till then.

Just after lunch, Officer Lewis appeared. She took him to her office and buzzed Elisabeth and Deborah to join them. Within a few minutes, Elisabeth arrived. Seconds after her, Deborah flounced in as if she were most inconvenienced to be there, until she saw Officer Lewis. Then she couldn't be more charming. She actually fawned over him. It was pathetic. Hilary tried to maintain some professional decorum, while Elisabeth wanted to escape. Officer Lewis appeared unaffected.

Hilary quickly ran through the matters that she had attended to for the benefit of both Officer Lewis and Deborah, and told

Officer Lewis that Deborah would now be the lawyer assigned to have conduct of Paulette's estate file.

Officer Lewis said, "I haven't been able to find any next of kin other than Helga. You can proceed with cleaning out Paulette's apartment and authorizing disposition of her remains, as dental records received from Swift Current have confirmed her identity."

Hilary felt at ease with Elisabeth handling the file. She had done many estates over the years and was perfectly competent.

Deborah's name was paged over the intercom, and that was her queue to become important again. She rose to the occasion. Elisabeth followed behind.

Officer Lewis said to Hilary, "You'll probably never have an employee die on the bus on the way to work again."

"I hope not. Thank you for making this situation easier for us to handle," Hilary volunteered.

For the first time, she noticed a jagged little scar just on the edge of his cheekbone near his eye.

"How was your vacation?" Hilary asked, as they walked down the hallway toward the reception area.

"You know I actually had fun!"

He seemed very genuine.

"I'm sure you will have many more happy times to come," she said delicately.

He felt exposed suddenly and fell back on his policeman demeanour. "Well, the investigation of the death of Paulette McNeil is over. The police don't need to be involved anymore. The Coroner's office will issue a death certificate. I will arrange for it, along with any personal effects we have, to be delivered to you."

When Elisabeth received Paulette's death certificate, Coroner's report and personal effects, she arranged for Paulette's remains to be cremated and sent back to Swift Current to be scattered over Paulette's husband's grave. She could only guess what Paulette would have wanted and, since Paulette had many years to remarry and never did, Elisabeth wanted to think it was because she had loved him to the end.

Documents were placed in Paulette's estate file and Paulette's purse, wallet and clothing were discarded.

* * *

Time rolled by and the firm of McDowell Hill continued to flourish. There was the occasional blip, but nothing too worrisome. Conveyancing cycled in its predictable fashion. The market was strong and the economy was booming.

In late October of 1981, Denise Shelton, whose specialty was administrative law, and whose forte was interpreting legislation, knocked on the door to Andrew McDowell's office.

"Come in Denise," Andrew beckoned. "What brings you here?"

"I have some news, Andrew, and I wanted you to be the first to know. Last May, after I won the taxation case on behalf of British Columbia's biggest logging company, it was suggested that I apply for a judgeship. At first I was reluctant, because I didn't feel I had enough experience and thought that I may be too young, but after encouragement from Madam Justice Tyler, I reconsidered and allowed my name to stand. I've just received word that I will be officially appointed to the Bench as of December 1st." Denise tried to stifle her excitement, but it was spilling into the room anyway.

"Denise," Andrew said, as he walked around the side of his desk, "I'm so proud of you! This is great news for you personally. It's hell for us of course, because we'll have to lose you, but what an achievement! Youngest woman in British Columbia to be appointed to the Bench! I'm so happy for you!"

It seemed like he already knew.

"This calls for an announcement and a celebration! Do you mind if we tell the staff now?" Andrew asked.

"No, I don't mind at all. I think we should. I wouldn't want to be victimized by any rumours!" Her wide smile said everything.

Andrew lifted his telephone and spoke to Toby. "Please page the entire staff and tell them there will be a meeting in the boardroom at 4:00 p.m. Everyone must attend." He hung up the receiver and soon could hear Toby's voice on the inter-office paging system.

At precisely 4:00 p.m., lawyers and staff started filing into the boardroom. No one knew what to expect. Everyone found a seat and chatted quietly. When Andrew entered the room, silence fell and all eyes fixed on him.

"Ladies and gentlemen," he started, "I have an important announcement. This will be a crowning glory for the firm of McDowell Hill and a crowning achievement for Denise Shelton, who has today been appointed a judge of the Supreme Court of British Columbia.

Congratulations, Denise. We are all so proud of you!"

All applauded Denise's remarkable achievement.

By the time five o'clock rolled around, the caterer had delivered appetizers and Andrew had broken out the stock of fine wines and imported beers he kept just for such special occasions. As the evening passed, those who had commitments drifted away. Those that did not stayed to party.

The next morning, those who arrived early started cleaning up the debris.

* * *

Denise's official call would be November 20th. This involved a swearing-in ceremony at the Law Courts in Vancouver and a huge dinner and gala evening at a posh hotel. The "who's who" of British Columbia law and politics would be there, as well as other selected guests.

The business operations of McDowell Hill shifted into high gear after Denise's announcement. Not only that, some manoeuvring and politicking began amongst the junior partners, speculating on who would replace Denise, how much they would earn, and where they would fit in the scheme of things generally.

Denise wrapped up as many matters as she could; the rest were re-assigned. By November 15th, Denise's office was bare. There had been a couple of office discussions as to how Denise's position would be filled, and what kind of a candidate they anticipated recruiting, but no decisions were actually made and no specific plan was put in place.

Finally, November 20th rolled around. Hilary arranged for limousines to pick up those attending Denise's ceremony from the ferry and take them to the hotel. The whole office was excited and happy for Denise's success.

The ceremonies at the Law Courts were impeccably proper. Denise assumed her responsibility with honour, grace, and dignity. She would do well.

The Pan Pacific Hotel hosted the gala and the meal was truly magnificent.

It was indeed Denise's night to shine. Usually she appeared studious and dowdy, with untameable hair, no makeup, and lost in thought most of the time. But this night, she was radiant in a strapless, steel grey, shimmering gown. She wore an exquisite diamond necklace and earrings set in platinum. Her hair was piled high on her head. She was dazzling! No one had ever noticed how elegant she could be. She was vivacious, gracious, and social. She held a glass of champagne to her lips and sipped delicately.

Edward Barton, another of the promising partners of McDowell Hill, graduated from the University of Victoria Law School and had been specifically recruited to join the firm. Ward, as he was known to his friends, grew up in Victoria. He was an athlete, a scholar, and the son of one of British Columbia's self-made millionaires. He was good looking, charming, and had all the attributes required for public relations.

As he entered the hotel lobby, he caught a glimpse of his reflection in the mirrored glass door. In a James Bond gesture, he straightened his tie, ran his fingers through his hair, and assumed a confident arrogance. He did look very handsome in his jet black tux, and he knew it.

Later in the evening, after the formalities and too many martinis, Ward approached Denise's table, where she sat with her parents, her mentor Madam Justice Tyler, and two of the Supreme Court judges and their wives. Denise invited Ward to join them, and she introduced him as a partner in her former firm. He said that he merely came to offer his congratulations and to persuade her to dance. She hesitated and said that she didn't dance. He reassured her, as he took her arm and almost dragged her to the floor. Just as they began to dance, the music changed to a slow waltz. They intertwined their arms. After a minute of slow music, Ward thought the time was right, and in a bold move, he pressed his cheek against her ear, nuzzling her hair and trying to kiss her neck.

Denise dropped her arms, backed up, and stared wide-eyed at him. "Three words, Ward, and they are not 'light my fire'! Try your stupid tricks on someone else," she wheeled around and headed for her table.

Ward shook his head, raised his outstretched arms, and shrugged his shoulders in disbelief. What the fuck! Bitch!

Just as he turned to walk away, his wife, Jackie, appeared. "What was that all about?"

"She said that she didn't want to dance anymore. Her feet were hurting her."

"Ward, it's ten to two. Can we go to the hotel now? I'm tired."

"Sure, you always want to leave just when the fun starts!" In his finest theatrical form, he stomped over to the table, grabbed his jacket from the back of the chair with one hand and tore open his tie and collar with the other. He made for the door. Jackie looked at her feet.

In a voice that was too loud, Ward yelled, "Well, are you coming? You want to go, so let's go!"

When she caught up with him, he said, "Why did you wear that dress? You look like a fucking hillbilly!"

She stifled a reply, because she knew it would not matter what she said. He was drunk.

* * *

Denise's appointment was another opportunity for the firm of McDowell Hill to promote its name and fame. They should be able to get good mileage out of this, although they were operating at near peak capacity already. Frank and Andrew knew that some planning was needed for future development, especially now that Denise was gone. They rolled over some ideas at a lunch that lasted well into the afternoon.

Andrew commented to Frank, "As much as I dislike criminal work, Dan has built himself quite an empire. He's been asking for a junior. That may be a direction we could head. Surprisingly, his accounts receivable aren't that bad. We should look at his competition and see if we can either bring it in or wipe it out. Dan probably has some ideas of his own. I think we need to talk to him."

Andrew pulled his calendar from his briefcase and scribbled a few notes on a blank page, under the word "Agenda", which he printed neatly at the top.

"What else?" Frank asked Andrew.

"I hate to point out the obvious, but with Denise gone, we don't have a woman partner. Deborah is not interested in being a partner. She's only biding her time until her husband is finished here and they can move on. We need a couple of good women candidates to consider."

Andrew was determined to continue being the captain of the most successful law firm in Victoria.

Just as the waitress was bringing the check, their wives walked into the restaurant. Andrew waved them over. Frank thought Melissa looked tired, but they both approached the table with enthusiasm.

"Playing golf today ladies?" Frank asked.

"We already played," said Melissa, "and I shot my best game ever!"

"Take a rest, you're getting too good for me," Frank teased his wife.

"What are you boys scheming about?" Andrew's wife asked, as Andrew clicked the lock on his briefcase. Lenore had been a lawyer's wife for nearly thirty years. She knew the game. He laughed and pecked her on the cheek. "You know, honey, you always have to have Plan A and Plan B in this business. We have to go and close up shop. You two have a lovely afternoon. See you tonight."

Luckily for Andrew and Frank, Lenore and Melissa were just as good friends as they were partners. Their success in both areas lay in the fact that none of them ever crossed into each other's territory.

CHAPTER FOUR

Elisabeth typed up the agenda for the partners meeting, set for Wednesday morning at eight. She arranged for a continental breakfast to be delivered. Document packages containing financial statements from the last fiscal year and the most recent quarter, and the latest batch of resumes from prospective lawyers, were carefully assembled for each partner.

Elisabeth handed Andrew a copy of the final agenda on Tuesday afternoon and Andrew wandered down to Frank's office just to give him a head's up.

The next morning, Frank reluctantly left the house at 7:30. He knew he could not miss the partners meeting, but Melissa wasn't well; she was feeling dizzy and weak. She assured Frank she would be fine. She would call her sister if she needed anything. "Go!" she urged him. "You have business to attend to. I'll be fine. I'll just lounge in bed until I feel better."

By the time he parked his car, he was rolling over in his mind all the points he wanted to bring up at the meeting.

Everyone arrived on time.

Trust Deborah to point out that Ward was wearing the same suit that morning as he had worn the day before. He graced her with one of his best sneers.

Everybody sat flipping through the pages of the financial information with one hand and a coffee mug in the other. Andrew always arrived last. He loved to make grand entrances. He also loved to make everything look easy, when, in fact, it was usually the product of a highly polished rehearsal.

The financials didn't look bad so far this year. Everyone took their medicine when it came to accounts receivable. Criminal had forty more active files this year than the previous year and Dan Moody wanted to interview and hire his junior within three months. No one wanted to mess in this area. No one knew exactly what made a good criminal lawyer. But they all agreed the workload now demanded immediate attention. Dan could interview and select his junior, this time, but the standard rule was strongly reinforced: absolutely no hiring without the partners unanimous approval.

Ward said, "I've just done some work for a talent agent. Don't forget the new performing arts theatre will be opening soon. I think the entertainment industry holds some promise. Most of the work would probably be in either contract preparation or dispute."

Andrew added that he'd had a few calls inquiring about medical malpractice. "We have two large hospitals in Victoria— one of them a training hospital. There are a gaggle of medical specialists in virtually every field that serve all of Vancouver Island and more. We also have a huge retirement population. Maybe that's an area where we could expand."

Frank opened the discussion of an articled student. "The University of Victoria Faculty of Law has approached us many times, but we have never taken a student. I think it could be an excellent way to assess prospective junior lawyers without having to make too much of a commitment."

Everyone knew that Deborah would never stay much more than a couple of years, and when she left, the solicitor's department would be reduced to Frank alone.

On a final note, Andrew said—with some reluctance—that Deborah had requested her own secretary. Deborah had always been very critical of the support staff. In Deborah's opinion, the only truly competent one was Hilary. What Deborah did not know was that Hilary had no intention of ever working for her, or even with her.

Andrew announced that he would be taking some time off over the next three months and that Elisabeth would probably be available for some extra work.

At the end of the meeting, the results were summarized and the next partnership meeting was scheduled for the first of February.

At 10:30 a.m., the boardroom door opened and everyone migrated to his respective office, elated with the prospects of continued success for the firm of McDowell Hill.

* * *

Dan arranged for an advertisement to be placed in the Lawyers Magazine, and was overwhelmed with responses. One, however, stood out above the rest. He phoned Jason Grieco and invited him to lunch. Jason sported a solid gold stud earring and a spider web tattooed on the back of his right hand. Together they would make a perfect team.

Frank contacted the Dean at the University of Victoria Law School and asked him to refer suitable candidates for the articling position, from those students who anticipated a solicitor's practise. His approach to hiring was different than Dan's. He asked Hilary to arrange an office interview for each person who submitted a resume. He spent a couple of weeks consumed in scrutinizing resumes, conducting interviews, and doing extensive reference checks. Some of the secretaries started a pool, betting on who would be the successful candidate.

At Hilary's suggestion, Frank considered a young woman who had started off being a legal secretary and ended up in law school. Hilary pointed out that she was obviously ambitious and would come equipped with some useful skills. Frank had Hilary telephone Maria Ross for a second appointment. Hilary liked her. What more could Frank ask?

* * *

Frank appeared from his office with an ashen face. He was extremely distressed.

"What's wrong?" Hilary immediately asked.

"I have to go," Frank replied. "I just got a call from Melissa's sister; she took Melissa to the hospital."

"Are you okay to drive? Do you want me to call a cab for you?"

"No. No thanks. I'll be fine. Just keep a lid on things here for me. I don't know how long I'll be. I'll call in." He fled for the elevator.

Hilary checked Frank's calendar and the files on his desk. Fortunately it was late in the day and there were no more appointments scheduled.

Around eight thirty that night, Hilary called Frank at home. She knew visiting hours at the hospital ended at eight. There was no answer. She didn't leave a message, but she was worried.

Frank didn't come in the next day either, but she covered him off in her usual efficient manner. It was Friday and she hoped she would hear something from him before the weekend.

***

Monday morning rolled around and everyone in the office was asking about Frank, and if Melissa was recovering. All Hilary could say was that she had not heard anything yet. At three o'clock Frank phoned.

"Hi Frank. What's happening? How is Melissa?"

"The last few days have been complete hell, Hilary."

She could hear the tension and tiredness in his voice.

"Melissa had a mastectomy this morning. She's not in any danger at the moment, and the doctors are optimistic about her recovery, but it scares the crap out of me!"

"Frank, don't worry about a thing here," Hilary said. "Just stay with Melissa and be her support. She needs you. Give her my love, and tell her we are all sending positive thoughts her way. If you need anything, anything at all, please phone me."

A small group had gathered around Hilary's desk, waiting to hear the news. Hilary hung up the phone and made the announcement. Toby circulated an envelope and everybody chipped in ten bucks for a beautiful bouquet of flowers and a fruit bowl. Hilary delivered them to the hospital on her way home.

***

Maria Ross was learning more at McDowell Hill than she had learned in the last year of law school. Hilary thanked her lucky stars that Frank had chosen her.

Deborah, on the other hand, was insufferable. She was picky and critical over trifles. She was arrogant and abusive.

At one point, Hilary marched into Alan's office and spoke to him in no uncertain terms. "You need to talk to Deborah about the way she's treating staff members and her inexcusable behaviour. Deborah is always at Elisabeth. Always! She undermines and invalidates her at every opportunity. She is turning a perfectly competent legal secretary into a neurotic, hysterical woman who second-guesses herself at every turn! Make her lay off!"

I'm no good at this stuff, Alan thought. His way of handling anyone who got in his way was to out-yell them. He knew that it never solved anything, but he usually did it anyway.

Five minutes before lunch, Hilary rang Alan's office. "She's at it again. You have to stop her! None of us can stand it anymore. Frank's home taking care of Melissa, Andrew's on vacation ... you are the only one with the authority to do something! Please, Alan, don't let this go too far," Hilary begged.

Alan jumped up from his desk and steamed toward Elisabeth's desk, where Deborah was in full swing. "Enough!" he bellowed from halfway across the room.

The whole office fell silent.

Deborah shoved past him and muttered, loud enough for him and everyone else to hear, "She is so stupid; I don't know how she ever got a job here!"

Elisabeth immediately burst into tears!

Alan stood in the centre of the room, totally perplexed. Eventually he made his way back to his office. He was not convinced that he had 'handled' the situation, but at least he'd made it stop for the moment.

Elisabeth was grateful for the intervention, but she didn't want to have anything more to do with Deborah.

* * *

The following week they were at each other's throats again. Elisabeth brought up the subject of Paulette McNeil's file.

"Deborah, you have never given me any instructions as to what you want me to do on the file. Do you want me to advise the appropriate authorities of Paulette's passing? Do you want me to destroy her documents? What about an income tax clearance?"

"Are you fucking stupid?" Deborah yelled at Elisabeth.

"These things need to be done, Deborah," Elisabeth implored.

"Not fucking now!" was Deborah's vehement response. "Can you not see that I have work up to my eyeballs that is far more important than finalizing the estate of a dead person who had nothing? Are you truly too stupid to figure that out?"

"Fine then!" Elisabeth snarled. "Forget I ever asked!" she shrieked, as she snatched the file from Deborah's hand and flung it toward the trash can.

Alan was on the run again, but he was too late. The fireworks were over. Deborah was back in her office pretending like nothing happened. Elisabeth was in the bathroom in tears.

Hilary went into the bathroom. She put her arm around Elisabeth. "You know you can't fight with her. She always has to have the last word. Why don't you go home for a while and compose yourself. Have a cup of tea. Deborah will be gone soon enough, and we won't have to put up with her anymore. Besides that, Andrew will be back soon and you'll be busy working for him again. You won't have to have anything to do with her."

"I don't know why I do this anymore. All I ever wanted was to have a little business of my own. A tea room maybe. It would have been so easy. I just never had the money to get it going, and now I think I'm too old," Elisabeth confided to Hilary. "Life would have been so much easier."

After silently retrieving Paulette's file from the floor, reorganizing it and placing it in the bottom drawer of her filing cabinet, Elisabeth pulled on her coat. She was still crying. Hilary could see her out the window walking home with her head down, occasionally dabbing at her eyes with a Kleenex. Hilary was angry. She wanted to take on Deborah herself, but she thought she was no match for her, and, as much as she loved Elisabeth, she could not risk losing her own job.

* * *

Christmas holidays were rapidly approaching and there was lots of excitement in the office. Andrew and Lenore were off to Hawaii for the holidays. Frank and Melissa, who was slowly recovering, were having a family Christmas. Hilary and her family were going to the hockey tournament in Seattle on Boxing Day, for four days. Everyone had plans.

In an unprecedented surprise, Andrew announced, at 10:00 a.m. on Christmas Eve, that since the firm had enjoyed such a good year financially, most of the staff would be given the time off between Christmas and New Year. He had already arranged for two junior lawyers to staff the office during the break. The office closed at noon in a frenzy of excitement. Everyone hugged each other and wished each other season's greetings, but by 12:15, there was not a soul in sight.

CHAPTER FIVE

At the law firm of McDowell Hill, the first day back in the New Year was horrendous. Everyone wondered how a week off, even at that time of the year, could create such a backlog. Hilary spent all day returning calls, booking appointments, and talking to accountants whose clients were trying to find tax shelters for the previous year's income.

Deborah was enlisted to calm the storm, but she was in a foul mood. At noon, Hilary overheard Deborah in the cafeteria telling Ward that she had spent her Christmas vacation in Vale, but her husband had spent his in Maui, golfing. Perhaps that was the reason she was so cantankerous.

Elisabeth tried her hardest to steer clear of Deborah at any time, especially since the blowouts they'd been having, but that day, Andrew had asked her specifically to retrieve a file that he had given Deborah to review.

Near the end of the day, Elisabeth grabbed the files that she wanted to put in accounting for closing procedures, and thought she would stop by Deborah's office on the way. The 'closed door policy' of the firm was to just knock and enter. Elisabeth did just that. Balancing her files in one arm, she made a quick rap on the door, twisted the knob, and walked in.

Deborah was sitting on the edge of the far side of her desk, with her back to the door. Her legs were wrapped around Ward's waist in a scissor-lock. She leaned back on her hands. Ward looked up and stepped back.

Elisabeth was aghast! Disgust and revulsion glued her feet to the floor. Her mouth groped for the words "Excuse me!" but no sound came out.

Ward looked utterly ridiculous in his black Italian suit jacket, silk tie, and crisp white shirt, with his pants around his ankles and an enormous stupid grin smeared across his face.

Elisabeth looked to the doorway, hoping her feet would take her in that direction, but it was too late.

In one deft move, Deborah flipped the dangling pantyhose from her toe, slipped off the desk, smoothed her skirt over her hips, and charged toward Elisabeth. An angry hiss leaked from her curled lips. Elisabeth tried to move, but before she could, Deborah pushed her hard and screamed, "You stupid, stupid idiot!"

Elisabeth toppled over, her arm bent underneath her still clutching the pile of files. She hit the floor hard. Hilary heard the thud, and the crack of Elisabeth's collarbone breaking, from her desk in the next office.

Sandra, who had been coming down the hall, witnessed the whole altercation.

Hilary dashed out of her office in time to see Ward step over Elisabeth and retreat to his own office. He was still fumbling with his belt buckle.

Hilary crouched beside Elisabeth. She gingerly took the files out of Elisabeth's grip and shoved them aside. "Call 911, Sandra!" Hilary yelled. "Right now!"

Deborah hovered over Elisabeth and Hilary. "She fell. She tripped over her own clumsy feet!"

"Don't lie, Deborah! I saw you push her!" Sandra said.

"Sandra, go and watch for the ambulance!" Hilary commanded. "Deborah, just get away!"

Deborah started for Andrew's office. She wanted to tell her side of the confrontation first, but Andrew would not give her the opportunity. He strode down the hall.

The ambulance attendants were getting ready to place Elisabeth on the stretcher.

"Hilary, you go with her to the hospital. Make sure everything is taken care of. Deborah, get in my office! Sit there and don't move!"

No one had ever seen Andrew so angry. He knew he had to do some immediate damage control.

Deborah was sitting in his office when Andrew got back from watching Elisabeth being loaded into the ambulance. He ignored Deborah for the moment and picked up the phone. He called his old friend, James Norgate, General Hospital's chief administrator. James came on the line.

"James, this is Andrew McDowell calling. I need to get right to the point here. I need your help. You know I don't like to ask favours, but this is an unusual situation. One of our employees was just injured in an accident at the office a few minutes ago. She is on her way to you by ambulance. She should be arriving there any moment. She is my secretary, Elisabeth Nielsen. I want her to have a private room and the best care. Do whatever it takes. I will be in your debt," Andrew spoke directly, thinking of the $100,000 donation the firm of McDowell Hill had made to the Hospital Foundation.

"Say no more, Andrew," he answered. "I understand completely." James knew the meaning of the word 'litigation'.

Andrew hung up the phone and turned to Deborah. "I don't want to hear anything from you right now! You better hope to hell she does not sue us or I'll have your head in the wringer!" Andrew angrily admonished. "Tomorrow you are going to that hospital and you are going to apologize to Elisabeth for everything that happened. And you're going to mean it. Her sick-pay is coming out of your pocket and any care that she may need that is not covered by medical you'll be paying! You will make sure she has a nice new robe and slippers and flowers every day she is in that hospital and that she wants for absolutely nothing. Do you understand me?"

Deborah knew he meant business. She also knew she had taken an enormous risk and lost. She tried to appear remorseful.

"Do not set foot in these offices until I call you. Now get your purse and coat and get out of here. I have clean up to do thanks to you," Andrew said vehemently.

As soon as Andrew was sure Deborah was out of the office, he interrupted Frank.

Of course, the office was buzzing with speculation about what had happened.

Andrew quickly enlightened Frank, and said. "I want you to talk to Ward. I am too angry right now to be objective and we need to nip this in the bud. Find out from him exactly what he thinks happened. It is 4:30 right now, and I want to talk to the staff before they go home. I don't want Ward at the meeting; perhaps you can take him out for a drink. Maybe that will loosen him up enough for him to tell you the real truth rather than the glossy version."

Andrew grabbed Frank's phone and called Toby. "Please make an announcement for everyone to gather immediately in the boardroom."

The staff filed into the boardroom in absolute silence. Each person knew there were going to be serious repercussions following the day's events. Andrew strained to maintain his composure.

"Ladies and gentlemen, we have had a very unfortunate incident occur today. Elisabeth was injured in a fall. We do not know how serious her injuries are, nor do we yet know the circumstances that led to this incident. I assure you that there will be a full investigation. In order to protect the reputation of our law firm, I would ask that you not discuss this matter amongst yourselves or with anyone outside this firm until we know the facts. If you have any questions or observations to make, please feel at ease to speak to me. I will let you know Elisabeth's condition as soon as I receive word. Thank you for your discretion and support."

Just as silently as the staff had filed in, they filed out.

Andrew phoned Lenore and told her that he was going to be late and that he would explain later. He hurried to the hospital.

Hilary was in the emergency waiting room. He sat down heavily beside her. "Any news," he asked.

"She has a broken collarbone and a dislocated shoulder. She is in surgery right now. They said it would be a couple of hours before she would be in recovery. I thought I would wait. She doesn't have anyone else," Hilary said.

Andrew sat motionless. His breathing was laboured.

Hilary flipped through a magazine, but she couldn't really concentrate on the articles. She got up to phone home and make sure everything was okay, and told her husband she would be late.

After about an hour, Frank arrived.

"Have either of you had anything to eat yet? Do you want to go for something in the cafeteria while we wait?"

Hilary and Andrew looked at each other and then stood up. They followed Frank to the cafeteria, loaded a few sandwiches on a tray, and poured coffee into three Styrofoam cups. Andrew picked a table in the corner near the door.

"Hilary, you probably know just as much, if not more, about what happened today as either of us does," Frank said. "You can hear whatever we have to say, and I hope you will feel free to speak. This incident could have disastrous consequences for the firm. From what I know so far, if the details got out, our firm would be the laughing stock of all Victoria."

"I just can't believe it," Hilary shook her head. "Everyone knew there was no love lost between Elisabeth and Deborah, and most people thought that Deborah antagonized Elisabeth unmercifully. Andrew, when you were away on vacation and Frank was off taking care of Melissa, I had to have Alan calm Deborah down a couple of times. She was at Elisabeth all the time. I never thought it would come to this, though."

"Did you get a chance to talk to Ward? What did he have to say?" Andrew asked Frank.

"He said that he was getting a little action when Elisabeth walked in unexpectedly. If Elisabeth knocked, he didn't hear. He said the window was open and there was a lot of noise from the street. Apparently, when Deborah saw Elisabeth, she went berserk. He said he wasn't sure if Deborah actually pushed her or if Elisabeth just tripped over her own feet trying to get out of Deborah's way."

"Apparently Sandra was in the hall at the time it happened. She said that she saw Deborah push Elisabeth and that's what caused Elisabeth to fall," Hilary confirmed.

Andrew shook his head in disgust. "Jesus Christ."

The mood around the offices of McDowell Hill the next morning was very somber. Andrew called everyone together for a quick briefing on Elisabeth's condition.

"Elisabeth has a broken collarbone and a dislocated shoulder. She had some surgery to reset the shoulder and pin the collarbone," he said. "The doctors feel she will be out of the hospital in about a week, but she will probably be convalescing at home for about three months. I would encourage everyone to try to visit her to keep up her spirits."

* * *

Andrew visited Elisabeth every day she was in the hospital. She had been a devoted and outstanding employee. He also wanted to check to make sure Deborah was following his instructions.

Many staff members had baked cookies, cakes, and even lasagna, to stock Elisabeth's freezer in preparation for her return home.

As diplomatically as possible, Andrew had brought up the subject of the fall. "For the sake of the firm's reputation, if anyone asks you what happened, please just say that you fell and injured yourself. Don't worry about a thing. I have arranged for a home-care nurse at night for when you get home, for as long as you need. And, when you're better, your job will be waiting for you."

Elisabeth complied with his request. Somehow she felt partially responsible for what happened. Perhaps she should have waited for Deborah to answer her knock. Perhaps she should have checked with Deborah by phone first, to see if it was convenient to pick up the file. Perhaps she should have moved quicker. The thought never entered her mind that she could sue her employer, or that she could have criminal charges laid against Deborah for assaulting her.

During her stay in the hospital, Elisabeth watched the soap operas, game shows, and talk shows on the television Deborah had rented. Sometimes she would talk on the phone to well-wishers or chat with the steady stream of friends, co-workers, and acquaintances that came to visit.

At first when Deborah would visit, she was all business and no talk. On Friday, however, Deborah made a most sincere apology for her indiscretion, not only with Ward, but also in her actions toward Elisabeth.

Elisabeth almost believed her.

After Elisabeth was released from the hospital, Deborah went every single day to Elisabeth's house just before noon. She made her a sandwich or a bowl of soup. They shared a pot of tea. Deborah was a hard nut to crack, Elisabeth thought. She was tough on the outside but as the days passed, Elisabeth began to see that, despite her outward success, Deborah was a very unhappy person. Elisabeth thought that, even though she was the one who had paid the price for Deborah's anger, she could forgive her but she would never trust her.

* * *

The following Friday, Andrew telephoned Deborah. He asked her to come to the office on Saturday afternoon at two. All of the partners were present, with the exception of Ward Barton. No one dressed for the occasion. Most wore golf shirts and shorts or Levi's. A couple had cracked open beers; others had pop or coffee. The atmosphere was casual and Deborah was grateful for that. She really didn't want any confrontation. She was embarrassed enough about her actions. She didn't want to have to defend them.

"Thanks for coming Deborah," Frank said, when she entered the room. "If you would like a drink, help yourself."

"Thank you, no."

"All right Deborah," Frank began, "we don't want this to be an inquisition. We would just like to hear your side of the story, please."

"Well," she said, as she looked at her hands folded in her lap, "Elisabeth interrupted me at a most inopportune time and I allowed myself to become angry with her. I did not mean to hurt her or even push her down. All I meant to do was push her out the door. I felt she had no business coming in when I had not answered her knock."

"So you admit that you did push her?" Dan asked.

"Yes, I did, but like I said before, I didn't mean to hurt her."

Dan continued. "It is well known around the office that you disliked Elisabeth. Is that a fair comment?"

"Well, I used to get very frustrated with her sometimes. She always seemed to be able to ask a question that put me on the spot. I believe it was me though who would get antagonistic." Tears gathered at the edges of her eyes, but she would not cry. "I have sincerely apologized to Elisabeth, and I sincerely apologize to each and every member of this firm—lawyers and support staff. I truly regret my actions."

"Deborah your actions have thrown this firm into turmoil. Your bad temper and angry outbursts have gotten out of control. If you agree to anger management counselling, we will retain your services for a trial period of six months, to be extended at the conclusion of the trial period, upon mutual agreement. If you lose control of yourself even once during that time, your employment with this firm will be terminated without further notice. If you do not agree to the counselling, you leave us no option but to terminate your employment forthwith," Andrew said, unhappily. "Deborah, you are a competent lawyer, and it is our fervent wish to help you as you appear to be having some difficulty in your life. We hope you will decide to remain in our employ, but the choice is yours."

Deborah sat silently as she weighed her decision.

"I would like to try to stay," she answered, in a tone barely above a whisper.

"Excellent!" Andrew clapped his hands together once. "We'll see everyone Monday."

Deborah returned to work. For the first few weeks, she spent most of her time locked in her office. She would leave just before noon to go to Elisabeth's to make her lunch and return promptly at one o'clock. She was very diligent. She was polite to every person she had contact with, yet somewhat aloof. She began seeing an anger management therapist, and honestly tried to gain some insight and benefits from the sessions.

The staff liked the new Deborah better than the old one. Finally, the tensions began to ease.

Elisabeth eventually recovered, and upon assurances received from both Andrew and Frank, that Deborah would never again accost or assault her, Elisabeth returned to work. Elisabeth made every effort to avoid Deborah, but if their paths crossed, Deborah made every effort to be congenial.

Upon reflection, Andrew had accomplished his mission. Damage control contained the incident to the immediate office, without adverse publicity.

* * *

Frank was definitely back in the groove, orchestrating some of the most complex acquisitions and take-overs he had ever done. Melissa was pronounced cancer free and Frank was making up for lost time.

Alan was hardly ever in the office during the day, because he was usually in court, but he spent long hours in the evening pouring over the details of his files. When he was involved in a trial, sometimes his staff would go for days without seeing him. They would know he had been there at night, though, because he would leave cryptic little notes with instructions clipped to the front covers of each file.

Dan Moody and Jason Grieco were embroiled in defending a 32-year-old man of diminished mental capacity, who allegedly sexually molested and murdered a 12-year-old girl. The case was splashed all over the newspapers, as the accused was the son of a member of the legislative assembly.

Ward was another matter. While he attracted a lot of work for the firm, he rarely did any. The legal assistants or other lawyers did most of the work, while Ward took the credit. He often appeared in the office unshaven and somewhat dishevelled, and not before eleven o'clock. There were reports that he frequented nightclubs until the early hours of the morning, buying drinks for pretty young girls.

Deborah kept her head down, did her work competently, and maintained a low profile.

CHAPTER SIX

In early March, 1984, the real estate market picked up dramatically, not just in the residential sector but in the commercial sector as well. Interest rates had fallen to the lowest ever, and everyone who could was trying to capitalize.

Ward pulled in a deal that involved the sale of an exclusive wilderness resort and marina on an island just off the east coast of Vancouver Island, with an astronomical $16,000,000 price tag. One of the shareholders of the company that owned the resort was a friend of Ward's father. The purchaser was a company represented by a Vancouver firm, with the purchase being funded by offshore money. The sale was set to close on April 18th.

As was Ward's practise of late, he left the copy of the contract of purchase and sale lying on his desk and neglected to open a file or even begin the process required to complete the transaction. Not only that, he had received a letter by fax from the purchaser's lawyer, requesting due diligence search authorizations, that he ignored.

On April 13th, the Friday before the closing, Toby received a call from the Vancouver law firm asking to speak to someone in the Commercial Conveyancing Department.

"Conveyancing Department. This is Sandra."

"Hello, this is Eleanor Johnson calling from the law firm of Burrard & Company in Vancouver. Our firm acts on behalf of the purchasers of Wilderness Island Resort and Marina. We are told that you act on behalf of the vendor, Wilderness Holdings Ltd. I wonder if you have had the chance to have the due diligence authorizations that I faxed over to you a couple of weeks ago, regarding the sale of Wilderness Island Resort and Marina, signed by the vendor?"

"I'm not familiar with the file," Sandra replied. "Please hold a moment and I will try to find the person who has conduct of that matter." She pressed hold on her phone and headed for the master file list. There was no "Wilderness Holdings Ltd." or "Wilderness Island Resort" on file.

Sandra went back on the line, "Eleanor, let me take your number and I will locate the file and have someone call you back shortly. When is the closing date?"

"Closing is April 18th, the Wednesday before Good Friday. If you have the authorizations signed, can you fax them to me please?" Eleanor asked. "I am getting a little anxious about the time frame. Do you think you can help me today?"

"I'll do my best."

Sandra hung up the phone and rifled through the loose papers on her desk looking for the correspondence, just in case someone dropped it there and she hadn't seen it. Nothing.

Sixteen million dollars! That sounds like a Frank file. She checked with Hilary. She had not received anything. Hilary looked on Frank's desk, but did not see anything there either.

Sandra checked with Deborah, just in case she'd received the authorizations. Deborah denied receiving anything.

Elisabeth had a suggestion. "Sandra, phone Eleanor and ask her to fax copies of the documents again. You don't need to make any apologies, just say we are unable to locate the documents, and that we understand the urgency as the closing date is rapidly approaching. I'm sure she will be only too happy to fax them, since she is anxious to close the transaction too."

Sandra made the call, and within minutes was back at Elisabeth's desk. She dangled the copy of the contract of purchase and sale between her thumb and index finger, as if she were holding a wriggling snake that she didn't really want to touch.

"Elisabeth, help! This is far too complicated for me! It's not residential. I don't even know where to start on this one. Sixteen million and closing April 18th! There is no way I can do this. If I had more time and someone to help me, maybe I could, but not this time. Besides that, I have a whole stack of residential closings on my own files over the next few days."

Elisabeth relieved Sandra of the paper evidencing the monster deal, and read over it quickly. Sure enough, the letter to which the authorizations were attached was addressed to Ward.

"Leave it with me, Sandra, I'll take care of it," Elisabeth said.

Normally Elisabeth wouldn't go through anyone's office, but she figured that if Ward wasn't on top of his workload, she had every right. She marched into his office and started turning over papers on his desk. Pushed to one side was the contract of purchase and sale; underneath was the copy of the letter with the authorizations. The fax date on the authorizations was March 29th.

Ward appeared in the doorway. "Elisabeth, what are looking for?"

"Ward, we got a call today from the law firm of Burrard & Company, asking about the Wilderness Island Resort transaction. I found the fax and due diligence authorizations on your desk. They were faxed to us on March 29th! Why didn't you tell us about this matter? It closes next Wednesday! There isn't even a file open!"

"Fuck!" Ward spit out.

"You better get going on this right now, if you want to close on time. You need to take these authorizations to the vendor and get them signed this afternoon. They need to be faxed to Vancouver before five tonight. You'll also need to find someone who can work on this file. I don't really have time for this one and neither does Sandra or Hilary," Elisabeth informed him tersely.

"Who's the vendor?" Ward asked.

"Are you on top of this or not?" Elisabeth asked in an exasperated tone. "It looks like it's Wilderness Holdings Ltd. but I have not read all the documentation. You need to get this under control, Ward, and fast, or you're going to miss the closing!"

Everyone knew that you could never miss a closing date without leaving your client exposed to litigation. Elisabeth stuffed the documentation into Ward's hands and returned to her desk.

Ward buzzed Toby on the intercom and said, "If Gina calls, tell her I had an emergency and I'll catch up with her later."

He left the office with the authorizations.

At four o'clock, Ward returned with the signed authorizations in hand and dropped them on Elisabeth's desk, then he plunged into Frank's office and announced, "I have an important transaction to close rather quickly and I need you to assign Hilary to close it." He did not see Hilary behind him.

"I don't think so Ward," she said, surprising him. "You left the matter too long. I don't have time. I have a full workload right now, and I have things to do before Frank leaves on vacation. Remember? Most of the partners are going to Phoenix for a few days golfing over Easter."

"Oh, right," Ward replied, as if he had forgotten. He had declined to go because he said Jackie didn't golf well.

He turned again to Frank. "Is there anyone else who can do it?"

"What exactly is it, Ward?" Frank asked. Hilary excused herself and Frank nodded his consent. Hilary didn't care to hear the rest of the conversation. She had other matters that required her attention.

Lucky Elisabeth, Hilary thought, as she saw Frank and Ward emerge from Frank's office, and start speaking to her in a very animated way.

Elisabeth protested, citing the fact that she had her own workload to clear before her upcoming vacation, but she lost. They both knew she could manage it. Ward was not about to turn the transaction away. He needed someone with some expertise. Elisabeth acquiesced, and in her usual efficient manner, instructed that the file be opened, obtained copies of the searches of the real property from Eleanor, ordered tax searches from the Surveyor of Taxes, and requested payout statements—on an urgent basis—from the prior mortgage holders.

Late in the day, Elisabeth contacted Eleanor again and asked her if she needed anything else from the vendor's side to complete the paperwork. The documents would be flown over on the floatplane as soon as they were ready. She left a note for Ward, telling him that she would alert his clients that they would be required to sign the documents on Tuesday, and that he should be available to attend on the signing and payout the following day.

On Monday afternoon a box containing all the documentation to be signed regarding the sale of Wilderness Island Resort and Marina was dropped on Elisabeth's desk by the courier. Elisabeth opened the box, sorted through the documents, and began reading the covering letter from Burrard & Company. She highlighted certain portions of the letter, and flagged specific items in the documents. She buzzed Ward. No answer. She left a message on his desk: 'Ward, I need to see you regarding the documentation for the Wilderness Island Resort transaction. Please call me as soon as you get in.'

Elisabeth rang reception, "Hi Toby. What is Ward's schedule like for the next two days? Is he going to be in the office?"

"He is not marked out, but lately he hasn't been coming in before eleven, and he disappears by three. I will leave a note for him to see you."

"Thanks, Toby. Please mark it 'urgent.'"

At five to five, Elisabeth thought she would try Ward at his home. "Hi Jackie, this is Elisabeth from the office. Is Ward there?"

"No, he told me he had a very important transaction that he was working on and would be busy with his clients for the next few days. He could be up at the marina," Jackie added, hesitantly.

"Thank you. If you hear from Ward, would you ask him to phone me immediately? I am working on the documentation for that transaction right now, and I need to speak to him."

"Yes, sure, Elisabeth, but I can't guarantee he'll get the message."

Elisabeth reread the copy of the contract of purchase and sale. There was no telephone number for the vendor. She called the realtor to get a contact name and number. She dialled the number she was given for Wilderness Island Resort and Marina. "Hello, may I speak to Joe Piquette, please?"

"Hold on a sec," the voice responded, and without covering the mouthpiece, yelled in her ear, "Joe! It's for you!"

She heard a click. "Joe here."

"Yes, hello Joe. My name is Elisabeth Nielsen, and I work for the law offices of McDowell Hill in Victoria, for Ward Barton, the lawyer who is handling the sale of Wilderness Island Resort and Marina. I need some information from you to complete the documents. Do you have a few minutes to answer some questions for me?"

"Yeah, sure. What do you need?"

Finally, Elisabeth thought, someone who knows what they're doing!

"First of all, Joe, I need to know who will be signing the documentation on behalf of the company, and I need them in my office tomorrow for signing."

"Tomorrow? The realtor said Wednesday—that Wednesday would be the closing day."

"Well, I need the documents signed at least the day before the money actually changes hands. But, besides that, and even before the documents are ready for signing, I need some other things. Let me review these things with you, and we can work out the matter of signing later," Elisabeth suggested.

"Sure," Joe mumbled.

"For a start, I need a copy of the most recent financial statements for the resort and marina. Then I need an equipment list with serial numbers. Are there any vehicles being sold? If so, I need copies of the vehicle registrations..." She went on and on with the list of information she required.

After twenty minutes, Joe said that he would make the necessary arrangements to get the information to her by fax the following day. Joe also said that he and the company's Secretary, Herb Myers, would fly in on Tuesday afternoon, for signing at Ward's office at three o'clock. Elisabeth knew this would be cutting it fine, but what could she do?

Information started pouring in the next day, just as Joe had promised. Elisabeth spent the whole morning integrating the information into the documentation, and composing the numerous letters required to complete the transaction.

By ten to twelve, Ward was still not in the office.

Elisabeth approached Frank. "You know Ward's file on the sale of Wilderness Island Resort and Marina? I have not been able to contact Ward. I've left messages for him everywhere. The vendors are coming to the office at three o'clock today to sign documentation relating to the sale. If Ward doesn't show up, can you attend on them?"

"Attend on a sixteen million dollar deal that I know nothing about this afternoon?" Frank asked in amazement, and accidentally bounced the stapler too hard on his desk. Elisabeth could tell he was ticked.

"I know," she shrugged, "but what can I do? No one else can handle it. I've done up a memo setting out everything that I can see. Ward may show up just in time, but even then, he doesn't know the details of the file, and someone will have to walk him through it anyway."

"WHAT THE HELL'S THE MATTER WITH HIM?" Frank actually shouted! He took a few deep breaths and tried to calm himself.

"Leave it on my desk so I can take a look at it. And try to find Ward!"

* * *

Joe Piquette and Herb Meyers sauntered into the law offices of McDowell Hill just before three o'clock. Joe carried a briefcase. He wore a checkered, red and black flannel shirt with orange suspenders holding up his faded blue jeans.

Herb smelled faintly like a cross between dead fish and diesel. His fingernails were lined with stains from working on too many engines in the holds of too many fishing boats.

The two of them would be quite rich by Thursday afternoon.

Joe and Herb were the directors and officers, President and Secretary, respectively. They also owned all the voting shares of the vendor company. Ward's father's friend was the majority shareholder of the non-voting shares. He too would do nicely from the sale.

Wilderness Island Resort and Marina had been an old whaling station in the early 1900s. Eventually the marina had become a satellite port for the Vancouver, Seattle, and San Francisco Yacht Clubs. Joe and Herb had built the marina themselves. They had hewn timber from the forest on the Island, brought in an old portable mill to saw the logs into planks for the floats and lumber for the two houses. They built the barn from the mill tailings.

Every summer for the last fifteen years, without fail, Joe and Herb would make their way to the Island with wives and kids in tow. It had been a labour of love, but there comes a time to move on. The partners' children were beginning to venture out on their own, and the Island held little appeal for them anymore. Joe and his wife wanted to move farther north. They loved rugged wilderness and desolation. Herb and his wife, whose children had left home, planned to stay on at Wilderness Island Resort, performing marine repairs, managing the shop, gas bar, and floats. He and his wife would be caretakers in the winter months.

Elisabeth went to the reception area, "Joe Piquette?" she asked, making eye contact. Joe rose.

"Hello, I'm Elisabeth. I spoke to you on the telephone."

Herb stood up too, "And you must be Herb," she said, as she turned and shook both men's hands.

"Unfortunately Mr. Barton has not yet returned to the office." She hoped neither one of them noticed the little lie. "In his absence, Frank Hill, one of our senior partners, will be attending on you to sign the documents. Sometimes in this business, you just don't know when you will be delayed. I am sure you'll find Mr. Hill very competent and knowledgeable. Please ask him any questions you may have."

"Toby, if Mr. Barton returns, would you please send him to Mr. Hill's office? Tell him his clients from Wilderness Island Resort are with Mr. Hill."

Elisabeth led the way to Frank's office. The stack of documents sitting in the middle of Frank's desk was staggering. Elisabeth introduced Frank.

"Sit down, gentlemen," Frank said, as he flourished his hand toward the chairs in front of his desk. "It's really not as bad as it looks. This seems to be a very clean transaction, considering the amount of money involved. I want to start by reviewing the details."

Frank went through each point covered in the contract of purchase and sale in detail. Then he went to the Vendor's Statement of Adjustments. He reviewed specifically the adjustments to the sale price, and explained thoroughly the calculation of each item that was adjusted. "The company will net $14,400,750." He made it sound so simple. "We will make our trust cheque payable to the vendor company: Wilderness Holdings Ltd. What would you like us to do with the cheque when it is ready? We can deposit it to your company bank account, or you can pick it up."

Joe and Herb looked at each other and spoke for a few moments in hushed tones. Finally, Herb nodded. "Frank, I think you would save us some trouble if you would have it deposited into the company's bank account. That way no one has to hang around down here or make a special trip to pick up the cheque. Our accountant will be calculating the division of sale proceeds, and winding up the company before we really see any of the money anyway."

"Elisabeth could you add that to the Direction to Pay, please?" Frank instructed.

"Well, gentlemen, we can begin to sign." Frank handed each of them a pen. Just as they were about to start, Ward breezed through the door.

"Joe! Herb!" he greeted them with an enthusiastic smile, "I am so sorry I couldn't be here earlier. I was delayed in Vancouver this morning. I had another transaction to close that bogged down in the details. I knew you were here though, because I saw the float plane anchored to the dock in the harbour when I arrived. You know, I think I might have to get a small plane of my own. I'll have to speak to you later about that. Maybe you can give me some tips. I'm happy to see Frank is taking good care of you."

He pulled up a chair. "Please continue. I'll just listen, as I don't know what Frank has covered so far." Elisabeth's wry smile caught Ward's eye, but he ignored her, because he thought no one else had noticed.

Frank wanted to punch him. He could be so arrogant sometimes. At least Ward looked presentable Frank thought, but he did seem a bit too exuberant though.

By 5:00 p.m., everything was signed, sealed, and delivered to Elisabeth's desk.

Joe, Herb, and Ward were on the way out for an early dinner before Joe and Herb had to fly home. "Would you join us for dinner tonight, Frank?" Ward asked.

"Thanks for the invitation. I would really like to hear more about the Island. It sounds like a wonderful place. Unfortunately I have another commitment for this evening. It was very nice to meet both of you. I admire the way you built up such a resort to the extent you did. It takes a lot of hard work," Frank observed. "Perhaps I'll be up that way in the boat this summer. If I am, I'll be sure to stop in for a tour." He shook hands with both Joe and Herb.

"I will see you later Ward," Frank pointedly commanded.

Elisabeth put the finishing touches on the letter to Burrard & Company, and presented it to Frank for signing.

"Nice work Elisabeth."

"Thank you Frank, at least you appreciate it!" she said, happy for the compliment.

Elisabeth pulled all the documents together, bundled them into an enormous package and wrapped them in brown paper.

She filled out the courier waybill and addressed the package. By the time she was finished, it was 5:30. She dashed home for her car, clutching the heavy bundle so that she could deliver the entire package to Loomis Courier before the 6:00 p.m. cut-off for overnight delivery to Vancouver. Fortunately she had a $20 bill in her purse so she could pay the courier.

On her way home, she made some mental notes: to have accounting reimburse her for the $20 courier fee; to make sure Ward was going to be around to sign the cheques, when it was time to pay out; and to phone Joe for the company's bank account number for deposit of the sale proceeds.

* * *

Elisabeth collapsed in a heap on the couch when she got home. She was thoroughly exhausted and ravenously hungry. After a moment's rest, she stuck her head in the fridge and grazed through the leftovers. There would be no going back to the office tonight. She was too tired, and besides that, in all the panic of the last week, she had not even thought about packing for her vacation.

Maybe she shouldn't go on vacation. Maybe she should just stay home and pretend she went on vacation. She would have peace and quiet. She could regain her energy. But then, she had always wanted to go to Toronto and this was the perfect opportunity. All these thoughts were jumbled in her mind. She had been invited to her second cousin's wedding, and other members of the family had actually asked her to travel and stay with them in Toronto. This was something she had always wanted. She would actually get to really participate in being a family. The thought warmed her. All the plans were in place and she already had her ticket. She could not bail out now. She really did want to go.

She sat at the kitchen table, writing a list of all the things she needed for her trip. Then she got down her suitcase from the top shelf in the closet, and wiped the dust off. She set out each outfit, and the accessories and shoes that she would need. Last, she packed her makeup bag and left it on the bathroom sink for the morning. The plan was to fly out Saturday morning, the day before Easter Sunday, and stay for ten days. The wedding was the following Saturday.

She could remember, so clearly, the day the bride, Amber, had been born, and how beautiful she had been...

At 11:30 p.m., she crawled into bed and counted two more days of work to go before her vacation. It promised to be eventful. She still had to close the Wilderness Island Resort transaction, with little or no help from Ward, she thought acrimoniously.

Elisabeth fell quickly to sleep that night, but woke all too often, turning over the Wilderness Island Resort transaction in her mind. Had she covered every little detail? Were the documents signed properly? She reminded herself to check the payout calculations first thing when she got to the office in the morning. When 7:00 a.m. rolled around, she was not ready to get up, but the alarm bleated relentlessly!

When Elisabeth arrived at work, there was a huge pile of doughnuts and pastries at the coffee machine. Andrew, the kind soul, had stopped at the bakery on the way in. The staff descended on them like a pack of hungry wolves, and before ten o'clock there was not a single one left!

The office bustled as most of the lawyers and their wives were off to Phoenix for five days of golfing. The plane left at two o'clock from Vancouver International. Some were taking the ferry to Vancouver; others had made arrangements to fly to Vancouver. The only lawyers not attending were Ward Barton, Deborah Ruxton, and Maria Ross.

"Andrew, I will be on vacation starting Tuesday, so I won't be here when you return," Elisabeth reminded him.

"You have a great time, Elisabeth!" he said. Andrew was in fine spirits and excited about his golf trip.

Just after 10:00 a.m., Elisabeth got a call. "Hi, Elisabeth, this is Eleanor, from Burrard & Company, in Vancouver. I just wanted to let you know that I got the document package and everything is a 'go' for later today. I should have the money to you by 2:00 p.m. Thank you so much for all your help and cooperation," Eleanor gushed, knowing full well the amount of effort that had been required, not to mention the stress!

"That's great!" Elisabeth said. "Please fax me something to confirm the deposit to our trust account as soon as you can. If you have any problems at all, please let me know."

As soon as Elisabeth hung up, she started looking for Ward. He was not in the office yet, so she phoned his house. Much to her amazement, he answered!

"Ward Barton."

"Hi, Ward, this is Elisabeth. I just wanted to be sure that you would be around today to sign the cheques for the closing on the Wilderness Island Resort deal. I should have the money by 2:00 p.m. No other lawyers will be around. Both Deborah and Maria will be here part of the day, but neither of them has signing authority on the trust account. You're it today!" she warned.

"Not a problem. I'm on my way there now."

At noon, no lawyers were left in the office except for Deborah and Maria. Ward had not shown up and Elisabeth was trying not to panic. Most of the staff met for lunch at the Chinese restaurant across the street from the office. Everyone fudged a bit in taking their time coming back to the office.

At two o'clock, there was still no Ward. Elisabeth was in a panic now. She instructed Toby to find him any way she could, even if she had to send someone to search for him. Deborah announced that she was leaving, because she was catching the three o'clock ferry to Vancouver.

Elisabeth sent Maria to all the usual spots that she thought Ward frequented. "He drives a dark blue BMW," Toby told Maria.

Elisabeth nodded, and offered some suggestions. "Try the Oak Bay Marina Pub, or the Snug, or maybe even the Golf Club. Just find him! And if you do find him, bring him back to the office and do not take 'no' for an answer, I don't care how drunk he is, as long as he can sign his name! I'll phone around looking for him too."

The money arrived right on schedule just as Eleanor had promised. Elisabeth hurried to the Accounting Department and made sure that Joan, the bookkeeper, receipted in the funds. She had cheque requisitions all set to go, and left them with Joan too. "I have to get these cheques out of here today. The cheque for Business Development Bank has interest ticking on it, and they want it by four o'clock today," Elisabeth informed her. "I have to deposit Wilderness Holdings Ltd.'s cheque to its bank account."

"Where is Ward to sign the cheques?" Joan asked.

"I don't know. He promised me he would be here. We're running out of time!" Elisabeth said, with a very nervous edge in her voice.

"I'll bring the cheques to you as soon as I've done them," Joan told her.

Elisabeth made her way back to her desk. Toby had every single person in the office out looking for Ward.

At twenty after three, Ward phoned in. He was immediately put through to Elisabeth.

"Where are you, Ward? I need you here now!"

"I'm sorry Elisabeth, I just completely forgot!"

"Well, you have to get here now! I cannot pay out on your transaction until I have someone to sign the cheques!" Elisabeth didn't even try to hide her irritation.

"That's impossible. I'm on the ferry to Vancouver! Just sign the cheques for me. I trust you! Nothing will happen."

Elisabeth could hear Deborah twittering in the background. Elisabeth tensed her jaw muscles and clenched her teeth. "I am not signing your name to any trust cheque! You can forget that!" Elisabeth said curtly into the phone, a few decibels louder than normal. "Your deal can just wait until you can take your responsibility, and if your clients have a problem with that, you can take care of it yourself!"

Hilary could hear Elisabeth—actually, everyone could hear Elisabeth! She never raised her voice, so they paid attention. Hilary, Sandra, and Maria, gathered around Elisabeth's desk. She had a strangle-hold on the phone receiver.

"JUST SIGN THE DAMN CHEQUES, ELISABETH!" Ward yelled into the phone. "It's not your neck on the block! Nothing—believe me—nothing will happen! The money is there! It is owed to our client. What is the problem?" Ward's tone was taunting.

"The problem, Ward, is that I do not have signing authority on the trust account, and I do not think it is right that I should be signing your name to a trust cheque for millions of dollars! That sounds like forgery to me!" Elisabeth shrilled into the phone.

"FOR CHRIST SAKE! JUST SIGN THE DAMN CHEQUES!" Ward was incensed now. "What do you expect me to do? Walk on water? I can't get there! But that doesn't mean we can't close the transaction. Just do it!"

Elisabeth clicked the speaker button on. "Say that one more time, Ward?" Elisabeth emphatically requested.

"Sign the damn cheques, Elisabeth!" Ward heard his voice reverberate through the offices of McDowell Hill.

"Ward, Hilary, Sandra, and Maria are here. They have all heard you tell me to sign the cheques. If anything happens to me, because of your instructions, they will be my witnesses." "Just sign the damn cheques now!" Ward said, and hung up on her.

"What do I do?" Elisabeth asked, as she surveyed the faces of Hilary, Sandra, and Maria.

Hilary spoke quietly. "We've all heard Ward's instructions to you. It's a calculated risk, but the chances of this transaction taking a turn for the worst are slim. I think you sign the cheques and make a note in the file. We will all initial the note, and keep a copy so that, even if someone destroys the original in the file, there will be copies around."

Elisabeth acquiesced. "I don't like it, but I guess I have no alternative."

Within just a few minutes, the cheques were signed and a note made for the file documenting Elisabeth's conversation with Ward that was dated and signed by all.

"Do you need any more help before I go Elisabeth?" Hilary asked.

"No, don't worry. I just have a few loose ends to tidy up on the Wilderness Island Resort file, and I'll be on my way too."

Before Toby left, she called the courier to pick up the cheque for the Business Development Bank.

Elisabeth tidied up her desk, stuffed the envelope with the cheque for Wilderness Holdings Ltd. into her purse, for deposit at the bank, set the office alarm, and locked the doors to the law firm of McDowell Hill carefully behind her. She had taken her car to work that day, even though she only lived two blocks away, but she thought she might need it.

At twenty after five, Elisabeth pulled her car into her parking space and walked slowly up the stairs. Once inside, she tossed her purse on the closet floor and wearily hung up her coat. She poured herself a small glass of sherry, like her mother used to do when she'd had a difficult day. Plunking herself down on the couch and kicking off her shoes, she actually put her feet on the coffee table and clicked on the news. The icon of Canadian news broadcasting, Lloyd Robertson, slowly came into focus. On her old TV, his voice was clear before his image was. Before she could focus on anything he was saying, his comforting familiarity magnified her exhaustion from the hectic week, and she feel soundly asleep.

A couple of hours later Elisabeth woke to a ringing telephone.

"Hello," she answered, in a voice filled with forced cheer, especially since she was not expecting any calls.

"Hi Auntie Elisabeth," the caller said. She searched her memory bank for someone who would call her that.

"This is Mike. I just wanted to touch base with you. I heard you were going to Toronto for Amber's wedding. I can't make it, but I wanted to ask you to say hello to everyone for me."

"Oh, Mike!" she said, "Of course, I will. It's too bad you can't make it to the wedding. I really miss seeing you. How is your sister?"

"She's fine. You'll see her there. She is living in Calgary now. She's got one of those highfalutin' jobs in the oil industry."

Her late cousin would have been so proud of her daughter, she thought; on the other hand, Mike had always been a handful. He was such a lovely, friendly boy, but he just could not seem to stay out of trouble. He always tried to take the easy way, and couldn't say no to anything. The last time she had seen him was when she'd caught a glimpse of him in Dan's office one day. Dan had defended him on a drug-trafficking charge. She was so shocked and disappointed at the time that she couldn't bring herself to say hello to him. Dan got him off though. She didn't know if that was good or bad—good that he did not have to serve any jail time, but bad that he never learned his lesson to stay away from trouble.

"Well, you take care of yourself, Mike. Thanks for phoning."

"I'll be going down East later in the year," he said. "I have a friend in Montreal that I want to visit. He runs a dry-cleaning business on the corner of Peele and Stanley Streets, right downtown. He's been after me for years to visit him!" She sensed that he was exaggerating. He rattled on. "I'll stop off in Toronto to see the happy couple then."

"That sounds good Mike. I'm sure a nice trip like that would do you good ... something nice for you to look forward to," she said. "Thanks again for calling."

"You have a safe trip, Auntie!" Mike said, and hung up the phone.

* * *

Hoping for a peaceful night sleep without worrying about details left unfinished, Elisabeth finished packing her suitcase, even though she wasn't leaving until Saturday. She wanted to be sure she didn't forget anything. She hung the outfit she wanted to wear on the plane on the knob of the closet door, and wandered restlessly around her apartment, puttering here and there and making sure everything was neat and tidy.

She even phoned Yellow Taxi to order a taxi in advance, which would take her to the bus for the six-thirty Saturday morning ferry, and ordered a wake-up call for five thirty, just in case her alarm failed.

Unexpectedly, a wave of nostalgia swept over her. Perhaps Mike's phone call was the trigger. She examined the wedding picture of her mother and father, which she kept on top of the television. They looked so young and happy. She stared into their eyes, trying to see the people that had made her. All she had of her father now was in her eyes. Perhaps that was why she liked the colour blue so much. Her father had always praised her bright blue eyes, because they were so much like his own. He used to say that he could see her soul through her eyes, and when she was 6 years old, she thought that was most profound. In the picture, he looked to be a strapping, handsome man, but her memory of him was that of a thin man with shaking hands too big for his frail arms, and of course, his own piercing blue eyes. He died one day when she was at school. Her mother never recovered from his death, even though she had nursed him every day since his return home after the Second World War. She kissed the picture tenderly. She would always carry her parents in her heart.

She crawled into bed at ten o'clock and clicked on the TV. She didn't think she would be able to sleep, because the excitement about her impending trip was overtaking her nostalgia. Charlton Heston appeared in all his grandeur on the screen. She recognized the picture instantly: The Ten Commandments. Of course, it was almost Easter. Somewhere near the parting of the Red Sea, she dozed off, despite the loud, dramatic music.

Whenever Elisabeth was overtired, under stress, or anxious, she would have the same recurring dream, in which she was searching for her lost love. In her dream, she would scan crowds of faceless strangers looking for his face. Would she recognize him? She'd become frantic when she couldn't find him in the crowd, and she would wake in a breathless panic. The thought of her impending trip to Toronto and the complicated sale of Wilderness Island Resort, had left her stressed and her nerves jangled; so, of course, it was inevitable that the dream would manifest that night of all nights!

Elisabeth jolted awake to the brazen reality of the TV blaring that annoying, crackling, off-air broadcast sound and the test pattern for CHEK TV reflecting off the walls of her bedroom.

That dream was almost as heartbreaking as her reality. Years before, her girlfriends had persuaded her to go on a camping trip to Long Beach. It was 1954. She was 22. The drive from Victoria to Port Alberni took four hours. The drive from Port Alberni to Tofino took six long, slow hours. The dangerous road was a twisted logging road full of dust and potholes etched perilously into the sides of steep mountains falling away to deep jagged canyons. The road was only accessible to public traffic on weekends. When she got to Long Beach, the sight was breathtaking! She had never seen anything like it! She discovered there was a whole world out there waiting for her to explore.

She sat in the sun on the pier in Tofino with her friends, eating a sandwich and just watching life happen, when a fishing boat chugged toward the dock. A young man emerged from the hold and tossed a rope over the bow onto the dock. His muscles tensed as he leaned over the side of the boat to fasten the rope. His thick brown hair was streaked with blond from the sun. After he fastened the rope, he turned and looked up at the pier. He put his hand over his brow to shade his eyes, as he looked toward some of her friends, now fooling boisterously on the pier. His eyes met hers and, for an instant, it seemed like she had known him forever. She looked away, almost frightened by the intensity.

She and her friends made their way back to the beach later in the evening. They laid their tarps on the sand, up against the logs on the beach, and built a fire. As the sun set, the stars appeared one by one in the night sky. A full moon rose over the expansive ocean. It was a perfect night, like a masterpiece of a painting she had never seen before. The tide receded and a brightly lit sandy playground unfolded before them. They chased each other down to the ocean and plunged themselves in the icy water. They screamed and laughed. They splashed and frolicked in the water until their feet were purple and frozen, even though the day had been hot. Headlights appeared on the beach, and they scampered back from the water to their campsite, and cloaked themselves in towels and blankets waiting for the headlights to pass. The car contained other young people with the same thoughts in mind, and they relaxed when the car parked and others jumped out and darted for the water. When they were warm, they too were off for another dip in the ocean under the brilliant moonlight. Suddenly the young man from the dock caught Elisabeth's hand in the froth of the surf.

"I've been looking for you," he said. That night, they walked hand in hand at first, and then arm in arm, the entire length of the beach. They shared stories of their youth and her first most delicate, passionate kiss ever. They dragged their sleeping bags together and fell asleep beside each other, listening to the pounding surf.

As if it were yesterday, a pang of utter sadness pierced her heart as she remembered that time. She and Mark had spent the rest of the week together, exploring and hiking, lost in each other's thoughts and expectations, hopes and dreams. They parted company on the last day of her vacation. He asked for her phone number and address. He told her he would call her as soon as he was in port. It could be Tofino, Port Alberni, or maybe even Sooke.

She remembered the drive home: the scenery from the car window was shadowy; the conversation with her friends stilted and meaningless.

Every time Mark was in port, he called. They would meet and spend their precious time together.

When they were together, the days flew by, but when they were apart, the days seemed endless.

Mark needed to go home. Fishing season was over, he missed his family and Thanksgiving was coming. He stayed overnight at Elisabeth's house. Her mother was filled with trepidation about the relationship, but she stayed quiet.

Elisabeth looked at his sleeping form curled under the quilt on the couch. He was the most beautiful person she had ever seen. She touched his shoulder and his curly hair.

"Mark, it's time to get up, if you want to make the first ferry," she said gently.

He pulled her toward him, and whispered, "I love you Elisabeth."

Her mother slipped into the kitchen and started filling two cereal bowls.

"You don't need to do that, Mom," Elisabeth said softly to her. "I can fix breakfast for Mark, and then I will drive him to the ferry. I'll be back right after that, and maybe we can go to the Dutch Bakery when I get home."

"Thank you, dear, that would be nice." She handed Elisabeth the quart of milk. "I'll be ready when you get back," she said, as she turned away. She did not want Elisabeth to see the tears in her eyes. She passed through the living room where Mark was folding the quilt. She gave him a hug, wished him a safe trip, and turned up the stairs to her room.

At the ferry terminal, Mark kissed Elisabeth goodbye. "I'll be back as soon as soon as the fishing season starts again. Next time I go home, I want you to come with me."

He flung his backpack over his shoulder, and disappeared up the ramp.

* * *

The last time she was in Tofino she was on a retreat with her Church. She was 34. She didn't really want to go. There were still too many memories there, but she felt obliged. It was mid-January. West Coast rain poured from the sky. The fog was a thick heavy blanket. She walked the wharves, looking for his fishing boat, the Pacifica, hoping to make even a thread of a connection. She combed the beach alone in a fierce gale. She looked out across the Pacific Ocean, in its raging thunderous beauty, while the wind whipped up waves that crashed the shore with fury. She found no trace of him. No connection. Nothing.

She did not know for sure if he was alive or dead. She only knew that he never came back for her. Eventually, she had realized that she would never find his face in the crowds of faceless strangers. It was pointless to wonder what her life would have been like if he had found her.

Now she was wide awake. She checked the clock. She got up and buzzed a cup of water in the microwave. She sipped the steaming liquid. She wondered if Toronto would meet her expectations. Her youthful plans of adventuring and travelling the globe had morphed into working, waiting, and caring for her mother. She remembered her mother's illness—how sick she had been for so long, and how her death had come as a relief from her suffering.

Loneliness was at her window again.

CHAPTER SEVEN

The sharp ring of her telephone scared her. Who would phone at 4:00 a.m.? Probably a drunk with the wrong number? She slowly picked up the receiver and whispered a quiet hello.

"Hello Elisabeth? This is Ward from the office. I just had a call from the police. The burglar alarm is going off at the office. They think someone is trying to break in. Since you live so close, could you go over and check it out?"

"What?" she said, in absolute shock. "Me?"

"Yes. You only live two blocks from there. The police will probably be there by the time you get there."

"Me?" She was still incredulous. "You want me to get dressed, walk over there in the dark, at four o'clock in the morning, and search for a burglar? Are you out of your mind? The alarm never works properly anyway."

"Goddamn it, Elisabeth, do you care about the place or not?"

"That is not the point! Of course I care, but what would happen to me if I confronted a burglar or some other weirdo on the street at this time of the night?"

"Well you're wasting so much time now with this stupid conversation that if a burglar were actually there, he'd be gone by now with whatever valuables happen to be there! Just head over there now and make sure nothing is missing. You know the place better than anyone."

"Ward, would you send your mother over there?"

"Jesus Christ, Elisabeth! If I lived closer, I'd go myself. The police just called me to say the alarm was activated. They should be there by now," he repeated tersely. "Just go or maybe you won't have a job come tomorrow morning!"

"Oh really! Well that's just fine, isn't it?"

"What is wrong with you? Why are you such a coward?"

Indeed, why am I such a coward? Elisabeth asked herself and wished she could just tell him exactly what she really thought. She slammed the phone down, pulled on her slacks, which were folded neatly over her dressing-table chair, and struggled into her warmest sweater. She slipped on her winter boots and pulled her winter jacket from the closet. Just before she went out the door, she went back to the bedroom to retrieve her flashlight from her night-table drawer.

Pulling her purse out of the closet in a flustered rush, she glimpsed the corner of an envelope sticking out of the front pocket. Much to her absolute dismay, she was horrified to realize that she had forgotten to take Wilderness Holdings Ltd.'s cheque to the bank! How could she have missed a payout date? How could she? She was instantly plunged into frenzy. Her heart was beating faster that it should have. What was she going to do? Ward would be so mad at her, and she would have to tell Frank and Andrew that she had let the firm down. How could she be so stupid? Perhaps it was true; she really was that stupid! Now, everything Deborah had said about her was true. It was all true! Ward's threat would come true. She wouldn't have a job come

9:00 a.m. How could she afford to live without a job? A panic beyond logic seized her!

Elisabeth grabbed her purse, and in a complete fog, stumbled down the stairs and out onto the street. She ran to the office. She completely forgot about the alleged burglar. The alarm was not ringing. She extracted the key from her purse, and with swift precision, opened the door.

Dim lights from the photocopy machine and the switchboard glowed green in the darkness.

She didn't even look for any burglar. No burglar could do any worse than what Ward was going to do to her when he found out she had missed the payout date.

How would she live? How could she possibly survive? She had relatively little in savings, and virtually no inheritance left. No pension plan. No one would ever hire her again, especially when they found out what she had done, or rather, hadn't done!

She switched on the lights and the blaze from the fluorescents burned off any fog in her brain. She fumbled in the bottom drawer of her filing cabinet, and extracted a file, which she shoved into a shopping bag she kept under her desk.

If the police had been there, she didn't see them. If anything was amiss, she didn't know. She walked straight home. Adrenalin coursed through her veins. She took the stairs two at a time.

By the time Elisabeth got home, she felt like a different person. She felt like a shadow of herself. Her reflection in the bathroom mirror looked like her, even dressed like her, but she did not know this person.

Safe inside her apartment, she brushed her teeth and washed her face. She made her lunch for work and set it on the counter in the same red plastic bag she always used. The clock said 5:30 a.m. She zipped her suitcase and carried it out to her car, started the engine, and sat in the car, letting it idle until she felt the heater blow warm, and then she backed carefully out of her parking spot. She didn't know where she was going or why she was even driving. She drove by her high school, and then by the apartment where she and her mother used to live. She drove by the first shopping mall Victoria ever had, and thought of how many times she had been there. She drove by the new hotel under construction—the one she had just disbursed the second construction draw for—and somehow knew she would never see the inside. Two hours evaporated before she pulled into McDonald's drive-thru, and ordered a coffee and a Sausage McMuffin, which she took to the office to eat at her desk.

She did not feel the least little bit tired or reticent, incapable or incompetent.

She marched into the office as if she owned the place. Nothing was amiss in the office after the burglar alarm had gone off in the middle of the night. It never did work properly. She did not have time for chit chat on Thursday morning. She had work to do. The office was extraordinarily quiet, since all the lawyers were away golfing. At 9:30, she told Toby that she had to go home for a few minutes and that she would be back by 10:30.

On the main floor of the office building, at her dentist's office, she asked a favour of her friend: "May I use your phone to make a personal call. I don't feel comfortable talking about my personal business in my own office, where everyone can hear."

"Of course, Elisabeth," her friend said. "Go into the dentist's office. He isn't here today. I'll close the door for you so you can speak in private."

Elisabeth telephoned the law firm of Stevens and Heinrich in Toronto, and asked to speak to the conveyancing secretary. She was put through to Tammy Allen.

"Tammy, my name is Deborah Ruxton. I'm a lawyer with the firm of McDowell Hill in Victoria, British Columbia. I'm referring one of my clients, Paulette McNeil, to your firm. Our firm had dealings with your firm on a recent transaction, involving the mortgaging of a hotel here in Victoria, so I thought your firm would be perfect to represent my client. Paulette McNeil is anticipating buying a small apartment building in Toronto, with some funds she is receiving from an estate. Miss McNeil would like to retain your firm to act for her in the purchase. She will be in Toronto next week, and would like to come to your office to give you the particulars of her purchase. I would like to make an appointment for her to attend there."

"Certainly," Tammy replied, "I think the best person for her to see would be Mr. Stevens."

"Yes. That would be fine. I will direct deposit the money she is receiving from the estate to your trust account, for you to hold in trust, so that you won't have to worry about certified cheques or the timing of funding for her purchase transaction. Can Ms. McNeil have an appointment for Tuesday? She will give you the particulars of the transaction when she attends, along with a copy of the contract of purchase and sale. I believe she is doing the final negotiations this weekend, and will have a firm contract to deliver to you on Tuesday. The funds will be sufficient, I'm sure, to complete her purchase, and are to be held in your trust account payable at her direction. I will confirm all of this by covering letter."

"Tuesday, April 24th, at 11:00 a.m.," Tammy confirmed.

Bank account particulars were provided, and names, addresses, and telephone numbers were exchanged.

Elisabeth returned to her office.

She switched on her IBM Selectric typewriter that was her faithful friend. She slit open the envelope that contained the cheque for Wilderness Holdings Ltd., and rolled the cheque into the typewriter. Very carefully, like she had done hundreds or maybe even a thousand times before when having to make corrections to legal documents, she positioned the cheque precisely, and lifted off the name of the payee so meticulously that it was never evident. In its place, she typed 'Stevens and Heinrich, In Trust'. She placed the cheque and the old envelope in her purse. She lifted the typewriter ribbon and correction tape out of the typewriter, and replaced them with new ones. She pulled open the bottom drawer of her desk, extracted a tattered old plastic bag, and dropped in the ribbon and correction tape.

For the rest of the day, Elisabeth appeared completely absorbed in her work. She didn't socialize at all, even though the mood of the office was light and carefree without any slave drivers around.

At one thirty, a call came to the office from Mr. Stevens, asking for Deborah. Toby asked if anyone knew anything about the call. Elisabeth said she did, and spoke to Mr. Stevens. She confirmed that Deborah Ruxton had, in fact, called Tammy Allen, but that she had left the office for the rest of the day. Elisabeth confirmed the details of the appointment for Paulette McNeil with Mr. Stevens. She also confirmed that the money would be in Stevens and Heinrich's trust account by Tuesday morning. If anyone at McDowell Hill heard anything, they thought that it was in the ordinary course of business.

Elisabeth left the office at three o'clock to go to the bank to deposit the cheque to the trust account of Stevens and Heinrich — nothing unusual at all.

Near the end of the day, Elisabeth went to Hilary's desk. "Hilary, remember I'm going on vacation? I really want to thank you for all you've done for me ... for being my friend and always helping me. I will never forget your kindness."

It seemed a weird thing for Elisabeth to say, but Hilary didn't think much of it. Perhaps Elisabeth was just nervous about flying, and wanted to say goodbye in case the plane crashed. A bit odd, but she could understand it.

"Have a wonderful time on your vacation. See you when you get back. Now, let's get out of here. It's a long weekend!"

Elisabeth pulled on her coat, and retrieved her purse and the loose change in her top desk drawer. She also took home the extra pair of shoes she had living under her desk.

* * *

When Elisabeth finally became fully aware of her surroundings, she was parked, overlooking the Strait of Juan de Fuca. The Cascade Mountains were glistening in the fading sun. A brisk breeze blew off the water and the whitecaps danced furiously. She felt this strange detachment. She saw a stranger's hand reach into the bag and remove the typewriter ribbon and correction cartridge, open the car door, and then walk around to the front of the car. There wasn't a soul in sight, as she flung both objects into the surf at the foot of the rocks below. She got back into the car, drove down to Clover Point, and sat, by herself, watching the seagulls swoop, glide, and soar. At any other time, she would have been afraid to be there by herself, all alone in her car, but this time she wasn't.

When she returned home, she tidied her apartment to perfection, pulled her suitcase out of the trunk of her car, put her shoes in the closet, methodically washed, dried, and put away her breakfast dishes, and dusted the TV screen.

Curiously, she fished the silver dollar that her father had given her from her jewellery box, and dropped it into her purse like it was her good-luck charm.

* * *

Good Friday was a lost day in Elisabeth's life. She huddled in bed until she needed to eat. Restlessly, she shifted about her apartment raiding the cupboards of junk food; channel-changing on TV; sorting threads by colour for her needlepoint project, although she knew she was leaving it behind; and trying to read, unable to focus or concentrate on anything. Church service was avoided on the pretext of illness, although she knew she would be expected. One moment she felt distracted, then impatient, then exhausted, but, then again, she stayed up very late watching an old episode of Perry Mason. Finally around 2:00 a.m., she switched off the TV and stared in the dark at the ceiling in her bedroom until morning was announced by the dispatcher at the taxi company: "The time is 5:30 a.m., Saturday, April 21st. This is your wakeup call." She was not sure if she had been asleep.

Somehow, she was no longer the least bit excited about the wedding, but she was very anxious to get to Toronto.

She had one medium-size suitcase and a handbag. She pulled the suitcase to the front door, and straightened the mat after she had wheeled the case outside. Then she closed and locked the door. Even though she knew she would never set foot in her apartment again, there was not one ounce of hesitation or trepidation.

The cab driver greeted her and lifted her suitcase into the trunk.

CHAPTER EIGHT

Elisabeth sat silently on the ferry, peering out the window. A yellow haze glowed over the rugged North Shore Mountains, and the Vancouver skyline etched itself against the backdrop.

The airport was alive with commotion. She had no idea how to find her way around, so she found a man in a uniform. "Could you tell me where the Air Canada ticket counter is?"

"Domestic or International?"

"Toronto."

"Down one flight of stairs, turn right, walk a bit, and you'll see it on your left, ma'am."

"Thank you," she mumbled.

Without too much difficulty, she checked through the ticket counter and entered the waiting room for Flight 188A. She was early. She waited impatiently for her travel companions, Paul and Susan, to arrive. The aroma of morning coffee filled the waiting room and tantalized her. She convinced herself that she needed a cup. The waiting room began to fill with passengers, who chattered excitedly.

People of all ages, shapes, and sizes were going to squeeze themselves into the same airplane for a multitude of different reasons, but none of them with a reason like hers. She waved to Paul and Susan as they entered the waiting room.

Anxiety tugged at her as she headed down the tube to board the plane. She thought she would dread the take-off, but anticipation fended off any real fear. She had never been on a plane before. Imagine that, she thought. I've never been on a plane!

Paul slept most of the way.

Susan was non-stop chatter, reminiscing about so many things that ordinarily Elisabeth would have been delighted to talk about. Not to appear rude, she tried to hide her preoccupation. They ate lunch and she savoured a glass of wine that Susan insisted on treating her to. She looked out the window at the vast expanse of Canada and its different geographic regions. She knew they existed, but why hadn't she seen them until now? Susan was a tour guide, pointing out Mt. Baker far above the clouds, the Rocky Mountains, the City of Calgary, the vast prairies, the huge Great Lakes, and finally, the sprawling city of Toronto.

Her anxiousness reappeared during the landing, but once safely on the ground, she felt like a seasoned traveller. They collected their luggage and made for the exit. Paul hailed a cab and gave the driver the address: "132 St. Clair Street."

They arrived to a houseful of exuberant relatives and a banquet of food. She tried to feign interest, but was detached and preoccupied.

After the last dish was washed and dried, Elisabeth bid goodnight to everyone. Before parting for their separate sleeping places, it had been made clear to everyone that, on Sunday mornings, the rule was that the first person up was to plug in the coffee, and in the afternoon, those who were interested were going sightseeing.

Despite the fact that Elisabeth thought she should have trouble sleeping, because a million thoughts kept swirling through her head, once her head hit the pillow, her eyes closed like a kewpie doll. She slept very late, and by the time she got downstairs, all the young people had vanished. After a cup of coffee, she decided to take a solitary walk around the neighbourhood.

CHAPTER NINE

Even though Easter Monday was considered a holiday, Joe and Herb had agreed to meet at the plane at first light.

Herb had the plane fired up by the time Joe hurried down the dock.

Herb was all fired up too, and anxious to go, but not foolish enough to take any chances. He had filed his flight plan with the Comox Air Force Base. Flying on the West Coast in the spring could be difficult and dangerous, especially if there were any strong-wind warnings. Herb was a seasoned pilot, but that didn't mean he couldn't crash. He kept his plane in tip-top shape himself, and the engine hummed like a kitten's purr.

The flight would be about two hours and twenty minutes, and they should be in Victoria easily by nine.

The sky was clear with a light headwind. It was usually a little bumpy between Wilderness Island Resort and the coastline of Vancouver Island, but basically, Herb would follow the coastline of Vancouver Island from Campbell River to Victoria. He could fly across land, but he preferred keeping the land to his right and flying over the ocean. That way, he always knew exactly where he was. He had made the trip many times before.

Pods of orcas on their spring migration were visible in the strait—such a spectacular sight from the air.

The fishing fleet had an opening for herring, and fishing boats dotted the strait.

The coastal mountains still had quite a bit of snow on them, even though it was mid-April.

Herb radioed the float plane base in Victoria Harbour for clearance to land. There was always a lot of activity in the Victoria harbour, with two floatplane terminals, the Coho ferry, the Victoria/Seattle Clipper, and the first brave souls of the boating season out on an Easter weekend excursion. Most of the sailboats in the strait were under full sail, with enough gusting wind to make sailing interesting.

Herb made a perfect pinpoint landing and taxied to the wharf. Joe hopped onto the pontoon and flipped the rope to the dock attendant.

"How long can we stay tied up here?" Joe asked the attendant.

"You should be okay until about noon."

"No problem." Joe hoisted his briefcase onto the dock.

Herb reached into the toolbox in the back of the plane and extracted a heavy-duty wrench. He slid it into the narrow pocket of the pant leg of his work overalls. The weight of it made him look lopsided, but he was never one for appearances.

At the top of the floatplane ramp, Joe went to the payphone and phoned Ward's home.

"Hello," Jackie's tired voice filtered through the receiver.

"Hi Jackie. It's Joe Piquette. Is Ward at home?"

"No, he isn't, Joe. He's down at the boat at the Oak Bay Marina with Todd. He and Todd slept on the boat last night, so they could get an early morning start on giving the boat a good cleaning.

Ward thought it would be a good thing for him and Todd to do, so they could spend some time together. Is there a message?"

"No, no message. Herb and me are just in town and we hoped to be able to see him, to thank him for all the work he did for us, but we'll catch up to him later."

"Okay then," Jackie replied. Joe could hear a child crying in the background and a commotion in the kitchen. It sounded like Jackie was getting breakfast for the kids. He felt sorry for her.

Next, Joe phoned a taxi, and within a few minutes, they were heading for the Oak Bay Marina.

The coffee shop was full of people. You could hardly squeeze into the marina manager's office. Herb managed to catch his eye and asked over someone's head, "Do you know where Ward Barton's boat is?"

"Aisle 3, number 227."

Herb nodded.

Things looked pretty quiet on Ward's boat. Herb stepped aboard and knocked loudly on the cabin door.

A muffled young voice inside said, "Dad, wake up, someone's here. Dad! Dad!"

Ward stumbled to the door and pulled it open. He was clad in the dark blue ski underwear he'd been using as pyjamas. His hair was swirled into a big cowlick at the back. He was obviously not expecting company.

"Holy shit, what are you guys doin' here?" he asked, groggily.

Neither Herb nor Joe had planned to make a scene in front of anyone, but they intended to get what they came for.

Herb looked past Ward. "Hey Todd, would you mind going to the coffee shop and buying three coffees for us. Buy yourself something to eat for breakfast too, if you're hungry." Todd pulled on his jeans, zipped up his fleece jacket, and slipped on the new deck shoes his dad had bought him. Herb shoved a $20 bill in his hand.

"Well, I didn't expect to see you boys here today. What brings you to town?" Ward was quite astonished to see them.

"Ward, we don't have our money yet. It was supposed to be couriered to the company bank account. We expected it on Wednesday, Thursday at the latest, and it isn't there yet." Joe's voice was beginning to strain.

Ward looked confused. He shook his head, winced, and ran his hand through his hair. "I'm sure I signed the cheque and it was couriered to the bank. Maybe it's sitting on someone's desk waiting for deposit. Sometimes the banks get too damn busy, or they get careless. I can certainly follow up with my secretary and the bank as soon as I'm back to work—"

"No, not good enough," Joe snarled through his clenched jaw. "We're not talkin' pennies here, Mr. Barton. This is our money and we've come to collect it, now!"

"But what else can I do?" Ward asked. "The bank is closed today, so there's no way I can verify what happened to the cheque. I'll let you know as soon as I find out."

"Did you not hear Joe?" Herb said. "That's not good enough, Ward, and we think you can do better. You can write us a new cheque. Now. Today! You can always put a stop payment on the other cheque, since it hasn't shown up."

Herb reached down the length of his leg for the large shiny wrench, and flipped it end for end in his hand to make his point.

Ward got Herb's drift right away. "Let me get dressed and take Todd home first."

Ward's BMW was in the marina parking lot. Todd could sense that there was something going on, but the men silently sipped their coffee until Ward pulled up in front of his house to let Todd off.

"I'll be home later. I don't know what time," Ward said, and as soon as Todd had closed the car door, Ward peeled away from the curb.

The offices of McDowell Hill were located on the top four floors of the tallest building in Victoria. The lawyers' offices were impeccably decorated with carpet and rich furnishings. The boardroom had a huge, polished walnut table with twelve matching chairs. The library was perfectly organized, with large, comfortable reading chairs, lamps, and writing tables, with book stands and two photocopiers. Absolutely no clutter lay about on desks or tables. The reception area was bright, with large windows facing the harbour and soft leather furniture. In the far corner was a baby grand piano. Paintings of each of the Prime Ministers of Canada hung on the hallway walls. Two Emily Carr originals graced the walls of Andrew McDowell's office. Frank Hill went for the more conservative but flawless paintings of Robert Bateman.

Ward's office housed a collection of First Nations art that included several Bill Reid pieces, ranging from masks to plaques and even a portion of an original totem pole from the Haida Nation, possibly rescued or pilfered by persons unknown.

All the way to the office, Ward turned over in his mind how he could make this happen. When they got there, he scoured the office trying to find the file. The place was dead quiet. There was no one around to help him.

Herb grabbed him by the arm. "Let's try the bookkeeper's office."

Ward found a ring of keys in the bookkeeper's desk drawer and tried them on the row of fire-proof filing cabinets that lined one wall. By sheer luck, he opened one of the filing cabinets that had accordion folders full of blank cheques, each labelled by bank. He knew the bank where the cheque had been drawn, and he extracted a sheet of cheques, joined together in twos. He could only pray that he had the right account, and that he could fill it in correctly.

"Now, bear with me guys, I'm not very good at this," he half joked. No one laughed.

He wrote out the name of the payee, Wilderness Holdings Ltd. The cheque writer was located on a shelf behind the bookkeeper's desk. Ward wasn't sure how to use it, but he had seen the bookkeeper use it before, so he grabbed a piece of paper from the photocopier bin, and tried to set the figures on the cheque writer and line them up on the paper. After a couple of tries, he figured he had the hang of it.

Ward managed to produce a cheque payable to Wilderness Holdings Ltd., for the amount shown on the Vendor's Statement of Adjustments that Joe had produced from his briefcase. He signed the cheque and gave it to Herb.

"Thank you, Ward," Herb said. "We're sorry it had to come to this."

"Nice doing business with you," Joe said sarcastically.

Ward had to let them out of the building because of the security in place on weekends. Once on the street, Joe and Herb headed for the plane. Ward headed for the bar at the Strath. In ten minutes, he had three double scotches under his belt, but his hands were still shaking. He couldn't understand what had gone wrong. He went to the bathroom and splashed cold water on his face and hair. He ran his fingers through his hair until the cowlick relented and fell into a soft wave. He emerged from the washroom and hesitated for a moment. He thought of Todd and wondered if he had said anything to his mom about what had happened at the boat. For an instant, he thought about going home to try to explain things to Todd, but dismissed the thought. Todd would be okay, but Jackie would be all over him with her incessant questions. He picked a seat at the far end of the bar and ordered a Heineken and a corn-beef sandwich.

A few people wandered in over the lunch hour, but no one he knew. He downed a few more Heinekens.

At last, some excitement. A group of young men and women, who had been practising in the park for a slow-pitch team, ploughed through the door. Their exuberance was catching. Ward sent over two jugs of beer and eventually wandered over to chat. He was beginning to feel a little more relaxed after his morning incident, and after a couple more Heinekens, decided he would be able to work everything out on Tuesday.

Monday turned out to be a cloudless warm day and it had drawn people out of their winter doldrums, although Ward couldn't tell, because he had parked himself on a bar stool in the dingiest corner of the Strathcona Pub for the entire afternoon.

One of the girls on the slow pitch team had definite potential in Ward's eyes. She was slim, tall, and blonde, with a wide smile and perfect teeth.

Dinner hour brought the Strath even more to life, and by eight o'clock the place was rocking. They had live music every night, and this particular night showcased a blues band that really did rock the place. By 10:00 p.m., if you left your chair, you'd never get a place to sit back down.

Jayla kept trying to resist Ward's advances. He wasn't really her type. She thought he was too old for her, and he kept trying to impress her by talking about his boat and his cars and his salary. She wanted to hang with her group, but Ward had a different idea. He wanted her to go for a drive. She didn't want to. She knew he had been drinking for at least as long as she had been there, and while she was young, she was not that foolish.

By the last call, Ward was a sloppy drunk. Two of Jayla's teammates lured Ward out to the back alley. Ward wanted to be 'cool' and impress his new friends, but the boys decided to make sure he wouldn't be bothering Jayla anymore that night.

A couple of quick punches, a hard shove, and a slew-foot later, Ward was face down behind a big blue heavy metal garbage bin.

Much later, when the clean-up crew came on, and the garbage from the Strath was being put out, they found Ward still on the ground. An ambulance took him to General Hospital.

CHAPTER TEN

On Monday, Elisabeth allowed herself to be talked into going to the Hockey Hall of Fame. For years, she had followed hockey, knew every player, and was a die-hard Maple Leafs fan. Now it all seemed so foreign to her. Who were these people? Did they make a difference in the world? She endured the tour while the tour guide's spiel went in one ear and out the other, as her mother used to say. She went through the motions to please her cousin and her husband, but she really wasn't interested.

Elisabeth couldn't wait for Tuesday to arrive, and all the hubbub around the house did not distract her; she just found it irritating. She went upstairs to her room to read the cheap novel she found at the airport. This was better than trying to make small talk with a bunch of people, who now seemed like strangers to her, and in a few short days, would be.

Tuesday morning at breakfast, she announced that she had business in downtown Toronto. While she wanted to take the bus, Margaret insisted that Tom drive her. Elisabeth said that she had no idea how long she would be and that it would not be fair to make Tom wait perhaps all afternoon for her. They settled on

Tom driving her to Eaton's Centre and then she would take a cab back to the house when she was finished.

At the Eaton's Centre, Elisabeth found a hairdressing and makeup salon called 'Sherry's', and asked if anyone was available to do a cut right then. The most unlikely looking hairdresser she had ever seen called her to her station. She wore a bright blue smock and underneath had a very loose, fluorescent green moo-moo-style sleeveless top, with some really tight black pants that showed every bulge she had. She wore thongs on her feet, with fluorescent green toenail polish. Apparently, she had a headache, because she had drunk too much wine the night before. Her cheeks were puffy. Her name was Sherry.

Elisabeth was skeptical about her competence, but she couldn't be choosy. She pulled out a passport and showed the picture of Paulette McNeil to Sherry. She said that she had liked the hairdo and wondered if Sherry could do the same.

"Piece of cake, babe!" Sherry said.

Elisabeth shivered.

Elisabeth looked as chic and cosmopolitan as any woman thirty-pounds overweight can look. She wore her best black business suit, with a dark bottle-green wool coat, black shoes, and matching leather gloves, with a paisley scarf.

Before she set foot in the law firm of Stevens and Heinrich, Elisabeth had transformed into Paulette McNeil.

Once seated in Mr. Steven's office, Paulette showed him her letter of introduction from Deborah Ruxton, and explained in detail: "I was negotiating the purchase of a small apartment building; however, I have decided not to proceed. An inspection of the structure disclosed too many irregularities. Repairs would have to be made to improve the building and there are no long-term tenants. These things, along with some other smaller details, would have made the transaction less than profitable. I would like to have the money you hold in trust for me returned."

Since the money was not held on any undertakings, except to be payable at her direction, Mr. Stevens nodded. "I can have a cheque ready for you by the end of the day."

"Please take your account out of the funds, and courier the cheque to me at 132 St. Clair Street. Because the cheque will be quite large, would you please make the cheque drawn on the same bank that I use. I don't want any problems when it comes to cashing the cheque."

"Yes, I understand. I'll make sure the cheque is properly prepared for your convenience. Miss McNeil, if you ever need any legal services in the future, our firm would be very happy to serve you."

Mr. Stevens and Paulette shook hands when he led her into the firm's foyer. On the street Paulette transformed back into Elisabeth and caught a cab back to Tom and Margaret's house.

The courier delivered the cheque from Stevens and Heinrich right on schedule. The cheque was drawn on the correct bank.

The next day she headed for the bank.

Jordan Levie, a very dull-looking middle-aged man, called her name: "Paulette McNeil?" Paulette rose and followed him to his office.

"I haven't used my account at the bank in Victoria for some time," she explained and produced her bank books, "because I've been working abroad. I came to Toronto to close a real-estate transaction, which failed for a number of reasons, but I'll be receiving a cheque from Stevens and Heinrich—the lawyers across the street—for approximately $14,400,000. I want to make sure that there will be no problems when I get the cheque. Once the cheque is deposited, I would like to have $750,000 placed into my chequing account, $2,000,000 divided into $100,000 increments of GICs, and the balance placed into my savings account. I would also like to reactivate my Visa card. Could you handle that for me? Do you anticipate any problems? If so, you can always contact Mr. Stevens at Stevens and Heinrich."

Mr. Levie looked a bit bewildered, but she thought her impression was due to his over-sized, black-rimmed glasses that sat cockeyed on the bridge of his nose. He asked for identification and inspected her driver's licence and passport.

"I don't believe there will be any problems."

After her visit at the bank, Paulette had lunch at the bakery on the corner near the bank. She bought some biscotti to take back to Tom and Margaret's place. Then she poked in and out of a few shops before catching a cab and arriving back at Tom and Margaret's just in time for tea.

Wednesday evening was quiet at the house. Elisabeth retired early to her room, busily creating—in her mind—the story of Paulette McNeil. She knew that if she was ever going to pull off assuming Paulette's identity, she had to have an iron-clad story, with no room for deviation, which she could relate in a believable way without ever flinching or giving any indication of deception. She had the basics of the story in documentation already: a birth certificate, passport, driver's licence, medical card, income tax returns, and bank books, even the death certificates for Paulette's parents ... anything that Hilary had managed to mine out of Paulette's apartment. She memorized names, places, and dates. What she didn't memorize, she created and wrote in a small black journal.

The next day, Elisabeth, known to Mr. Levie as Paulette McNeil, went to the bank to deliver her cheque.

"I'd like to have all matters completed by next Tuesday, May 1 as that is when I am planning to leave Toronto."

"Certainly," he replied.

* * *

Time dragged by for Elisabeth. Her cousin and her husband took her on Friday to Niagara Falls. The Falls were truly spectacular, and for a few hours, she relaxed.

The wedding would, by any standard, be described as lovely. The reception was very exclusive, and the couple did look very happy, but her thoughts kept drifting away.

The whole family met at ten on Sunday morning for brunch, at the hotel where the reception had been held. She saw herself walk into the small banquet room, take her seat, and look around at everyone gathered there as if in slow motion. This time, she did not say how much she would like them to come visit her in Victoria, or how much she would look forward to their next occasion or family reunion. She did not make any sad goodbyes or promises she knew she would break. At the end of brunch, hugs and kisses went around, but she was emotionally distant.

According to her plan, she was supposed to return to Vancouver on Tuesday, on a one o'clock flight, direct from Toronto to Vancouver. She decided that she would let Tom and Margaret drive her to the airport, and let them think that she had left for home. Once inside the terminal, she located the Air Canada ticket booth and cashed in her ticket to Vancouver.

When she was sure Tom and Margaret were on their way home, she caught a cab back into Toronto to go and see Mr. Levie at the bank to pick up her GICs, updated bank books, re-instated Visa card, and confirm with him, that the deposits had been made to her accounts as instructed. Later in the evening after a bite of supper alone, she caught a cab to a hotel close to the airport, and gave her name at the front desk: Paulette McNeil.

Paulette made one last trip to Victoria on the 5:00 a.m. flight out of Toronto. She arrived in Vancouver, changed planes, and was in Victoria, in front of the bank at the intersection of Fort and Douglas Streets, at exactly 9:30 a.m. on May 7th.

This time and for the last time, she transformed back into Elisabeth. She was singularly focused on what she had to do. As soon as the door was unlocked, she headed straight for the customer service counter.

"Hi Elisabeth!" One of the customer-service representatives greeted her. "I heard you were on vacation."

"Yes," she replied, "I went to Toronto for a wedding. Before I left though, I had a transaction close with a rather large cheque. I need to know if that cheque cleared. Do you have our cancelled cheques ready?"

"Let me look," she replied.

Elisabeth knew they would be ready. The bank was always very good about adhering to its own rules.

Within a couple of minutes, the representative approached with the package in her hand.

Elisabeth casually flipped through the cheques. Fortunately the cheque payable to Stevens and Heinrich, in Trust, was penultimate in the pile.

She looked up and over at one of the other representatives she knew, a young woman who was sitting at her desk nearby. "Hi, Margaret. How are you doing?" she asked, smiling warmly and shifting everyone's focus onto her.

"Good. You changed your hairdo. It looks nice," she replied.

"Thanks." Elisabeth casually ran the fingers of one hand through her new shorter style, careful to keep her other hand firmly on the pile of cancelled cheques. "I needed a change I guess. I love your outfit!"

"Oh this?" The woman looked down at herself and, as the original representative expressed her agreement with its appeal, Elisabeth slipped the cheque into her pocket.

"The colour really brings out your eyes."

"Thanks."

Elisabeth shook her head, and quickly boxed the cheques into a stack—the way you would with a deck of cards—wrapped the statements around the cheques, twisted the rubber band around them, and handed them back.

"I don't see the cheque I'm looking for here," Elisabeth said. "I guess it hasn't cleared yet. I don't want to take the cheques with me. I'll let our bookkeeper pick them up and sign for them like she usually does. Thanks very much."

Out on the sidewalk, Elisabeth transformed into Paulette again, and walked a couple of blocks up the street, just in time to catch the bus to the Schwartz Bay Ferry Terminal. She was aghast at how simple that had been and alarmed at how devious she'd become.

On board the ferry, she sat outside, sheltered from the breeze, and sipped hot tea from a paper cup. When the voyage was well underway and her cup empty, she pulled the cancelled cheque from her pocket and turned it over and over in her hands, then she tore it into a million tiny pieces, went to the side-rail of the ferry, opened her hands carefully, and, as if setting a small bird free, let the tiny pieces of paper flutter away.

* * *

The return trip to Toronto was uneventful. Back at her hotel, she unpacked everything she had and examined the items closely. She decided to leave the outfit she had worn to the wedding in the closet when she left. She figured that she'd never wear it again, and that maybe whoever found it could use it.

In a drugstore near the airport, she purchased a package of Nice and Easy hair dye, two shades darker than her own colour, and a pair of reading glasses with dark brown rims. She decided to wear a wrinkle-proof casual skirt that made her look wider than she actually was, with a white shirt-style blouse and a pair of sensible shoes for her trip to London, England. Inside one of the shoes, she put her lucky silver dollar. She also wrapped a hotel towel around her waist and tucked it inside her skirt to make herself look bulkier than she was. How can I do this? she thought to herself. It's amazing what you can learn from watching too much TV!

She compared herself to Paulette's passport picture. The similarities were quite remarkable. Blue eyes, pale complexion, short ash blonde hair. Elisabeth was one inch shorter than Paulette. Elisabeth was twenty pounds heavier than Paulette, but the picture was four years old, so she didn't think her appearance was that far off. She could have shrunk from approaching old age and a twenty-pound weight gain over three pre-menopausal years was not altogether unusual.

She reviewed the story she had composed about Paulette McNeil's parents and her early life, practised writing her new signature, and finally, without compunction, shredded Elisabeth Nielsen's identification and identity. It was done. She was now and forever, irrevocably, Paulette McNeil.

At 10:30 p.m. she clicked on the TV news to say goodbye to Lloyd Robertson. A mindless movie followed the news and was the best sleeping pill she could have wanted.

On Wednesday, May 9th, she checked out of the hotel, paid cash, and caught the shuttle to the airport. She wandered around the airport shops and bought a bottle of sherry at the duty free liquor store. She had a grilled cheese sandwich for lunch, and checked in to her flight, which was to depart at seven and arrive six hours later in London. Paulette had no idea what she was going to do, but she thought she might find a place near where Elisabeth's pen pal lived, in Maidstone.

'Pen pal', those words seemed so juvenile, but Isabella Barley had been a very important person in Elisabeth's life. They used to share their intimate thoughts with each other, as if there was some security in the unknown, in much the same way that a total stranger tells another total stranger the story of their life while sitting beside them on a bus. For a fleet moment, she thought about the real Paulette McNeil sitting dead on the bus. She wondered if Paulette had ever told a stranger her story. She quickly shook away the thought, reminding herself that Paulette was alive and well and on her way to England.

Elisabeth's pen pal was the daughter of a friend of her father's, whom he had met in the war. Their respective fathers never lost touch and the daughters had started a correspondence when they were 7 years old.

It was puzzling to her now how such a relationship could exist between two people for all those years and yet they had never once met. Sometimes they would go for months without corresponding, and then, at other times, there would be a flurry of letters. It all depended on whether things were going good in their lives or not. She valued Isabella's opinions, because she seemed like such a sensible person. Isabella seemed to have all the things in life that she had wanted: a husband, her own business, two children, a vacation every year to the continent, security, intimacy, and love. The children were grown now, but Isabella used to send their school pictures every year. Isabella would wonder what happened to Elisabeth. Her letters would eventually be returned.

The new Paulette realized that she thought of Elisabeth as a completely different person from herself now—as though Elisabeth had been an old friend who had passed away.

* * *

Once aloft, dinner was served and a movie droned in the background. She tried to finish her cheap novel, but it was far too tedious. By midnight, the plane was quiet, the lights were dimmed, and she drifted off restlessly. About an hour away from

London, she could smell the coffee brewing. People were already coming to life when the captain's voice broke the reverie: "Ladies and gentlemen, we will be landing in London in approximately thirty minutes. The weather is drizzling. The temperature is nine degrees Celsius; fifty degrees Fahrenheit. Time of landing in London will be approximately midnight, May 9th. Thank you for flying Air Canada." The message was repeated in French.

Her nervousness about flying had evaporated. She knew that she would have to clear customs when she landed in London, but she was nonchalant, maybe even confident, that her identification was adequate to protect her new identity.

The customs officer looked briefly at her passport and then at her.

"What is the nature of your visit?"

"I'm here to visit an old friend."

"Your length of stay?"

"One month."

"Have a nice visit, ma'am."

She toted her carry-on bag to the carousel, where her larger suitcase would arrive, waited impatiently to collect it, and then headed out into the main airport. She was overwhelmed with the size and bustle of activity at Heathrow. After reading almost every sign she could find, she boarded a shuttle that made the rounds of several of the hotels near the airport. At the third hotel, she found a small but comfortable room. It was 1:20 a.m. She dropped her luggage inside the door, draped her coat over the back of a chair, and kicked off her not-so-comfortable shoes. Slipping Elisabeth's lucky silver dollar into the inside pocket of her coat, Paulette wearily crawled onto the bed. Within seconds, she fell into a dead sleep.

* * *

She awoke abruptly, and before anything, she needed to eat. A menu on the dresser showed a full English breakfast for four pounds. She showered, dressed, and headed downstairs. She had to wait a few minutes to be seated, unless she wanted to join another table, the hostess offered. She decided to wait. The hotel catered to patrons who just needed a place to sleep and eat. She was reluctant to ask for help. She knew that if she didn't learn to get around on her own, the plan would never work. She collected the bus and tube schedules, a map of London, and some of its suburbs, and a brochure on the highlights of London, and took them all back to her room. Check out was at noon.

Paulette decided she would go to Maidstone. True, it was where Isabella lived, but she didn't intend to ever visit or see her. She knew enough about her habits and haunts to avoid those places. Maidstone was simply a place where she had some connection, which made things easier to cope with somehow.

Maidstone, being only an hour from the airport, was an easy train trip. She wasn't used to the English accent, so she strained to understand the announcements on board. The scenery was lovely. The drizzle had stopped, and the sun emerged from behind some very fluffy clouds.

At a small tea shop on Pudding Lane, she chatted with a friendly, matronly woman who served her tea.

"I'm thinking of staying here for a few months," Paulette ventured. "Do you know of any places available? I don't want to stay in a hotel or anything too large."

"Well, as a matter of fact, there's a flat for rent over one of the shops just around the corner. I saw a sign in the window just a few days ago. I can't say what it's like, but you could check."

"Thank you, I will."

After Paulette drained her teapot and finished her scone, she dragged her suitcase around the corner to find "Melanie's Sweater Shop." Indeed, the sign was still there.

She approached the gentleman behind the counter at the back of the store.

"Excuse me, I understand from your sign that you have a place for rent. Is it still available?"

"Yes, it is," he replied in a thick English accent. He had kind eyes and a jolly smile. He wasn't like what she imagined most Englishmen to be: stoic and pompous.

"May I enquire about the size of the flat and the rent?"

"Well," he replied, "it's small actually; it is just two rooms and a bathroom. There isn't much of a kitchen. No oven or anything, though I suppose you could get a toaster oven."

"Is it possible to see it? I don't need a lot of space."

"Just a second, mum, I'll get the wife. She can show you." He pressed a buzzer on his side of the counter, and a few minutes later a very tall thin woman, with shockingly snow white hair and a smooth ruddy complexion, appeared.

"This lady would like to see the flat, Melanie."

"Yes," Melanie replied. She turned to Paulette. "Come along. Leave your case behind the counter. It'll be safe with Robert.

"Now, you might not find it suitable. You have to go through part of our place to get to the stairs. You would have the whole top floor, which used to be two bedrooms and a bathroom. We converted it to a sitting room with a bit of a counter, a hot plate with a small refrigerator, and a full bedroom. It has all the furniture you need included. The upstairs used to be our children's rooms, but they are grown up and married now, and we don't use the space. No use letting it go to waste."

"I don't need much at the moment," Paulette replied.

"There's no kitchen sink, but you could use a basin for your dishes and empty it in the bathroom. We're quiet people, except when the children come to visit with the grandchildren. They live close, so they don't stay overnight. During the weekdays and Saturdays, we are busy with the shop."

At the top of the stairs, Paulette recalled her carefully rehearsed package of information.

"I need a base to call home for a while. I have business in London, but it is far too busy for me there and an easy commute from here. I thought I would combine my trip with sightseeing and visiting as well. I don't know exactly how long I will be, at least six months though. I prefer to have my own place, rather than stay in a hotel. I may take side trips and be away a few days at a time, but I thought this kind of arrangement would work better for me."

Overall the flat was pleasant, clean, and certainly functional.

"This is perfect," Paulette said.

"Where are you from?" Melanie asked.

"Canada."

"You've come a long way then. I'm supposed to ask you for references. I expect the first and last week's rent in advance. I guess you don't have much to move in except your cases, do you? Oh, and one more thing," Melanie said, "We expect you to keep the place clean. No visitors after ten o'clock."

"Oh, of course. All I have to move in are the cases that are with me. I'll probably do a bit of grocery shopping and exploring the town." Paulette looked directly at Melanie, and shrugged apologetically. "I'm sorry, I don't have any references. I never thought to bring any letters of reference. I can pay three weeks rent right now in cash though. And I will pay every Wednesday after that, in cash as well."

"I think you look pretty reliable, but if there is any trouble, I'll be asking you to leave."

"It's a deal then," Paulette smiled. "I will take the flat starting today, if that is all right with you? Oh, by the way, my name is Paulette McNeil."

"My pleasure to meet you, Miss McNeil. I am Melanie Moore and that was my husband, Robert, you met downstairs."

"Please, call me Paulette. I hope you don't mind if I ask you questions about Maidstone from time to time, to help me get acquainted. Oh, and also, I will need keys."

"Robert will have some keys for you. The shop opens at 10:00 a.m. and we close at 6:00 p.m. Usually, Robert and I take turns during the lunch hour or we eat in the shop. I do have a young lady who comes from time to time, if I need help in the shop. Please be sure to lock the shop door if you are in and out other than business hours. I also keep the door to our flat locked, even during the day."

"Thank you. I can do that. Let me get the rent money for you," Paulette said, as she extracted her wallet from her purse and counted out the foreign money exactly, just as she had practised.

"Robert will be around with the keys after we close."

"Thank you very much, Melanie. I hope I am not too much of a bother."

"You are entitled to make the flat your home, Paulette. I hope you will be comfortable, and please, feel free to call on us if we can help you in any way at all."

Robert insisted on carrying her large suitcase upstairs.

Paulette spent an hour hanging up her clothes, looking in cupboards and drawers, and generally getting used to the place. She made a note of the precise address and then went out to buy a few groceries and find a bank, carefully noting directions.

Maidstone was enchanting, with its lush green lawns and pathways that wound along the river bank. Bright spring flowers bloomed prolifically and the sky was as blue as could be. She could have been in Victoria.

Paulette stopped at a bakery to buy some treats and a loaf of bread. She also bought a toaster and a crockpot, which she thought she couldn't live without.

She was home before 6:00 p.m. Robert gave her a key and she carried her bags upstairs. Melanie was busy in the kitchen. The sun was getting low in the sky by the time Paulette unpacked her groceries. She made herself a sandwich, had a bath, and crawled into bed. She slept soundly until 2:00 a.m., when she woke with a start in what seemed like another world. *How did I get here?*

One voice in her head felt truly justified: "They deserved what they got. I should not have had to put up with Deborah and Ward, or been made to feel inadequate and stupid, or be humiliated and insulted."

Another voice agreed: "I earned every cent of the money I took."

Now, all there was left to do was wait—wait until the police caught up with her ... wait until her conscience caught up with her ... wait until death.

She could face any consequences her actions might generate. If the police ever came, she would go peacefully. She would spend her time in jail, and if she didn't die there, she would be an old, old lady when she was released.

CHAPTER ELEVEN

Ward had a close call with death. By the time he was found and taken to the hospital, he had been unconscious for two or three hours.

"He has suffered a severely fractured skull, along with the resulting concussion," the doctor in charge of the emergency department told Jackie. "We are monitoring for any bleeding in his brain. He is missing a couple of molars. We have put him in a state of induced coma to mitigate any brain swelling. We don't know if he has suffered any long-term brain damage and that won't be evident for some time. He is very lucky to be alive."

On Tuesday morning, no one missed Ward at the office. No one even knew what happened until the papers hit the streets late Tuesday afternoon. Jackie and Ward's parents had been so absorbed in caring for the children, and being in a state of shock themselves, that they had not called Ward's office. These kinds of assaults didn't usually happen in Victoria. Everyone was shocked.

Wednesday morning, Hilary spoke to Jackie on the phone, to get an update on Ward's condition and to ask her if there was anything she or the firm could do. She also told Jackie that she would tell Frank as soon as he returned from Phoenix. In fact, she would call his house and leave a message. They were expected back from Phoenix later that day. Jackie was still too distraught to be logical.

* * *

When Frank finally arrived in the office, he instructed Hilary to go through Ward's files with Deborah so she could pick up Ward's work.

Frank and Andrew roared to the hospital to get first-hand news and see Jackie and Ward's father, Phillip.

On Wednesday afternoon at 4:00 p.m. Frank briefed the staff and assigned secretarial support for the workloads. Calls flooded the office, asking for information on Ward, since the hospital would not allow visitors or give out any details. Frank authorized reception to say, "Ward's condition is guarded. His family is with him, and they ask for your respect and privacy at this difficult time." If the callers asked about work, they were to be referred to Deborah.

Melissa went over to Jackie's and brought the children home with her. Jackie had enough to worry about. Ward's mother and father, Rhonda and Phillip, were numb. All of them were exhausted.

After a week, Ward slowly regained consciousness. He had great difficult speaking. His face was bruised and swollen. Both his eyes were black. His neck, left shoulder, and lower back ached, although there were only soft-tissue injuries. He had no recollection of what happened the day of his assault. He had to be reminded that he had slept on the sailboat with Todd. Anything after that was a complete void. Jackie and Todd reconstructed what had happened that morning, up until Todd was dropped off at the house.

His doctor's prognosis was that it would be a long and difficult rehabilitation.

The police investigation produced nothing. There had been no witnesses. It was unlikely that there would ever be any charges laid, unless some information came forward through TIPS, but that was unlikely.

The patrons at the Strath, who could be identified by the bartender, were interviewed by the police, along with all the staff. No one saw, heard, or knew anything. Most of them did say that Ward had been very drunk though.

Todd thought Joe and Herb had something to do with what happened to his father. He was sure of it. But who could he tell? He didn't want to tell his mother. She would only worry more. He wanted to tell the police, but he wasn't sure if he should. He became sullen, angry, and withdrawn.

Luckily for Ward, he had insurance that paid for all of his treatment and his lost income. Jackie and the children would not suffer financially.

Ward began a rigorous regimen of speech and physiotherapy.

* * *

On May 10th, Joan, the bookkeeper at McDowell Hill, picked up the cancelled cheques and bank statements for the month of April from the bank. McDowell Hill had one general account, one pooled trust account, and a multitude of interest-bearing accounts for various clients.

Joan had been the bookkeeper for at least ten years, and a very competent one. Every month she balanced to the penny. Each year at the annual audit, no discrepancies were ever found. She loved her work. It suited her fastidious nature.

That afternoon, for reasons unknown to her, she had great difficulty balancing the pooled trust account. She double checked her work. She kept being out of balance by $14,400,750. From the statement, it looked like the same cheque had cleared twice. There were two entries on the statement for the same amount: one payable to Wild H Ltd., and one payable to S&H. The bank often abbreviated the names of the payees, but she would know who they were from the cheque stub. She leafed through the cancelled cheques again and again, and then checked them against the cheque book, but there was no cheque stub for S&H. The cancelled cheques were not referenced by number on the statement. She figured she must be doing something wrong. At 4:30, she packed up her desk and thought that she had been staring at too many figures that day to make any sense of them. She would find the error the next day, even if it meant going to the bank to straighten it out. She left the office with a headache.

The next morning, she thought fresh eyes would spot the error right away, but she still could not make any sense out of the trust-account statement. At coffee break, she headed for the bank. McDowell Hill's account manager, Sebastien Sprott, went over the cancelled cheques and the bank statement with Joan. Either the bank had cleared the same cheque twice, or a cheque for the same amount had cleared and was missing.

Sebastien told Joan, "You have all the cancelled cheques. I will call the clearing department to find out if they are out of balance, and I'll let you know."

Joan headed back to the office more confused than when she left. This had never happened before!

She decided to wait until she heard from the bank, hopefully soon, as it was imperative that she balance the trust account as soon as possible.

After a couple of days of worrying, Joan called Sebastien for an update. The bank's response was that they were in balance, and that two items for the same amount had cleared on different days.

"Impossible!" Joan murmured.

Joan tracked down Hilary

"Can you give me a hand? For some reason I can't get the trust account to balance. I'm beginning to think it's me. Maybe I am too old for this job now," Joan offered as an excuse.

Joan went through the entire procedure under Hilary's scrutiny. Joan thought that, if she heard herself explaining the procedure to Hilary, something would click and she would figure out her error. No such luck!

"Joan, that particular transaction was Ward's, and Elisabeth did the documentation. Perhaps they can help," Hilary said. "When I have a minute, I'll check the file and see if I can see anything obvious."

Hilary found the file and she and Joan reviewed it. According to the cheque-book, one cheque had been issued to 'Wilderness Holdings Ltd.' on April 18th. That cheque had cleared the bank on April 24th. The other entry on the bank statement, payable to S & H, had cleared on April 27th, but there was no cheque stub in the cheque book and no cancelled cheque. No cheques were out of sequence. Joan checked the entire cheque book.

"Maybe we should wait until Elisabeth returns. She may have an explanation for it," Hilary suggested to Joan.

On Monday morning, three weeks after Ward's assault, Joan went to Elisabeth's desk and left a note:

'As soon as you are in the office, please come and see me regarding the Wilderness Island Resort file. It is urgent.
Thanks, Joan'

"Hilary, have you heard from Elisabeth? I thought she was supposed to be back from vacation by now," Joan said anxiously.

"No, I haven't heard a word, not even a postcard. I don't know exactly when she's supposed to be back. How long has she been away now?"

"Well, she left the long Easter weekend, and it's now May 15th, so a little over two weeks."

"Wow! That's not like Elisabeth! She's probably never taken more than two days off in a row ever before," Hilary joked.

"Well, I really need to see her to find out what happened on the Wilderness Island Resort file. I still cannot balance the trust account, and the bank says that their records are correct. I'm going to have to alert Andrew and Frank. I can't wait much longer."

Hilary could see that Joan was anxious.

"Well, I suggest you bring this to Frank's attention right away, Joan. You can't leave something like this unresolved for too long. I'm sure there is a reasonable explanation. Don't worry; I'm sure it will work out."

Joan's next stop was Frank's office.

"Frank, do you have a minute to see me?" Joan asked.

"Not unless it's something urgent," Frank was brusque.

"Well, it's not a matter of life and death, but it is very important that I talk to you soon about this matter."

"I'll come and see you as soon as I can," Frank said, putting her off.

The next morning, on his way to work, after he had breakfast with Phillip Barton, Frank reminded himself to see Joan, but as soon as he walked through the front door of McDowell Hill, the investigating officer from Ward's assault was waiting for him, and he had a stack of phone messages, some of them marked 'urgent'. He zoomed past Joan's door without a thought.

On Friday, Joan was not about to be put off again. It was now May 17th and she still had not balanced the trust account from April 30th. She wasn't happy. She had not been able to speak to Elisabeth about the matter, and she was beginning to fret.

She marched into Frank's office and closed the door. She decided to be direct.

"Frank, I have a problem. I cannot balance the trust account. I know it sounds crazy. I have never had this problem before, but I am out of balance by exactly the same amount as the Wilderness Holdings Ltd. cheque that was written. We are out of balance by $14,400,750. I have checked, and rechecked. I've had Hilary look at it. I've checked with the bank, and I just can't figure it out! Maybe I'm too old for this job now and the stress is too much! I just can't figure it out and it has me very worried!"

"What do you mean 'can't balance'?" Frank asked.

"Well from the bank statement, it looks like two cheques for the same amount cleared the bank, but I only have a cancelled cheque for one entry. I thought the bank had cleared the same cheque twice, but they assure me they did not. I went to the bank and checked with them myself. As far as I can see, I don't have any missing cheques. All the cheques are accounted for in the cheque book. I just can't figure it. It must be the bank!" Joan implored.

"How much again?" Frank asked.

"Fourteen million, four hundred thousand, and change."

"On the Wilderness Island Resort file ..." Frank said slowly, as the colour drained from his face.

"Yes," Joan said quietly.

"Shit!" Frank exclaimed as the thoughts of closing day blazed through his mind -- the day he covered Ward's ass by signing up his clients on that very deal!

Frank called Andrew's extension. "Can you come and see me right away?"

As Andrew walked through the doorway, coffee mug in hand, he knew instantly that something was terribly wrong. He closed the door.

"Now let me get this right," Frank looked at Joan, "Andrew, Joan says she cannot balance the trust account. She says she is out the exact amount of the payout to Wilderness Holdings. She says that our trust account is overdrawn by fourteen million dollars. That's right, isn't it Joan? Is that how you would explain it?"

"Yes. I have checked and double checked. I had Hilary look for the error. I went to the bank to check their records. I cannot reconcile the trust account. I just don't know what could have happened. It is like the same cheque cleared twice. At first I thought it was the bank's fault, but when I questioned them, they said its records are correct. They say there were two cheques, but I only have one. I just don't know what to do." Joan was getting a bit shaky.

"Well, I know what to do," Andrew said. "I'm going over to our accountant's office right now. I'll get him to come over and take a look. He can do this on the weekend, when no one else is around. I'll go and see him right now. Joan, will you be available this weekend, if necessary?"

"Yes, of course, Andrew."

"Don't worry. We'll get to the bottom of this," Frank assured her.

At exactly 9:00 a.m. on Saturday, Andrew, Frank, Joan, and Shawn Yee met at the offices of McDowell Hill.

Joan and Shawn went through every entry for the month of April, while Andrew and Frank strategized privately about what to do if, by some unthinkable conundrum, the trust account had been tampered with by someone.

At ten minutes to noon, Shawn confirmed, "From what I have observed of Joan's bookkeeping records, the trust account statement and the calculations I have made, the trust account cannot be reconciled. I think we have a serious problem here."

Shawn still remained slightly optimistic. "I will personally arrange a meeting with your account manager at the bank for Monday. I'll phone you on Monday morning and let you know the time. I'll be in touch."

Andrew and Frank stared silently at each other, trying to make sense of what happened.

Joan startled them. "Is it all right if I go home now?"

Frank, Andrew, and Joan emerged from the building onto the street, engulfed by the first really warm rays of sunshine since winter.

Joan was visibly upset as she said goodbye, and on her way to the bus, bought a large dark-chocolate bar for her trip home.

Frank and Andrew slipped over to the Union Club for a quiet lunch, some private conversation, and some straight-up Irish whiskey.

"I don't want to be pessimistic, but I have a bad feeling about this, Frank," Andrew whispered.

"Let's not panic until we have something to panic about," Frank consoled his friend, in low tones. "Shawn will launch an investigation with the bank on Monday. Maybe we should go to the hospital and see how Ward is; maybe he remembers and can tell us something. It must have something to do with his file. It is just too coincidental! No two cheques for the same amount would clear the bank so close to each other for such an unusual amount."

"You know we have an obligation to inform the partners and the Legal Services Bureau, and the sooner the better," Andrew said.

"I know, but what exactly do we say at this point, Andrew? It just sounds too absurd!" Frank scratched his forehead and rubbed his hair.

Andrew took a long swig of his whiskey. "We just state the facts. Do you think this is just a mistake, or do you think the trust account has actually been tampered with?"

"Who would tamper with the trust account?" Frank muttered. "Really, who?"

"Not Joan. Never. We know it wasn't you or me. Not Hilary or Sandra. None of the support staff. Certainly not Elisabeth. It would had to have been a lawyer. All indications point to Ward, but it doesn't make any sense." Andrew was puzzled. "He has a good income. Mind you, four children and a wife cost a lot. He does have an expensive lifestyle: big house, kids in private school, yacht, trips. Do you think he could be in financial trouble? I've heard rumours that he isn't happy at home and that he drinks and parties too much, but I don't think he would do that!"

"Yes, I've heard that too. But it doesn't make sense. You're not happy in your marriage, you get a divorce; you don't embezzle the trust account. I just can't imagine it." Frank shook his head.

"Well, there is also Deborah," Andrew suggested. "She wasn't too happy with us when we forced her into anger-management counselling. She hates Victoria; maybe she hates us too. Maybe she would like to see the firm destroyed, especially after I made her pay for Elisabeth's care. She was pretty embarrassed and humiliated.

"I know this sounds totally bizarre, but do you think we should have the office surveilled?" he asked. "How long would it take to set up? Could we get it done for Monday or would it have to wait until next weekend? By the end of the week, if this issue isn't resolved, we will have to inform the other partners and the Legal Services Bureau, maybe even the police." Andrew felt his blood pressure rising.

"Jesus Christ, let's hope to hell that Shawn can get to the bottom of this before the situation gets that far." Frank drained the last drop of whiskey from his glass.

"This is what I think our course of action should be, Frank. First of all, we shut down all bookkeeping on Monday. We wait for Shawn to contact the bank and see what progress he can make. We get our hands on the Wilderness Island Resort file, and we get anyone who worked on the file to write down everything they remember about it, because I'd lay odds, this situation has something to do with that file. Both of us must make every effort to be in the office constantly until this matter is resolved. If it isn't resolved by Wednesday, we will have to report the matter to the Legal Services Bureau. They will tell us the next step. I don't want anyone to learn of this problem. I am still hoping no one will ever have to learn about it."

"Maybe I should have Joan stay home on Monday," Frank said. "Ask her to say she's sick. That way, it will not look the least bit suspicious when we close the accounting department."

"Good idea." Andrew nodded.

"I'll go and see her. I don't want her to think that we think she is in any way responsible for this mess. I really don't think she had anything to do with this." Frank always wanted to see the best in everybody. Others would have suspected everyone, but not Frank.

* * *

The following Monday morning, Andrew asked Hilary to get the Wilderness Island Resort file for him. She retrieved it from Joan's office, where they had been studying it, and dropped it on his desk.

Andrew poured himself a cup of strong coffee, closed his office door, and put his telephone on 'do not disturb'. He disassembled the file and read every piece of correspondence from start to finish in chronological order. He was appalled to see the memo from Elisabeth in the file about how Ward had told her to sign the trust-account cheques. He summoned Frank to his office and showed him the memo. It had been signed by Elisabeth, Hilary, Sandra, and Maria, and dated the day of payout.

"Did you know about this Frank?"

"No. Ward was acting like such an asshole the day I signed up his clients. He left Elisabeth hanging, because he didn't show up to review the documents before he had to attend on the clients.

She got me involved, and I started to sign them up. Ward showed up about twenty minutes into the meeting and said he had been delayed in Vancouver. Frankly, I didn't believe him, but I was not about to call him on it in front of his clients. Afterwards, I didn't think it mattered that much, because things had gone so smoothly. I guess he did the same thing to Elisabeth on closing day too; just didn't show up."

"We need to speak to Elisabeth, but I think she's still on vacation. Maybe Hilary knows how things unfolded."

Andrew dialled Hilary's number, and within a few seconds she was seated in front of Andrew.

"Hilary, what can you tell us about the day the Wilderness Island Resort transaction closed?" Andrew slid the memo across his desk into her line of view.

"Well," Hilary started, "the condensed version is that Ward never showed up to sign the payout cheques. We had the whole office searching for him. We phoned all over Victoria looking for him. We even sent someone out looking for him—driving around to places he usually went, like his boat, the yacht club, and the golf club, but we couldn't find him. He had promised Elisabeth that he would be in the office to sign the cheques. All the other partners had left for Phoenix, so there was no one else to sign cheques. I guess Deborah met Ward on the three o'clock ferry to Vancouver, and told him he better call the office, because he called at about twenty after three. He and Elisabeth had a screaming match on the telephone. In the end, he told her to sign the cheques for him and that nothing would happen to her; it would be his neck on the block. It took a lot of convincing from Ward, and Elisabeth was still reluctant to do it, but she did in the end. There was no other way to close the deal, or else it would have had to wait until the following Tuesday, assuming Ward would even bother to show up then either."

Frank clenched his jaw as he and Andrew made eye contact.

"Frank, is this about Joan not being able to balance the trust account?" Hilary asked.

"Yes."

"What will happen now?"

"Well, we are reviewing our options. With Elisabeth still away, we won't be able to get her input until she returns. Ward is out of the question. He is still in the hospital and doesn't remember anything. He remembers seeing Herb and Joe when they signed the deal, but then he doesn't remember anything about the closing. He probably doesn't even remember yesterday. His doctor says he may never remember."

"When is Elisabeth due back?" Andrew asked. "Do we have a phone number where we could reach her?"

"I don't know exactly when Elisabeth is due back," Hilary said. "She went to Toronto for a wedding. She didn't leave a contact number with me and I don't even know the last name of the cousin that she was staying with. I'll ask around and see if anyone else knows."

"Hilary, not a word about this to anyone, please," Andrew admonished and begged at the same time.

"Yes, of course, Andrew. If there is anything I can do to help, please let me know. I'm sure there is a logical explanation."

Shawn Yee's appointment with the manager of the bank was for 11:00 am. McDowell Hill's account manager, Sebastien Sprott, was also there, as were Andrew and Frank. Shawn went through a detailed explanation, and his proposal to resolve the matter, which was for the bank to reverse the cheque they had obviously posted and deducted from the trust account twice. Sebastien phoned the manager of the clearing department in Vancouver, who was aware of the matter because of Joan's earlier query. The manager of the clearing department was adamant that he would not be reversing the second entry. He insisted there had been two cheques. He said that the clerks were also certain. There would be no reversing the entry. Sebastien, not wanting to anger one of his best customers, went above the manager of the clearing department in Vancouver to the national level in Montreal. He spoke to Doug Carter, who asked for information in writing and indicated that he would review the matter and respond as soon as he could.

Back at the offices of McDowell Hill, Andrew, still the captain of his ship, finally acknowledged reality. "Time is running out, Frank. We are going to have to go to the Legal Services Bureau. None of us can cover fourteen million dollars. This is not going to go away. We may lose the firm," he said, as he started vacantly out the window with an almost audible quiver in his voice.

Frank wanted to buy more time. Frank wanted to wait just one more day, until they heard from Doug Carter.

Andrew acquiesced.

On Wednesday, May 22nd, at precisely 9:40 a.m., Sebastien Sprott phoned Andrew.

"I'm sorry Andrew. The national clearing centre has refused the request to have the entry reversed. They are adamant that there were two cheques, even if they can't produce one of them. I have no alternative but to freeze your account until I hear from the Legal Services Bureau," Sebastien said with authority.

"Well that's it then, Frank." Andrew felt like the sands of time were shifting under his feet. "We have to call a meeting of the partners tonight at my house. Everyone must attend."

Frank felt a fire burning inside him.

Early that evening, cars started arriving at 1047 Beach Drive, an elegant ocean front estate, just a short stroll from the Victoria Golf Club. The wrought-iron gates were open. The lights were on. The light of a full moon skipped across the dark waters of Ross Bay. Andrew and Lenore employed a young man who did their gardening, attended to their cars, and maintained their property. He directed each car to its parking place and escorted each partner, whom he greeted by name, to the front door.

Inside, Andrew waited in the large formal living room, which was adorned with bronze sculptures and rich tapestries. Every partner was there, including Ward, who was accompanied by his father, and Shawn Yee, the firm's accountant.

No drinks were offered. No preliminary socializing graced the occasion. Andrew and Frank were grim. Ward and his father were somber. Once every one was seated, Andrew closed the elegant, scrolled French doors and turned to meet everyone's gaze.

"Gentlemen, once you have heard what I am about to say, I believe you will all concur that the reign of the law firm of McDowell Hill will be over.

"On May 17th, Joan, our bookkeeper, brought to my attention that she was unable to balance the trust account. There is a deficit of approximately fourteen million dollars. Our accountant, Shawn Yee, has done an audit of our books, and cannot locate the error. The bank was approached and they have searched their records and cannot find a discrepancy in their records that would account for this. Tomorrow morning, at 9:00 am, I will be contacting the Legal Services Bureau to advise them, and the firm will follow its direction."

Andrew gripped the back of an exquisite antique French provincial chair, which matched a small writing table nearby, and a visible shudder rippled through his body.

He began again. "Gentlemen, I am sure we will have many questions coursing through our minds over the next few days, about how this might have happened, but I am sure we will have opportunities to ask them after the Legal Services Bureau has made its review and recommendations."

Frank rose to his feet. Suddenly his face looked older than his years. "I don't think it will take long for word of the demise of McDowell Hill to hit the streets, but Andrew and I would appreciate everyone using the utmost discretion in discussing matters. I am certain a police investigation will follow."

One of the partners interrupted the silence. "I suggest that until the Legal Services Bureau has reviewed the situation, and made its recommendations, that we carry on as usual. What else can we do?"

"How long will it take for the Legal Services Bureau to act?" Alan asked.

"I just don't know," Andrew stated. "I will call the Legal Services Bureau myself tomorrow. I feel it is my responsibility. I will let all of you know, after I have spoken to them, what the procedure will be."

Frank nodded.

For a few minutes, the room fell silent as the partners realized that there was nothing they could do or say to make this situation go away, and each of them were trying to untangle their scrambled thoughts.

One by one, each got up and shook hands with Andrew and then Frank. Those who had not seen Ward since his hospital stay gave their regards to Ward and his father, and trudged toward the door.

* * *

The very next morning, the imperially slim Andrew McDowell, dressed in his dark navy suit, tailored white shirt, and tri-coloured tie, lifted the receiver and dialled the number of the Legal Services Bureau of British Columbia.

"Claims Department Manager, please," Andrew said.

"Clark Walton here."

"Mr. Walton, my name is Andrew McDowell of the firm of McDowell Hill, in Victoria. I must report a sensitive matter to you involving a large sum of money missing from our trust account."

"Are you familiar with our reporting procedures, Andrew," Clark's voice filtered through the receiver.

"No," Andrew answered simply.

"How much is missing, sir?"

"Approximately fourteen million dollars."

Clark raised his eyebrows. "I can fax you a form to fill in to start the process."

"No," Andrew said without hesitation. "I would prefer it if you sent someone to meet with me and the partners of our firm as soon as possible."

Clark was trying to find the listing of the law firm in his directory, to read the description of the firm of McDowell Hill before making any commitments.

"One moment, please Andrew. I am going to put you on hold."

Andrew wasn't used to being put on hold by anyone, but he figured he'd have a few new experiences ahead of him. He tried to remain calm and philosophical.

After a few long moments, Clark came back on the line. "Since this is an urgent matter, I can fly over on the one o'clock plane this afternoon and meet with you."

"Thank you, Clark. I will meet you at the plane."

"Yes, thank you."

Andrew could pick out Clark well before he arrived in the waiting room of the floatplane terminal. He was a slim, short, middle-aged man, dressed in a dark suit with a very large briefcase. He walked gingerly up the dock toward the terminal. He seemed unsure of his footing on the dock.

Andrew, forever bent on formality, approached him. "Clark Walton?"

"Yes. Andrew McDowell?" Clark extended his hand and Andrew grasped it firmly and sincerely.

"I hope you don't mind a short walk. Have you had lunch?" Andrew asked.

"I wouldn't call it lunch. I grabbed a muffin and a coffee for the plane," Clark revealed as they walked toward the Empress Hotel. Andrew offered a decent lunch, but Clark declined.

In a private meeting room, on a subterranean level of the Empress Hotel, Andrew, Frank, and the other partners of the firm of McDowell Hill, poured out what they knew of the fiasco to Clark Walton, in the desperate hope that he could do something to save the firm.

"Gentlemen," Clark said, "I see no alternative. On Friday you will issue every employee a layoff notice effective immediately. As of 5:00 p.m. tomorrow, all of the assets of the law firm of McDowell Hill will be managed by the Legal Services Bureau. Anyone who has money in trust will be notified. The firm of McDowell Hill will cease operation until a full investigation has been completed."

Clark continued. "Representatives from the Legal Services Bureau will be here Monday morning to work with all of you. From here, I will go to the police and alert their White Collar Crime Division. They will want to meet with each of you, including your employees."

Dan Moody asked Clark, "What happens now? I have court dates, trials, and clients, some of whom are in custody, or are on their way to trial or jail. I can't re-assign these matters on such short notice. Are we, as lawyers, allowed to set up practise again, and if so, when?"

"Good question, Dan. This will get complicated. At the moment, and subject to the written instructions of the Legal Services Bureau, since no lawyer of the firm has been identified as being responsible for the missing funds, I believe the Legal Services Bureau will allow each of you to resume practise on an individual basis, upon certain conditions to be set out by the Legal Services Bureau.

"Those conditions usually include such things as monthly reporting by each lawyer, to be scrutinized in detail by the Legal Services Bureau. All lawyers must remain in British Columbia, unless the Legal Services Bureau consents to a lawyer travelling outside this jurisdiction. As well, each lawyer of the firm must consent to an investigation of his or her personal finances and any companies in which he or she may have an interest. Much will depend upon the results of the investigations by the Legal Services Bureau and the police.

"Further, if the perpetrator is found, legal action will be taken against such individual that may result in disbarment and imprisonment. In that event, those lawyers not responsible for the disappearance of funds would then be allowed to return to practise unimpeded.

"Over the next few months, the Legal Services Bureau will collect McDowell Hill's accounts receivable, liquidate any assets of the firm, including funds held for future development of the firm, and moneys in any general accounts of the firm, and apply those to the outstanding balance of the trust account. Any shortfall will be made by a claim against the Legal Services Bureau insurance coverage, paid for by each member. This can be a lengthy process. Please keep in mind that this is a very brief synopsis of what will happen. There are many more details that will need to be worked out, such as how unbilled work in progress will be treated, among other things.

"The Legal Services Bureau will need a complete list of the names, addresses, and telephone numbers of each lawyer, associate, and employee of the firm.

"Since all active files are to be turned over to the Legal Services Bureau for assignment to a Trustee, appointed for the law firm of McDowell Hill, I would ask each of you to work closely with the representatives from the Legal Services Bureau who will be here on Monday."

The building that housed the firm of McDowell Hill was owned by a holding company comprised of the partners. Dan Moody was quick to say that he would continue to occupy his premises; he and Jason would operate as sole practitioners, and he would retain his support staff as his personal employees. He would put up a new sign, and it would be business as usual as soon as the Legal Services Bureau would permit.

Andrew and Frank wanted to occupy a portion of the existing premises too, and set up their own practises. Elisabeth, Hilary, Sandra, and Joan were claimed as their support staff. They also wanted to make arrangements for two of the junior lawyers to join them.

Ward was too weak and tired to think about what was going to happen to him. He was having trouble understanding the complications and implications. He even had difficulty following the conversation. Phillip was very anxious.

Friday was going to be one of the most difficult days of Andrew's life. He had to give up his dream, and not only that, he wanted the responsibility of telling his staff. Friday would be a very black day.

CHAPTER TWELVE

All of the partners were at the office by eight o'clock and huddled in the boardroom. Everybody had cleared their calendars and the office was unusually quiet. When Hilary came in, Frank asked her to order lunch for everyone, as there was going to be a meeting in the early afternoon.

Frank also instructed, "Toby, all lawyers have cancelled their appointments today. Please put the switchboard on answering service at noon, and to do a memo to the staff that everyone must attend a lunch and full staff meeting starting at noon."

The tone of the office was anything but jubilant. The partners looked secretive and the staff perplexed. Joan and Hilary both sensed the uneasiness but did not betray their oaths of silence. They were very worried.

"Joan, have you heard anything from Elisabeth?" Hilary asked.

"No. I expected her back weeks ago."

"How long has she been gone?" Hilary asked, but then answered her own question. "I know she left Easter weekend. That was five weeks ago! I know she has a lot of banked overtime and holiday leave, but she has never been away that long before.

I'm getting concerned. I'm going to see if I can track her down. Do you have a phone number for her in Toronto?"

"No. I tried to remember the name of her cousin that she went to see, but the only names I can remember are Paul and Susan. Paul lives in Vancouver and I think Susan lives in the States somewhere."

"I don't think either of them has the same last name as Elisabeth."

"I'm going to phone her at home again," Hilary declared.

She dialled Elisabeth's number. The phone rang and rang. No answer. Hilary asked the operator to check the number. The operator said that the phone appeared to be working; there was just no answer.

An hour before lunch, Hilary took a quick walk over to Elisabeth's apartment. She knocked on the door. No answer. At the foot of the stairs, near the entrance to the rose garden, Hilary saw Dick working in one of the flower beds.

"Dick, Hi! I'm Hilary. I work with Elisabeth. Do you know if she is home from her vacation yet?"

"I haven't seen her. Her car is still in the parking lot, and I don't think it's moved lately."

Hilary was more than a bit concerned. This was not at all like Elisabeth. First of all, she never took more than a few days' vacation at a time, and even then she would phone a couple of times to check in.

Hilary went to check out her car. She peered in the windows, but didn't see anything inside. Nothing looked unusual.

Hilary slipped across the street to St. Andrews Church. She went in the office entrance. A volunteer was shelving books in the library. Hilary asked the woman if she knew Elisabeth.

"Of course, everyone knows Elisabeth. She's such a wonderful person."

"Do you know if Elisabeth has been at Church the last couple of weeks?"

"I'm not sure," the volunteer said.

The minister overheard Hilary's question and came out of his office.

"Hello, are you asking about Elisabeth Nielsen? I know for certain that she's not been at Church, as she usually collects the hymnals and programs from the pews after the service, and I've really missed her help."

She shook his outstretched hand. "I'm Hilary Britt. I work with Elisabeth. If you see her, would you ask her to call her office or call me at home? The matter is quite urgent."

Hilary hurried back to the office and slipped into the boardroom to have a bite of lunch before the meeting. She wanted to talk to Andrew and Frank about Elisabeth. She was really beginning to worry about her and about what was going to happen.

The mood in the office perked up over lunch. The atmosphere was relaxed for a few moments, as staff speculated about the nature of the meeting: Work was still pouring in; perhaps another lawyer would be joining the firm, or another high-profile client had retained the services of McDowell Hill.

Andrew was always impeccably dressed. In his youth, his hair had been raven black. Now there were more than a few silver strands. He had few lines in his face for a man his age. He was slim, athletic, and confident. When he entered the room, the staff immediately diverted their attention to him, as they usually did; however, every single person in the room had to wonder what had happened to change his appearance almost overnight. His shoulders were stooped. His hair seemed almost white. His bucolic complexion was pallid. His eyes were not the sparkling green they usually were. He looked tired and sad. Staff suddenly feared the worst.

"Ladies and gentlemen," Andrew began, "I am especially grateful to each one of you for your devotion, dedication, and hard work. Without each of you, I would not have been able to enjoy the many things in life that I have been blessed with, and it grieves me to tell you what I have to say today.

"The doors of McDowell Hill are closing today at three o'clock. The firm will not reopen. Each employee will be given a record of employment, a letter of reference, and a cheque for three months' pay. Many of you are entitled to more; however, the firm is now under management by the Legal Services Bureau of British Columbia. Any claim you may have for your full severance entitlement will be adjudicated by the Legal Services Bureau. This is merely an interim measure. Thank you for each and every moment of service and dedication. I am proud to know all of you."

He paused for a solemn moment, and then continued. "I think you deserve to know why this has come to pass—especially because in the weeks and perhaps months to follow there will be a police investigation. Our trust account could not be balanced at the end of April, and we have been unable to determine whether it is an error or if the trust account has been tampered with by persons unknown.

"The firm's files and records will be relinquished to the Legal Services Bureau. I ask that you give the representatives of the Legal Services Bureau and the police, who will now be investigating this matter, your full cooperation."

"YOU GUYS ARE A BUNCH OF FUCKING IDIOTS!" Deborah screamed and hurled her glass as hard as she could against the wall, where it bounced onto the table and then smashed into shards on the floor. She headed for the door.

Frank stepped into her path to block her exit.

"Shut the fuck up!" he breathed into her face, his voice just slightly above a whisper. Alan grabbed her by the shoulders and headed her for the closest chair.

Andrew's eyes welled with tears.

It was Frank's turn to speak. "This has been a very difficult decision for all the partners. We are still hopeful that an audit will determine the missing money is from an error and not the result of tampering or embezzlement. We will be holding a meeting of partners and interested parties weekly, and I extend an invitation to each of you to attend. I suggest that everyone clean personal items out of desks. Staff must be out of the building by three today, as the Legal Services Bureau will come in after that to confiscate our records. If anyone has any questions or information, or wishes to talk about any aspect of these unfortunate circumstances, please call me."

No one could believe what they had heard. The silence as each contemplated the new reality was haunting. Frank and Andrew retreated to Andrew's office. Alan locked the front doors of McDowell Hill. Toby was instructed to put a new message on the answering machine:

'To reach any lawyer from the firm of McDowell Hill, please contact Clark Walton at the Legal Services Bureau of British Columbia at 604 478 9531.'

Frank came to Hilary's desk and asked her to come into Andrew's office.

"Hilary, the plan at the moment is for Andrew and me to carry on business on a reduced scale. We feel we have an obligation to our clients, and we don't want to leave them in the lurch. Two junior lawyers, hopefully, will join us. We would like you to continue your employment with us. We don't know how long this will be, and a lot depends on the result of the investigation by the Legal Services Bureau and the police. We'll have to work closely with the Legal Services Bureau and we need you. Are you with us?"

Without hesitation, Hilary replied, "Yes, of course, don't worry about the details. I'll be here Monday morning or whenever the

Legal Services Bureau allows. I still can't believe all this. There must be some explanation." She shook her head, trying to make sense of it all.

"As soon as we can, we will need to set up an absolutely fresh bookkeeping system for each lawyer. We will need new letterhead, a new phone system, and whatever else we need to get up and running."

"Yes, Frank. I'll figure out everything we need and we can start attending to these things as soon as we can. You know, I am beginning to really worry about Elisabeth. No one has heard a word from her and it's been at least five weeks. None of us remember the name of her cousin in Toronto. She was supposed to stay with her. I went around to her apartment earlier today. No one is there. Her car is still in the car park. It doesn't look like it's moved. Dick, her apartment manager, said he hasn't seen her. I'm getting really worried." Hilary nervously spun her wedding ring around her finger.

"Let's not worry about her for a few days yet. I'll try calling her on the weekend or maybe I'll get Melissa to call her. Maybe we'll see her at Church on Sunday. Don't worry yet."

"Oh yes, I called at the Church too and the minister said that she definitely has not been at Church, because he'd missed her."

"Well, let's wait a bit. We have enough other things to worry about."

Under the organizational skills of one of the junior partners, several people were wandering over to the Irish Times, to drown their shock in some Guinness and blarney. Hilary wanted to join them. Joan declined. She didn't want to be questioned about the details, and Clark Walton had made it clear that no one was to discuss the matter, except with the police.

At 4:30, Clark Walton, two movers, Shawn Yee, Andrew, Frank, and Joan, who had been asked to stay behind, started packing the accounting records of McDowell Hill into boxes for a move to a small office on Yates Street, where Clark had arranged for the audit team of the Legal Services Bureau and the police to begin work.

Joan was the first person to be questioned by the lead investigator. She was helpful and cooperative and answered every question. Her meticulous records were easy to follow, clear, concise, and accurate, except for the one entry that led to the downfall of McDowell Hill.

The audit team continued to question each lawyer and every staff member from the firm. Ward posed a special problem. While he was making progress with his speech, his memory of the events since the day of his assault was not improving.

Two officers from the audit team, Eric McDonald and Barbara Smith, accompanied by another member, left on Friday by police boat from Campbell River for Wilderness Island Resort, to interview Herb.

Herb and his wife, Anita, had stayed at Wilderness Island Resort to care take the marina, cabins, and store. There was a lot to do with summer approaching.

According to Herb, Joe Piquette and his wife, Lise, had already bought a piece of property on a small island just south of Morseby Island—very rugged and undeveloped. They were working with a property developer from Vancouver and the local Indian band office to come up with a plan. They were living on their boat and going to Sandspit for supplies as needed.

"What can you tell me about the Wilderness Island Resort sale transaction, Herb?" Eric asked. Barbara recorded Herb's answers.

"Well, everything seemed to go smoothly until the payout. We were promised that our cheque would be deposited to the company bank account either late Wednesday afternoon or the Thursday before Easter. I checked our account late Thursday afternoon and there was no deposit. Joe and I were pissed. That's a lot of money. We flew down on Monday and caught up with

Ward. We told Ward that we didn't get our money and that we wanted the cheque replaced. He had some story about how the bank might not have processed it, and how he couldn't check on it. We told him that was bull. We made him write us a replacement cheque right then and there. That's all we wanted. We told him he could put a stop payment on the one he originally issued. It never did show up."

"Do you have your bank statement for the month of April for Wilderness Holdings Ltd.?"

"Yeah, probably," Herb answered. "Anita does the bookkeeping. She probably has it filed already."

"May I see it?"

Anita retrieved it and Eric and Barbara scrutinized it.

"I'd like a copy for our records," Barbara asked.

Anita hurried away to wrestle with the ancient photocopier, and then produced the copy in an envelope for Barbara.

Herb said that he would try to get a message to Joe to call either Eric or Clark at his first opportunity. The investigating team decided that further corroboration of Herb's information by Joe could wait for a while.

Meanwhile, other members of the team worked on tracing the cheques that had cleared the bank in April, and questioned staff members at the branch, the clearing centre and head office; not only that, all lawyers and staff of McDowell Hill were subjected to intense scrutiny.

On Barbara's return to the Yates Street office, she began cataloguing the records of McDowell Hill. She opened a box that contained the folders of blank cheques. In one of the bank folder, she found a sheet with a missing cheque.

She noted the number and searched for the bank statement that Joan had failed to balance. She shuffled through the cancelled cheques until she found the one that had cleared. The number was the same as the one that was missing from the sheet. This was the cheque that Ward had written and signed!

The cheque stub in the cheque book that was written to Wilderness Holdings Ltd. was the one that Ward had told Elisabeth to sign—the one Ward was supposed to put a stop-payment on.

Barbara called Eric. Now they had proof there were two cheques that cleared the account.

Eric called Andrew, "Hello Andrew, this is Eric McDonald from the audit team. We are making headway. We can confirm that there were two cheques and both cleared within days of each other."

Andrew was puzzled, "How did this happen?"

"It would be easier to show you than explain it to you on the phone. I'm at the Yates Street office now if you want to come down."

"Yes, thanks, I'll be there shortly."

Andrew called Frank and Joan and they excitedly slipped out of the office onto View Street for the short walk to Yates Street. In a way, this was good news, but there was trepidation in their steps.

Barbara showed them the missing page from the blank cheques.

Joan couldn't understand how she could have missed the cheque number. "I was so intent on trying to make the trust account balance that I thought the cheque from the cheque book was the one that cleared. It never occurred to me to look anywhere else for a different cheque, certainly not in the blank cheques. I'm sure I didn't write the cheque that came from the missing page or I would have remembered. It had to be someone who had access to those cheques."

"Actually, it was Ward who wrote the cheque. He wrote it as a replacement for the cheque that Wilderness Holdings Ltd. didn't receive," Eric explained.

"Ward?" Joan said with doubt. "Ward has never written a cheque in his life! People do that for him!"

Eric explained about his conversation with Herb and how Herb said it had happened.

"Well, what happened to the cheque from the chequebook, the one that Elisabeth signed for Ward?" Andrew asked.

"That is the question, Andrew. That is the cheque that's missing. If we find out what happened to that cheque, we'll have the puzzle solved. I think our next step is to have a serious conversation with Ward."

Joan asked, "How is it that, on the statement, the cheque that Ward wrote says the payee is Wild H Ltd., while the first one that I wrote shows as S & H, I know I wrote that cheque to Wilderness Holdings Ltd. That is how I recorded it on the cheque stub. Who is S & H?"

"No one has been able to figure that out," said Shawn. "As you know, the cancelled cheque can't be found."

"We have another member of our team checking the bank records of Wilderness Holdings Ltd., to make sure that they did not negotiate both cheques. They could have cashed one and sent the other someplace else," Eric confirmed.

Barbara made a note to trace the money from the time it cleared until they could find the proceeds. The trail should lead them to the person or persons who ultimately ended up with the money. This could be a long and tedious process.

Andrew and Frank had growing concerns and suspicions about Ward's involvement. Later that evening, in the privacy of Frank's home, Andrew and Frank decided that the police should be the first to question Ward. They felt bad, because Ward appeared so fragile since his assault, but they were angry with him for his conduct. They felt sorry for his father, who had unfailing confidence in Ward and defended him at every turn of events. It would be a bitter day if it turned out that Ward had the missing money. Friendships would end. This was a matter better left to the police.

Ward swore to God that he could not remember writing the second cheque. Eric showed him a photocopy of the second cheque stub, and he admitted that it was his handwriting.

Eric wanted to choke Ward a little tighter. He thought he could squeeze more out of him, but Ward's doctor had forbidden it, along with hypnotizing Ward. The doctor said that if Ward was ever going to remember anything, it was going to be by healing, and the only thing he needed now was time to heal.

The investigative team scrutinized Ward's bank accounts and investments, and even Jackie's; then they went after his boat. They got an order to pull it out of the water and an investigative team went over the vessel inch by inch with Ward and Phillip in attendance.

Ward was confused, lost, and scared. Over the next couple of weeks, sometimes he seemed to make good progress, and then he would seem to lapse. Jackie fought to keep her family together and give Ward the space he needed for his recovery. She tried desperately to connect with him, to show him affection and caring, but he seemed so distant and indifferent.

Phillip took him to a criminal lawyer in Vancouver. Phillip knew Ward was the police's prime suspect, given his conduct and implication in the events that led to the missing funds. They flew over on the floatplane, and were at the offices of one of Vancouver's best criminal lawyers promptly at ten.

Phillip did most of the talking. Ward sat uncomfortably. Sometimes he seemed to have difficulty following the conversation. He answered questions as best he could, but he had so many memory gaps, the lawyer at first doubted his sincerity. Ward was twitchy and distracted. He didn't seem to have the ability to concentrate. He was now painfully thin and his expensive clothes hung on him like those of a scarecrow. William Dean, Bill to his friends, colleagues, and some clients, invited them to lunch at the Terminal Club and they taxied from his office. Bill watched Ward carefully to get a sense of who he was. He began to think Ward wasn't faking. He seemed disoriented and his balance was unsteady. Phillip looked strained and desperate.

After lunch, they returned to Bill's office. Bill explained, "I'll get the police reports and study them, then I'll contact the Legal Services Bureau, but on the face of it, since Ward has not been formally charged, I think there is probably insufficient evidence. Any evidence so far is circumstantial.

"Don't worry. Ward, I want you to concentrate on your recovery. I don't want either of you to talk to anyone about anything, not even the police, without me being present," Bill advised. "Try to keep a low profile."

Ward knew that it was very hard to work on recovery in a home with four kids—two sets of twins—especially when Jackie insisted he participate in childcare and chores. He had always managed to escape these things by saying he had to work, but if he stayed home, she didn't allow him any excuses. She expected him to pull his weight, sick or not, recovering or not.

He fretted about his own recovery. He was getting frustrated, because he could not gauge his own improvement. He had not had a drink since the night of his assault. He really wanted to escape to the bar and feel the warmth of a good glass of scotch in his belly. He wondered if he just wanted to escape from Jackie. One minute she was all over him trying to nurse him. The next minute she was nagging him to help. He felt himself pulling away from her.

He wanted to be the kind of parent to Todd that his father was to him. Todd and Janet were ten now, and he took great pride in their accomplishments. Todd played every sport and was very smart in school. Janet took ballet lessons and had a certain grace about her that came naturally; not only that, she was an exceptional student. Carla and Erica were five and in kindergarten.

Going on vacation as a family was impossible. Even going out to dinner was hard. He'd watch Jackie with the kids. She was a good mother, but then she'd dart him a look that would wither his admiration and make him look away.

He decided to try getting up at seven in the morning with Jackie and putting out the bowls for cereal, and preparing the fruit. He would help Carla and Erica get dressed for kindergarten. Afterward he would clear the table and load the dishwasher. Jackie seemed oblivious to his help. She was busy cleaning, or in the laundry room stewing the mound of laundry they produced.

Every weekday, Ward would meet with the speech therapist. In a relaxed, quiet environment, he began to feel he was making progress. He could converse with the therapist. At home he stuck mostly with one word answers or colloquial phrases that slipped easily from his lips. If there was tension, stress, or expectations, the words tumbled away from him.

Some days he would meet his father for lunch or he would make sandwiches for himself and Jackie. The younger twins would be down for their nap and he and Jackie would sit on the back porch. He tried to feel close to her; he tried to show her some affection, but she was always busy. He tried to do some work in the yard, but his shoulder ached with any strenuous movement.

* * *

Andrew McDowell and Frank Hill, along with the staff they took with them, were back in business. Andrew had been very reticent about jumping back into business so soon after the collapse of McDowell Hill. He blamed himself for not being more attentive to business matters and he worried about what others thought, but if either he or Frank ever thought that the scandal would diminish their business, they were mistaken. Business perked right along almost as if nothing had happened. Frank and Hilary orchestrated the revitalization of the firm and managed the office while each lawyer handled clients directly.

Eric McDonald had an appointment with Frank and Andrew, and anyone else who might be interested, at two o'clock Monday afternoon, to brief them on the investigation.

After pleasantries were exchanged, Eric asked, "Have you seen anything unusual in the transfer of records? Has anything come to light that might mean something?"

"No. Apart from the whole incident revolving around the Wilderness Holdings Ltd. cheques, there's been nothing," Andrew replied. "Not one thing that Frank or I could identify."

Hilary agreed. "As far as the records or files go, there's nothing. What does concern me now, a great deal, is Elisabeth. She went on vacation over six weeks ago and we've not heard from her. She hasn't returned. This is very unusual. She has never taken this much time off before. I have checked her apartment and made inquiries with her landlord and her Church and no one knows where she is."

Eric directed his gaze to Andrew, "What do you think happened to her? Any idea where she could be? This could be significant. You never mentioned this before."

"We have been hoping to hear from her, so we just kept pushing this aside in all the turmoil. She could have gotten sick on her vacation, I suppose, or perhaps she just decided to stay a little longer. She was going to Toronto to a family wedding. She doesn't have much of a family, and what she does have, she doesn't see very often. She could have gone to visit someone else after the wedding; although we would have thought she'd let us know. She does have a bank of vacation entitlement."

Eric frowned. "Do you think that her absence could have anything to do with the Wilderness Island Resort matter?"

Frank and Andrew said almost in unison, "Certainly not!"

"I think it's time we found out where this Elisabeth is. She could have some vital information. She did most of the work on the file in question," Eric said, as he turned to Hilary. "Where do we start?" he asked.

"Well, since I can't remember the name of the relative she went to see in Toronto, we could search her apartment for an address book. I think I would recognize the name if I heard it. She does have a relative here in town. He was a client of Dan's at one point. Dan got him off a drug charge a few years ago. I can't remember his name either but Dan might. All I know for sure is that she was taking the ferry on Friday or Saturday of the Easter weekend, to catch the plane from Vancouver to Toronto. I am sure Air Canada could verify her departure date."

Hilary provided Eric with Elisabeth's full name, address, and birth date, and arranged to meet him at Elisabeth's apartment at four o'clock that afternoon.

Back at the tiny office on Yates Street, Eric went over the new information with Barbara and asked her to check with Dan about Elisabeth's relative. Eric phoned a friend in Vancouver, gave him the details, and asked him to check with Air Canada and get back to him as soon as possible.

"Do you think the two events are related?" Barbara asked Eric.

"The timing is certainly suspicious and needs to be investigated thoroughly, but I'm not ready to jump to any conclusions that are not fact based."

At Elisabeth's apartment, the building manager opened the door for Hilary, Eric, and two police officers from the Missing Persons Division. Hilary and Dick stood in the hall outside while Eric instructed the team. Dick asked Hilary, "Did something happen to Elisabeth?"

"Not that we know of," Hilary said in a quiet voice. "She just hasn't shown up for work, and no one has been able to get in touch with her since she left on vacation."

"Well, I hope nothing has happened to her. You know I don't like that cousin of hers. He comes to see her sometimes. He's a little punk, if you ask me."

"Who would that be?" Eric asked Dick.

"I can't remember his name, but he drives a black Camaro with a white racing stripe. The car is really loud and all banged up."

"Yes, I know who you mean," Hilary said. "But I can't remember his name either."

Eric phoned the Victoria detachment and asked them to locate owners of black Camaros in Victoria, and to get a list to his Yates Street office.

On the bookcase in the living room was a picture of Elisabeth when she had been crowned runner-up in the Miss Victoria contest. She was 17. Hilary noted that it was a very old picture of her—too old to use to identify her. She knew that the Church had a more recent picture of her pouring tea at its Christmas celebration. She would get it for Eric.

At the foot of the stairs, Dick held a stack of mail that had accumulated for Elisabeth while she'd been away. He was now just as worried about Elisabeth as anyone else. He handed it to Eric. "There might be something in here that can help you."

Eric had been a cop for thirty years; he had worked in every area of investigations. Although he was eligible for retirement, he wasn't ready, so he had transferred over to the White Collar Crime Division. He knew that one little smidgen of anything could be the key to solving a case. He had to be careful not to get ahead of himself. One step at a time, he reminded himself, as he blocked the excitement over this avenue of the investigation.

Over the next couple of days, Air Canada confirmed Elisabeth's departure from Vancouver International Airport on Saturday April 21st.

CHAPTER THIRTEEN

Mike Parker, Elisabeth's cousin—who was known to police—had been located and brought in for questioning.

"Mike," Eric said, "This isn't about anything you might have done. We are trying to locate Elisabeth Nielsen. She has been missing for about a month. Can you tell us anything about her?"

Mike was visibly upset. He was more interested in asking questions than in answering them.

"Do you know what happened to her? Where she is? I hope nothing is wrong!"

"Mike, we want to know if you know where she might be. She left Vancouver International Airport on April 21st. That much we know. Do you know where she was going?"

"Yes, to my cousin Amber's wedding in Toronto."

"What is Amber's full name?"

"Amber Parker. She was marrying Gilles King."

"Do you know where Elisabeth was staying?"

"I think she was staying with Amber's mom and dad. I don't know exactly where they live in Toronto, but I have their phone number. I think I still have the wedding invitation. I didn't go. Not enough money."

"Let's go to your house right now, so that you can get the phone number and the wedding invitation. Thanks for your cooperation, Mike." Eric wanted to act swiftly on this.

Eric flew out to Toronto later that evening.

As soon as he landed in Toronto, he ate a greasy breakfast at the airport and then went to a hotel close to the airport and got a single room. He showered, brushed his teeth, and squeezed some eye drops into his eyes. A member of the local detachment, Patrick Weir, picked him up at eight thirty and took him to the station. He briefed the officer on his case and the two of them, after a swing through Tim Horton's, went to Margaret and Tom Parker's house.

* * *

"Tom, there's a police car stopped in the driveway, and two men coming up the sidewalk!" Margaret said.

There was a knock on the front door, and Tom opened it.

"Can I help you?" he asked.

"Yes, I am Eric McDonald. This is Officer Weir. We have some questions to ask you about Elisabeth Nielsen. May we come in?"

Tom, without hesitation, pulled open the door. Margaret stood in the doorway between the kitchen and living room. Both of them were still in their dressing gowns. Margaret said that she would like to change. Tom followed her upstairs. A few minutes later they came back down.

Margaret asked, in a fearful voice, "What is this about?"

"Elisabeth Nielsen, whom we believe is your cousin, has been reported missing by her employer," Eric explained. "She did not arrive home after the wedding she attended here in Toronto.

We are here to ask you if you have any information that might assist us."

Margaret lowered herself onto the couch and Tom sat beside her. Both were perplexed.

"Have you had any contact with her since the wedding, or heard anything about her from anyone else?"

"No," Margaret said. "Nothing at all."

"Not since we dropped her off at the airport a few days later," Tom agreed. "We just assumed she was back home."

"Can you tell us about her visit during her stay for the wedding?"

Tom nodded. "Elisabeth stayed with us. It was her first visit to Toronto, so we took her sightseeing, and, of course, to the wedding. It was a wonderful visit and a very happy occasion."

"Did she seem concerned about anything or agitated at all?" Eric asked.

"She did seem a little tired when she arrived, but nothing unusual. She seemed very happy to be included, and she was a wonderful house guest. She helped with meal preparation and fit right into our routine," Margaret volunteered.

"Did she get any phone calls or meet with any strangers when she was here?"

Margaret and Tom looked at each other and tried to read each other's minds.

"Not that we know of," Margaret answered. "We ate out quite a bit, and went to the Hockey Hall of Fame, and to the rehearsal dinner, the wedding, and the reception, as well as a brunch the following day. One day we went to Niagara Falls. We drove her to the airport and dropped her off. She did go downtown to do some business and shopping. I think she bought a sweater and a book to read. She wanted to take the bus." Margaret shook her head. "A city, even Toronto, can be unsafe when you don't know your way around. Tom drove her downtown a couple of times to the Eaton's Centre, but she took a cab back here both times."

"What day did she fly out?"

She glanced at her husband, who shrugged. "I'm not sure. Let me look at the calendar." Tom went into the kitchen and flipped the calendar back to April. "Okay," Tom called from the kitchen, "it was the May 1st."

Tom came back into the room.

Eric stood up. "All right. Well, thank you for your assistance. I am going to be in Toronto for a few more days before I return to Victoria. If you hear anything, or can think of anything that might help, please call me."

He handed Tom his card.

Tears streamed down Margaret's face as she got up from the couch.

"Call us any time if you have any more questions," Tom said, as he followed Eric and Patrick to the front door, "or if you have any information for us. Please let us know. We love Elisabeth. She's really a wonderful person." Tom gripped Margaret tightly around the waist with one arm and held the door for them with the other.

As soon as Tom closed the door, Margaret burst into sobs.

* * *

Eric and Patrick drove to the airport. Inside, at the Air Canada terminal, Patrick asked to speak to the manager of the Domestic Departure Terminal. He confirmed that Elisabeth Nielsen had cashed in her return ticket to Vancouver on the day of her scheduled departure. She did not rebook at that time. It would take a while to ascertain if she had booked a ticket to Vancouver on any other day. Patrick asked the manager to let him know, as soon as possible, what the records disclosed, one way or the other.

Patrick dropped Eric at his hotel.

Eric ordered a steak dinner and a bottle of beer from room service, and withdrew the mound of Elisabeth's mail from his briefcase.

He separated it into three piles: junk, bills, and personal correspondence. There weren't many pieces of personal mail. There was a thank-you note from Amber and Gilles, birthday cards from Margaret and Amber, and a handwritten note from the President of the Women's Christian Society, thanking her for the work she had done during the year at their fundraising bazaars and white elephant sales. Bills consisted of the usual hydro and phone, and requests for donations from United Way, Sick Children's Hospital, Champs, and the Boys and Girls Club. He tore open the phone bill to check for long distance calls. There were two to Toronto; both of them to Margaret and Tom.

Amber and Gilles lived in Toronto. They were both teachers. He made arrangements to call on them later that evening. In the meantime, he took a nap.

The brief meeting with Amber and Gilles disclosed nothing, except the realization that he was not clear on who was related to whom. They all called each other cousins, uncles, and aunts. He decided to go back to Margaret's the next day and make a family tree to figure it all out.

He carefully bundled up Elisabeth's mail and packed it into his suitcase. He made a note to check the bus depot and train station the next day, to see if Elisabeth had booked any other kind of transportation home. Several airlines flew out of Toronto, but only Air Canada had direct flights to Vancouver. If nothing came of his investigation with Air Canada, he would consider contacting other airlines.

He called Patrick and asked him to check hospitals and morgues.

He phoned Barbara for an update.

His gut told him that Elisabeth's disappearance and the money were related to Ward. He let his imagination run wild trying to connect some dots. Perhaps Ward's memory loss was not because he couldn't remember but because he didn't want to. He wanted to have another meeting with the partners of McDowell Hill when he got back to Victoria—all of them, except Ward. Someone had to know something or have some suspicions.

When Eric got back to Victoria, he had a private interview with each of the partners, Joan, and Hilary. He reviewed the Wilderness Island Resort file himself and saw the note from Elisabeth about Ward's verbal directions for Elisabeth to sign the first cheque with Ward's signature. Hilary had said that Ward had called Elisabeth from the ferry on payout day, and that Deborah Ruxton had been with Ward. Eric decided he wanted to interview Deborah.

Since the firm's dissolution, Deborah had not wasted any time obtaining the consent of the Legal Services Bureau, packing her belongings, and kissing Victoria goodbye. Her ex-husband was still in Victoria. From him, Eric learned that Deborah had gone to a firm in Los Angeles, and from his point of view, that was a good place for her. Eric wanted to go there to interview her himself, but there wasn't much left in the budget to finance that kind of travel expense. He contacted a person in the Los Angeles police detachment nearest the address he had for her, and asked her to interview Deborah. He asked her to send him the tape.

A week later, the tape arrived in Eric's Yates Street office. Eric found Deborah's voice and phony accent irritating, and he disliked her the moment he heard her speak. All that aside, she did not appear to know anything, or implicate anyone from the firm or herself. When asked if she knew what might have happened to the money, she said that Elisabeth was too stupid to take it and Ward had no reason to take it.

Did she keep in touch with anyone after she left Victoria? No.

What was her relationship with Ward? They were colleagues.

She did, however, say something interesting about banking in general, something to the effect of a bank employee having access to both cheques. He thought her off-handed, cynical comment just might have merit in this investigation, since all other leads seemed to go nowhere. Always follow the money, he thought.

Within the next week, he learned that Elisabeth had not returned home on any Air Canada flight, and she had not taken the train or the bus. He didn't believe she had returned home or ever would for that matter.

There was a chance that she had met with foul play, and he issued an alert to all police detachments in the Toronto area, and along her homeward-bound route, to see if anyone knew anything about her or her whereabouts.

He called on Andrew and Frank, and told them that he had interviewed Margaret and Tom and that everything had been normal with Elisabeth's visit. He then told them about the wedding and his interview with Amber and Gilles, the bride and groom. He also told them about the tape of Deborah Ruxton's interview. After they discussed it all for a few minutes, he let them know that he was intensifying his investigation of the banking procedures. There was a possibility that an unscrupulous bank employee had liquidated one of the cheques when two cheques for the same amount, payable to the same company, were presented for clearing at nearly the same time, without a stop-payment in place on either cheque. There were sufficient funds in the account to technically cover clearing both cheques, since the account was a pooled trust account.

Andrew and Frank had to acknowledge that anything was possible.

Then Eric told them that he had interviewed each partner and employee of McDowell Hill again to no avail. He asked them directly if they thought Ward was lying. Could his memory loss be a convenience to cover up his guilt?

Andrew and Frank did not want to believe this; they did not even want to think it, but they had to acknowledge that this too was possible.

If Ward had taken the money, what would he have done with it? It was not in any of his bank accounts. It was not in the records of McDowell Hill under a different name. Could it be in a different bank account, under a different name? Off shore? Hidden in his locker at the gym? At the bus depot? Perhaps it was at his house or in the trunk of his car? Maybe he put it in one of his father's accounts, or a fake company. Or maybe he used it to pay off someone? It's hard to hide that amount of money.

Eric wanted to get a court order to search Ward's house.

Andrew and Frank objected, but after Clark Walton from the Legal Services Bureau was consulted, the order was issued and executed. Andrew and Frank were sick about the situation. For God's sake, Andrew thought, I'm Todd's godfather.

At precisely nine the following morning, a team of investigative officers, headed by Eric, arrived at Ward's home, warrant in hand. Jackie answered the door with Erica on her hip. Ward was upstairs getting ready to go to speech therapy. Jackie reluctantly opened the door to them, but her frustration and anger with Ward quickly exploded! She had to be restrained and calmed. Then she put Carla and Erica in the stroller and stormed over to her parents' house.

Ward sat slumped in a chair at the kitchen table while the search team scoured the house. Then Eric asked him to open the trunk of his car. Nothing. He asked Ward to take him to his gym. Ward got in the car with Eric and drove to the gym. Ward was getting agitated and his speech was getting garbled. He opened his locker. Again, nothing.

Eric drove Ward home. The phone was ringing and Ward answered. He half snarled, half garbled something that sounded like, "Not today!" and hung up.

Eric didn't know what to say. Ward was obviously distressed. Eric called Ward's father. Phillip was furious with the court order, and immediately phoned Ward's lawyer in Vancouver.

Eric and the team retreated from the house disappointed.

Phillip took Ward out for something to eat and dropped him off at the house around three o'clock. Ward tried the front door, but his key wouldn't work. He went around to the back. He could see Jackie in the kitchen and he motioned to her. She opened the door and handed him his gym bag.

"Ward, I can't handle this," she said. "Please go and stay with your parents. I'm sorry. I can't do this anymore."

Her father stood behind her at the door for support.

Ward grabbed his bag, stared piercingly at her for what seemed like a lifetime, and headed to the yacht club.

He walked down the ramp to his boat and stowed his bag, then headed to the lounge.

"Hey Ward! How you doing?" his pal at the bar called. "Haven't seen you for a while."

"It's been rough lately. I'll have the usual."

"Single malt, neat, coming right up."

Ward felt the smooth warm Scotch heat up his chest. He missed that feeling.

By 8:00 p.m., Ward had downed a couple of scotches, or maybe a few. He had a big headache and his body felt numb. His words were slurred, and when he spoke to anyone, he had trouble understanding himself.

He decided to go down to the boat. The fresh air cleared his brain a bit.

He checked the lines, rigging, and running lights. Before it got completely dark, he putted to the fuel dock. He filled up the fuel and water tanks, and then checked the charts. Sitting at the table, he made a list of groceries, and then caught a cab up to the grocery store on Fairfield Road. When he was done there, he went to the hardware store, and then to the liquor store.

He flipped around in his bunk trying to catch a few hours of sleep, and then finally, at 3:30 a.m., the Mystical Winds slipped quietly from its mooring and headed out under a small sail into the Strait of Juan de Fuca.

Sailing had become second nature to Ward, and the wind on his face felt good. He breathed in the cool moist air as he hoisted a larger sail. Just before Cape Flattery, a half-moon shone sporadically between the clouds. He had sailed these waters a million times and knew to be vigilant.

Near La Push, he found a secluded cove and anchored there. Under the early morning sun, and the gentle rocking of a calm sea, the marine blue stripe of the Mystical Winds turned blood red and the sailboat itself became the Mystical Winds II. The Canadian flag that flew off the stern became the Stars and Stripes. The next day, after the paint was dry, and Ward had eaten a can of cold beans, he tuned in for a weather report and headed out to sea. The Columbia River Bar required a wide swath and it wasn't until he was clear that he headed back to land near Coos Bay.

In a small marina at Coos Bay, Ward picked up a couple of university students who were more than willing to crew for him just for the experience, as long as he gave them food and cold beer. Destination: Gulf of Mexico.

CHAPTER FOURTEEN

Paulette woke up to a brilliant sunny sky and a flock of small birds twittering noisily in the spindly tree near her bedroom window. She had plans to go to London that day to wander through the aisles of Harrods. She planned to pack a lunch so that she could sit on one of those London park benches and people-watch. She was growing more accustomed to the streets of Maidstone, making her way to London and feeling safe in her new community. Every day that passed grew a little easier. She wondered if anyone would ever find her, or, for that matter, if they were even looking for her. If they didn't find her, what would she do? If they did, she knew she would go to jail for a very long time. Either way, she had no regrets and no plans.

She went to the library almost every day, and volunteered at the Garden Club. She had taken the historical walks about the area, and had become acquainted with a few people.

Paulette was also getting to know Melanie and Robert better, and had invited them to a picnic on Sunday at one of the Garden Club's shows. Melanie seemed like an old friend—one of those old souls you feel you have known forever.

A quick rap at the door jarred Paulette into action. Before she could imagine that it was the police coming to get her, Melanie called to her. Paulette pulled open the door as quick as she could.

"Paulette, something has happened to Robert; the ambulance is coming. Can you watch the shop for me?"

"Of course, Melanie. Go and take care of Robert. I'll do my best to keep things under control. Don't worry about a thing! Ring me with news or I'll worry."

Paulette followed Melanie down the stairs and into her suite. Robert sat at the kitchen table, wheezing heavily and grey as an old sheet.

The ambulance pulled up outside and Paulette ran to the door.

"This way," she directed the driver. She fetched Melanie's coat from the rack by the door, and then pulled Melanie back from the table to allow the medics to do their work. She helped Melanie into her coat. "Where's your purse? Do you have any money?" She tucked a couple of bills into Melanie's coat pocket before Melanie followed the stretcher out to the ambulance.

Paulette went back into Melanie's suite to check the kitchen and make sure the stove was off and the kettle unplugged. She took the dishes off the table, covered the food, and put it into the ice box. After making sure the doors were locked, she went upstairs to her own suite and started a pot of stew in the slow cooker, in case Melanie came home later and needed something to eat.

Paulette combed her hair, put on some lipstick, and changed into a skirt and sweater. Then she went downstairs to open the shop door and place the sign in the window.

A couple of neighbours popped in to check on things, because they had seen the ambulance. Paulette explained what she could, but there wasn't much to tell at this point.

To occupy herself, she shifted a few things around in the window display. She saw a pattern for a summer hat made from a kind of raffia that she decided to try. It was very simple.

She greeted the customers that came in and chatted with them. They were curious about her accent. Some asked about Melanie. She merely said that Melanie was away for the day. Every customer that came into the store that day bought either some yarn or a sweater. She felt quite successful, and at the end of the day, she had a tidy sum in Melanie's cash register.

At six o'clock, she closed the shop. She phoned the hospital and found out that Robert had been admitted. He was in Room 302 but was not allowed any visitors. She put a sandwich, an apple, and a chocolate bar in her bag, and then got a face cloth, Melanie's hairbrush, toothbrush and toothpaste from the bathroom. The hospital was about a twenty-minute walk away.

Since coming to England, Paulette had lost thirty pounds. She felt tremendously better. She didn't get any palpitations in her chest anymore, her knees didn't ache, and she had much more energy. She was sure no one from Victoria would ever recognize her. She asked the nurse on the third floor to see if Melanie was able to come to meet her in the lounge. A few minutes later, Melanie appeared, looking tired and worried.

"Melanie, how is he?"

"The doctor says his condition is guarded. He's had a heart attack, but they think he has other problems as well. They want to stabilize him before they do any tests. I'm going to stay."

Paulette hugged her. "Here are a few things for you. Have you called your children?"

"No, I haven't called the children yet; I should do that now."

"I saw a payphone in the hall around the corner."

A few minutes later, Melanie returned. "They're coming."

"Oh good. Well, don't worry about a thing at home. The shop is under control. Just call me if you need anything else."

For the next few nights, Melanie stayed at the hospital. Every day Paulette took food and a change of clothes for her.

Each day at the shop, Paulette made sales, reorganized displays, and greeted customers. She finished her hat and coordinated it with a casual sweater and slacks on the mannequin. The whole outfit sold before the end of the day, even though the slacks were for display only.

A couple of salespeople came in and Paulette bought some items for re-sale. Melanie had women in Ireland and Scotland who knit sweaters to sell in the shop. They got half of the sale price. Paulette kept perfect records of the transactions. After five days, Melanie's son brought her home. It was Saturday morning. Paulette had opened the shop already and there were several customers inside.

Melanie's son told Paulette that things were dire. He didn't think his dad would last much longer. He said his mother was very tired. Paulette re-assured Melanie that she was doing well at the shop and for Melanie to take care of herself and not to worry about the shop at all.

Robert died five weeks later.

* * *

Paulette had transformed the shop into a 'boutique' of unique items, ranging from the traditional sweater sets to sweater coats and evening wear. She accessorized the items with jewelry, bags, and scarves. If the merchandise didn't sell in three weeks, she put it on special. She asked Melanie's suppliers for special items that sold well, but absolutely no duplicates. The shop looked curious and intriguing. In the few weeks that Paulette had looked after things, she had made more money than Melanie had made in three months.

***

The funeral was dignified.

Paulette had not been in a church since she had left Victoria, and she felt like a hypocrite. At the first opportunity, she escaped to the street.

Eventually she entered the hall and helped set out the sandwich trays and condiments. She started the coffee urn and helped slice the cakes. She piled cookies on plates and set out napkins. Everything was ready for the gathering that followed.

She stayed to help clean up and walked the three blocks home. The lights were still on in Melanie's suite, but she didn't stop. The next morning, she opened the shop as usual, and at about ten thirty, Melanie brought her a cup of tea.

"Thank you for all your very hard work," Melanie said. "I could not have endured these last few weeks without your friendship and help."

"People's paths cross for a reason," Paulette told her. "I'm glad I was here to help you. It's made me think of my own future, and where I should go from here. It was my intention to return to Canada, but I really love it here."

"My sister in Lossiemouth has asked me to come and visit for a while," Melanie said. "I think you've spoken to her on the phone. She knits sweaters for the shop. Her name is Fiona."

"Oh, yes. She has a splendid sense of humour."

"Yes, that would be her! Full of fun and laughter! I think a visit with her would do us good. Would you come with me?"

"What about the shop though, Melanie?"

"My daughter-in-law said that she would look after things for a couple of weeks."

She thought about it for a moment. "Why not? I've never been to Scotland, though I've heard a lot about it."

"Well, it's set then. I was hoping to leave on Wednesday. That will give me a couple of days to do my laundry and catch up on some sleep if I can. I'll tell my daughter-in-law and sister."

"Thank you for your very kind invitation, Melanie. I'm looking forward to it already."

Paulette was excited about going to Scotland. She had been feeling anxious lately.

Melanie made the reservations and Paulette could hear her coming up the stairs before she actually knocked. Paulette dreaded the "knock". She always imagined that, if she got an unexpected knock on the door, it would be the police to take her away. Strange. She knew in her heart that what she had done was wrong, but her brain kept rationalizing the circumstances. She wondered, for a brief moment, if the lawyers had figured it out.

She snapped her suitcase shut, and shouted "Coming!"

The train to Glasgow was so fast that it was hard to focus on the scenery, but the bus ride from Glasgow to Lossiemouth was amazing. Melanie provided a running commentary, as Paulette sat silent and took in all there was to see, letting her mind wander to the stories she had heard about Scotland and its people. The colours, the smell of the ocean, and the wind when they left the bus were all as Paulette imagined. She loved the Scottish brogue of the locals.

Melanie's sister could have been Melanie's identical twin. They walked, talked, and laughed the same.

After dinner, Paulette was tired and excused herself. From the guest-bedroom window, she could see the lights of the town and even hear the ocean. She felt peaceful as she tucked herself into bed.

The next day, she wanted to give Melanie some time to spend with Fiona, so she caught the bus into town and wandered about the shops, had a cup of tea and a meat pie for lunch, and spent the afternoon people watching. As she rode the bus back to Fiona's, she stared blankly out the window, tired from her day. She was also caught up in silently reminiscing about her early years, and the stories her own mother used to tell her when she was a child. She would catch glimpses of the ocean that, in a way, seemed so familiar. She was amazed at her journey to this place and time.

The discoveries Paulette had made about herself over the past few months amazed her too. Did she really have the courage to take the money, or had it been desperation? Now she had taken travels she never dreamed possible. She had met people she never expected to meet. What surprised her most was her success at Melanie's shop.

Now she wanted to be free of the turmoil she felt every time someone looked at her too long, or the phone rang unexpectedly. Would she ever be free of the fear of the unexpected knock at the door? It was time that she started doing all the things she had ever wanted to do—all the things she had put off in her former life. Now was her time.

She stood up and grasped the overhead rail to steady herself. The views of the cliffs over Lossiemouth and the North Sea were spectacular. She remembered how much her own mother had wanted to go back to Scotland to visit, but had never gotten there.

The driver announced her stop and she wobbled to the door.

Out of the corner of her eye, she saw a real-estate "For Sale" sign. She couldn't be sure, but she thought the property it referred to was an older style cottage, perched near the top of the cliff with a narrow little lane winding through the bracken down to the cottage. She would have to ask Fiona more about it. It looked so interesting and inviting.

After the supper dishes had been cleared, and they were sitting down for tea, Fiona, Melanie, and she chatted about their day, and she asked Fiona about the cottage. Fiona said that she had heard it was for sale. The owners had moved into town to be closer to their children. She said that her husband could take her tomorrow to investigate it if she would like. They could all go; it would be an outing.

All night Paulette tossed and turned, thinking about the possibilities. What did she have to lose? She could use some of the money. Wasn't that what it was for?

The next morning, after breakfast, they all piled into the car, drove past the cottage, and found out the name of the real-estate company. Fiona's husband knew where the office was, and in no time Paulette was speaking with the agent. Just $135,000 in Canadian funds would buy the whole property. Arrangements were made for a viewing in the afternoon, and by five o'clock Paulette had made an offer. She loved the little cottage! If she had to die, she wanted it to be there. Even the furniture was included. It was a curious combination of rustic and luxury rolled into one.

Paulette could move in within a week.

Once Paulette and Melanie were back in Maidstone, and Paulette's belongings were packed up, Paulette decided to make a trip to Lucerne, Switzerland, to arrange for the money to buy the cottage and to put the money from her savings account into a Swiss bank account. The very wealthy clients of McDowell Hill often had Swiss accounts, and she thought that, because of the stringent privacy laws, this might be the right move. She contacted a travel agent, who made all the arrangements for her trip. She took all of her bank books, passport, birth certificate, and any other documents she felt might be useful. She didn't know exactly what to expect, especially when it came to language, but once in Lucerne, she was relieved that many people spoke English and her anxiety was for naught.

On the day of Paulette's departure, to move into her cottage in Lossiemouth, she promised Melanie that she would keep in touch and was certain that they would.

Paulette scrubbed the cottage from top to bottom. She spent the first few days sitting on the porch looking over the ocean, surveying the roll of every wave, listening to the rhythm of the sea, watching the sun glint off the water, the clouds delivering sprinkles of rain, and the wind stirring the whitecaps.

She found a copy of the Lossiemouth newspaper in her mailbox at the end of the driveway.

A market on the outskirts of Lossiemouth, just before you came into town, where she did her shopping, provided a map of the town and a bus schedule. She introduced herself to the check-out clerks and butcher.

The ringing phone interrupted her and she answered sharply, but it was just Fiona checking on her progress and asking her over for supper on Friday night. She would send her husband to pick her up.

CHAPTER FIFTEEN

Ward had not quite figured out how he was going to get the Mystical Winds II and her crew through the Panama Canal. He decided to lay over in Cabo San Lucas until he came up with a plan, checked the navigation charts, and did a safety check on the boat. The boys would probably have a great time, and he gave them each a bit of cash.

He began by unloading everything from the boat onto the dock and giving the boat a really good cleaning, inside and out. He carefully repacked and trashed anything that was not useful.

His Spanish was not good. He wished that he would have had the foresight to get a crew member who could speak fluently. Maybe he would look for someone to join them, just to get them through the Canal.

He thought the police might be after him by now, and he thought fleetingly of phoning his father to find out what might be going on, but he didn't want to have to provide any excuses or lies to justify his unforeseen departure from Victoria.

That night he went to the restaurant at the marina for his dinner and one drink. He didn't need any more head-pounding headaches. He came back to the boat to find the boys partying—music blaring, a couple of empty tequila bottles rolling back and forth across the deck, along with a couple of bikini-clad girls dancing wildly. He headed for his bunk and closed the door. The music died and the kids wandered off. Ward fell asleep and the next morning found his crew passed out on the deck in the bright sun. Fortunately it was not too hot yet.

Ward got out his vessel logbook to check that his boat met the minimum standards for a canal crossing, which the sailors in the lounge had told him about. The Mystical Winds II was a marvellous, fully-equipped vessel. He thought he had the necessary document for the boat, albeit slightly altered to accommodate the name change to 'Mystical Winds II', for himself and his crew. He would use the cash he took from his account, after he converted it to the local currency, to pay the fees and the line handlers, and rent the wraps.

Someone who had been through the canal a couple of times told him to contact the Panama Canal Yacht Club when he arrived. Apparently, they knew the current fees and what offices you needed to visit to get the necessary approvals. Once the paperwork was in order, you had to wait a few days for an official inspection of your boat. The crossing had to be completed within a day or you would pay extra.

Ward told the boys, "Be ready to leave tomorrow morning."

The seas were calm, but they kept relatively close to the coast rather than going out into the open ocean. It would be a few full days before they reached Panama.

During supper each night, Ward would tell the boys what they would have to do to make passage through the canal. He warned the boys about their behaviour. He wanted them to look like they all knew what they were doing, rather than fumbling their way along and drawing attention to themselves.

They stopped a couple of times for provisions, but since no one spoke Spanish, they always ended up with beans, a few fresh vegetables, and some fruit. They did stop for a chicken dinner one night and stayed in port until the morning, but there was no partying at that stop.

The boys pleaded for some time to go snorkeling, but Ward had an agenda he wanted to keep. When they got to the Gulf of Panama, they pulled into a small marina in between Panama City and San Meguelito, which they had learned about when they'd stopped in Cabo. He had the boys shine up the boat again while he went to Panama City to get more information on making the trip through the Canal.

Ward had a bearing about him that attracted certain attention. You could tell that he was well-heeled and had advantages in his life.

Arrangements were made for the boat inspection. A downpayment on the fees was paid. They should be through the Canal by the end of the week. He went back to brief the boys. Since they were there for a few days, he told them they could go sight-seeing, but not partying. He needed his crew to be available and ready once they got the word to go, not hungover or sleeping it off in the drunk-tank. He was not about to bail anybody out.

* * *

By now word had gotten around Victoria that Ward had skipped town, much to his father's utter embarrassment and humiliation. Ward's mother was taking the news particularly hard. She was angry with him for abandoning his wife and children. She tried to comfort Jackie, but Jackie was distant and angry too. In a way, Jackie felt relieved, but didn't want to admit it, especially to Ward's parents, who still vehemently defended him.

* * *

A claim had been made on the Legal Services Bureau insurance fund, and the police were still looking for leads. There was only circumstantial evidence against Ward, but fleeing Victoria looked very bad. If only they could find even one piece of substantial evidence. All indications pointed to something fishy with the Wilderness Island Resort transaction, but interview after interview gave no real clues.

Elisabeth's disappearance was a complete mystery even to the police. They had traced her to Toronto, but after that she was gone. Logically, she was involved somehow. On the other hand, if she disappeared in Toronto, she could have been the victim of foul play. No evidence, despite diligent work, emerged.

Eric McDonald wanted to post a bulletin for Ward as a person of interest, but the family and the partners of the former firm objected. Eric thought it might shake loose some leads, however insignificant they might be. Anything would be better than nothing.

CHAPTER SIXTEEN

Paulette woke up to the sound of loud knocking on the door, and a man shouting, "Hello? Hello? Anyone home?"

This is it, Paulette thought, the knock. They're here. She half-expected it to come someday; no point in fighting it. She had fallen asleep reading her book. She pulled on her jeans and shirt, found her purse, put on her jacket, and opened the door.

If these are the police, she thought, wouldn't they be in uniforms?

"Hello mum, sorry to disturb you, but it's the second of the month, and no one has told me where to pay my rent. I know you bought the place, but I don't even know your name." The gentleman before her waved his cheque book in one hand, and gripped the porch rail with the other.

"Oh, the rent cheque," Paulette echoed.

"Well, sorry, my name is Bruce McAllister. You know the house on the right-hand side of your driveway, when you turn off the road? I rent that house from the owner of this property."

"Really," Paulette replied. "Are you sure?"

"Very sure, mum; I've been paying rent here for nearly ten years."

"I only bought the cottage. I don't think I own that property. No one said I got more than the cottage, the driveway, and a chunk of property around the cottage. Are you sure?"

"Well, the previous owner owned quite a big chunk. Did anyone walk the property lines with you when you purchased?"

"No, not really. They showed me a map."

"Well, since you have your jacket on, come on. I'll show you what I think you own. The previous owner told me he sold everything."

Paulette stepped outside and closed the door behind her. A thought flashed through her mind that this might be a trick, and she held up, not following Bruce off the porch. He was dressed in work clothes and rubber boots.

"I thought a family lived in the house up on the corner?"

"Yes," he said, "I live there with my wife, Sarah, and my three children, Keith, Anne, and Liam. Maybe you've seen them? They wait out on the road every morning for the school bus to pick them up. They get home around four o'clock every day. Keith's the oldest. He's 16. Anne just turned 13, and Liam is 9."

Okay, Paulette thought, as she stepped off the porch.

Bruce led the way up the driveway, and at the top, near the road, he stretched out his arm to the left. "You see that telephone pole? I think your property line runs from that phone pole right down to the beach. We'll walk a bit the other way now, past the next telephone pole about a quarter of a mile down the road. You see a tall white peg through the grass there? That is your other property line. It goes on about a thirty degree angle to the left down to the beach. I think you have about six acres, in all, with the cottage and the house."

Amazing! Paulette thought.

"Hold off right now on the rent cheque. I want to check with my lawyer to make sure, before I take your money."

"Sure enough, mum, but I don't want to get evicted!" He exploded in a hearty laugh.

"By the way," she said, "I'm Paulette McNeil. Thank you for taking the time to come to see me. I didn't pay much for the property, and where I'm from, house and property values are high, so I didn't think my purchase would include that much land. I'll have to check this out to be sure. I'll let you know in the next couple of days."

As soon as Paulette got to the house, she organized herself for a quick trip into town. She thought her first stop should be Town Hall, to check out the plan of the land they had on file.

Sure enough, the clerk confirmed Bruce's description of the land. He made a copy of the plan for her.

Her next stop was the office of the lawyer who had handled her purchase. He checked the copy of the contract and the statement of adjustments. There was no mention of a rental house on the property. He phoned the seller's lawyer. Apparently, it was an oversight. The property was indeed approximately six acres. Because the tenant paid the rent to the end of the month, the seller didn't think an adjustment was necessary. The seller figured the new owner would eventually work it out.

Paulette kept asking, "Are you absolutely certain?"

She was assured that she was indeed the owner of the whole property, including the cottage, house, and six acres of waterfront property, although the beach was about forty feet down from the top of a rock cliff. There wasn't much arable land, and the rock was covered with broom, heather and bracken. A pebbly soil appeared in patches here and there. She had noticed a rickety old set of stairs down to the beach, but she had not had the courage to go down them to investigate. She was still getting used to the place.

On the way home, Paulette didn't need the bus driver to announce her stop anymore, and she scrambled up from her seat as soon as she saw her stop approaching. Once clear, she headed for Bruce's house.

Sarah answered the door, "Come in, come in. You must be Paulette. I'm Sarah. Would you like a cup of tea?"

"Yes, that would be wonderful," Paulette gratefully accepted. "What are you baking that smells so delicious in here?"

"Well," Sarah said, "I have about eight loaves of bread to do today. I bake bread once a week. We have three hungry children!"

Bruce appeared at the back door, kicked off his muddy boots, and came into the kitchen.

"Well, what did you find out?"

Paulette grinned happily. "I found out that everything you said was true."

"Well, then," Bruce said, "you'll want some rent cheques. What are you going to charge me? Is there an increase?"

"Just keep paying what you usually do. I'll find out about rents and read up on the rules for rental properties in Scotland. If there are to be any changes, I'll let you know."

Over tea and a piece of homemade bread with butter, Paulette, Bruce, and Sarah got to know each other. Sarah stayed home to look after the children. Sometimes she helped another woman who was a caterer, by baking and cooking. Bruce was a carpenter. More noise at the front door announced the arrival of Keith, Anne, and Liam home from school. They scrambled into the kitchen in search of food. Their rambunctiousness quickly ended when they saw Paulette at the table.

"Keith, Anne, and Liam, this is Paulette McNeil. She lives in the cottage and owns this house and the property."

Keith responded, "Yeah, hi."

Anne jabbed him in the ribs and said, "Very nice to meet you, Mrs. McNeil."

Liam, a little shyer, merely said, "Hello."

Paulette thanked Sarah and Bruce, took the rent cheques Bruce had made out, and put them in her purse.

"If you would like to walk about, or down the trail, or along the cliff," Bruce said, "I'd be happy to show you around. Anytime would work for me, really. I don't have much work right now. There is one place, in particular, I would like to show you that I think is something special on your property. Just let me know if you would like to see it. Be careful along the edge of the cliff. It can be slippery. And those stairs down to the beach, be very careful on those. I don't think they're safe anymore."

"Oh Dad," Keith snorted. "We use them all the time. There's nothing wrong with them."

Just like a teenager nowadays, Paulette thought. What does dad know anyway?

A couple of days later, Paulette's curiosity couldn't be contained. She saw Bruce in the yard and walked up the driveway.

Together they walked along the road to the beginning of the trail. The brush was quite dense on either side of the trail, but about fifty feet in, Paulette saw some massive blocks of granite, some huge decaying timbers, and up close, the remains of an old structure.

"What was it?" Paulette asked Bruce.

"I think it used to be a carriage house, a place in the old days where travellers could rest their horses, get some food to eat, and a place to sleep."

Scattered in the brush were various pieces of iron, old wooden wheels, an old stove, and horseshoes ... all sorts of stuff. She and Bruce speculated on what some of the pieces might be.

"Bruce, do you think we could do a cleanup here, assemble all the stuff we have lying around, and figure out if it is useful or just junk?"

"Sure," Bruce responded. "When do you want to start?"

"Right after lunch?" Paulette said.

Paulette grabbed a hunk of cheese and a piece of Italian salami from her fridge and wolfed them down, put on the gumboots she had bought at the thrift store in town, stuffed two apples in her pockets for a snack later and headed up the driveway. This is going to be fun.

Bruce was in the yard rummaging through the tool shed, looking for his scythe, rake, and any other useful tools.

As they cut grass and broom and rambling vines away from the remains of the structure, and salvaged pieces of god-knows-what from the landscape, she asked Bruce, "Do you think this structure could be rebuilt? What would it take?"

Bruce shrugged. "Anything is possible if you have enough money to throw at it."

What a coincidence, she thought.

"I have heard of a program," Bruce added, "sponsored by the government, to refurbish landmarks and heritage buildings, but I don't know exactly what's possible."

Paulette thought about taking another trip to town to find out if the property would qualify for any funding or if it fit the criteria.

Within the week they had cut back all the vegetation around the site of the old building, stacked timbers, logs, and wood in one area, anything metal that could be lifted in another, scrubbed the moss off the old quarried stone blocks, and found other bits and treasures among the debris.

Paulette made her weekly trip to town on Friday, and first went to the library to see if there were any archived pictures of her property that would show the kind of structure that used to be there. Then she went to the Town offices.

In the back of her mind, she thought that if she could rebuild the carriage house, perhaps she could open it as a bakery, or in her wildest dreams, the tea room she had always wanted. She made inquiries about the type of development authorized for the property. She didn't find any pictures at the library, but when she got home, she phoned the President of the Historical Society. Maybe he had some ideas.

Bruce was anxious to hear about her research, and again, at the kitchen table, as Sarah whipped around the kitchen making butter tarts and an applesauce cake, she disclosed her idea about a bakery or tea room. Bruce was miles ahead of her in planning the renewal of the structure. Sarah thought it was a good idea, but she wondered if people would come all the way from town.

Paulette thought that, if the product was good enough, they would. Also, there was getting to be more and more drive-by traffic, and in the summer there were lots of tourists. The program that Bruce talked about, to rebuild heritage structures, was still a possibility and she had received information in the mail about the program that she wanted to review.

Bruce drew up some plans to rebuild a structure that he imagined was what the former carriage house looked like, based on what he had seen of other carriage houses, using a lot of the materials he'd found at the site. Paulette was anxious to make it happen, but wanted to be sure that, once the structure was completed, it could be used for her purpose.

On the basis of the plans Bruce drew, Paulette and Bruce went to town for a building permit. Bruce was at least familiar with the requirements, and Paulette had money to fund the project. Even if a bakery or tea room didn't turn out to be profitable, Paulette was sure some business would find the premises suitable.

Bruce was concerned about the timing of construction. Bad weather was coming for the next couple of months, and after discussions with Paulette, they decided to put their plans on hold until spring.

* * *

One day, in passing, Paulette mentioned to Bruce, "I'd like to get a little dog to keep me company. Do you know where I could find one? I don't want a puppy. I want a dog that is fully grown that I don't have to train."

A few days later, Liam showed up on the porch and knocked on the door.

"My dad said you wanted a dog. Will this one do?"

In a small box, Liam had the most absolutely adorable little fur-ball that Paulette had ever seen. Her name was Irma. Liam set her on the kitchen floor and Irma immediately took over the house. She sniffed every corner, and even jumped on the couch to look out the window.

"Thank you so much, Liam. Do I owe you anything for her? She is absolutely adorable. I love her already," Paulette said, and immediately started planning her next trip to town for all the things she would need to make a home for Irma.

"Dad says you don't owe him anything. She is kind of cute. I like her," Liam noted.

* * *

On Halloween, well after dark, Keith and some of his friends were down on the beach. They lit a bonfire. Paulette could hear their music, laughter, and shrieks well into the night. At around 1:00 a.m., Paulette was rattling around in her kitchen, thinking about her plans for the bakery, when she heard the kids coming up the stairs. The trail to the stairs passed right by her cottage, but she didn't mind. Irma let out a couple of warning barks as she was supposed to do.

All of a sudden, she heard a scream. She raced outside. All of the kids had made it up the stairs, except Keith. He was standing motionless on the top step, too scared to move. Paulette raced to him.

"What's happening?" she shouted to him.

"The stairs are collapsing. I'm afraid to move or they'll give way altogether."

Paulette yelled at one boy, "Go get Keith's dad! Tell him to bring a rope. Hurry!"

Keith and Paulette could hear a couple of the stair treads clatter to the beach below. The rest of the staircase hung against the face of the cliff and groaned.

Paulette lay down on her belly on the edge of the cliff.

"Keith, grab my arm and jump!" Paulette yelled to him.

"No, I'm scared the stairs will give way altogether. I'm going to wait for dad."

Another tread clattered to the bottom and the remains of the stairway scraped against the side of the cliff.

"Now Keith!" Paulette implored.

Keith grabbed her arm and lurched forward as the remains of the stairway tumbled away beneath him. Keith's legs waved frantically, searching for some foothold, but the toes of his runners kept slipping off the wet mossy rocks.

"Hold on!" Paulette screamed. "Don't let go!"

Keith clutched her arm, praying she had the strength to hold him.

Bruce rushed to the edge and frantically grabbed at Keith. In the darkness, he found the belt on Keith's jeans and pulled him up until Keith could get his knee up and over the edge of the cliff. Bruce gave a tremendous heave and the two of them lay atop Paulette, exhausted by their efforts.

After a few gasps, Bruce grabbed Keith around the shoulders, and rolled off Paulette, crying and clutching at his son to hold him close. Keith's legs felt like Jell-O, and he clung to his dad for support. In the midst of their embrace, they looked down at Paulette, who lay on her side, moaning in pain.

Some of Keith's friends were transfixed!

Bruce yelled, "Someone go to the house and call an ambulance! Quick! And get the flashlights. Someone stand at the end of the driveway and direct the ambulance down here. Hurry up!"

Within a few minutes, they heard the wail of the siren and saw the flashing light approaching.

Keith held Paulette's hand, "Help's coming," he reassured her.

Sarah ran frantically down the driveway, screaming for Bruce and Keith. Anne and Liam were close behind her. Bruce caught Sarah in his arms and told her that he and Keith were all right, but that Paulette was hurt.

Sarah crouched down beside Paulette to help her, but Keith said, "I'll stay with her Mom. I owe her. She saved my life."

The ambulance attendants loaded Paulette into the ambulance. Keith got in with her. He waited in Emergency while the doctors assessed her condition. She had dislocated her bad shoulder. Her arm had stretched tendons and ligaments and some very bad bruising. They were x-raying her shoulder to see if she needed surgery.

"We will probably keep her for a few days. She's resting now. From what she told me, you are a very lucky young man," the doctor told Keith.

"Yes. Thank you. Please tell Miss McNeil that I'll be back tomorrow to see her."

Keith phoned his dad from the hospital. "Paulette is resting. Can you come and pick me up, Dad?"

The next morning at breakfast, Keith described what had happened at the hospital, and then said, "If it hadn't been for Paulette holding onto me, I would have fallen and probably died."

After breakfast Keith caught the bus back to the hospital. Paulette was awake, and propped up in bed with one shoulder visibly lower than the other. Her arm and shoulder were encased in a thick tensor bandage. She was sipping a cup of tea. She looked exhausted. Her hair was still tangled with little bits of grass and mud.

Keith smiled when he saw her.

"The nurses promised me a bath and a shampoo," she said, and managed a weak smile back at him.

"Is there anything I can do for you, Miss McNeil?" Keith asked.

"Yes. Don't call me Miss McNeil. Call me Polly or Paulette, please. The anaesthetic has made my eyes really blurry, and I'm too tired to read or watch TV. Do you have a book you could read to me?"

"No, I don't have anything. Do you want me to bring something from your house? You have a lot of books there."

"Well, next time you come, why don't you bring whatever book you're reading at school? You can read to me from that and it will do double duty. You won't have to read it again at home."

Keith wasn't even sure what book his class was reading. He never did his homework anyway, but the next day he told his teacher that he'd lost his book and got another one, stuffed it in his backpack, and arrived after school at the hospital with George Orwell's 1984.

"What a wonderful book! Have you read it before?" Paulette asked.

"No, never."

"How far have you read? Catch me up to where you are," Paulette asked.

"I haven't cracked it yet."

"Wonderful! Let's start."

Keith stammered along, but after a little while lapsed into a rhythm. He could see Paulette fade every once in a while. At the end of each chapter, she wanted to talk about what he thought the author meant. All of a sudden, it was six o'clock! He had never read so long! He phoned his mom from the hospital. When he got back to Paulette's room, she was having supper. Even though she was drugged for pain, she was so enthusiastic and grateful for his company that he told her he would be back the next day. Sure enough, after school she was eager to pick up where they left off.

Within three days they had finished the book, and he had to admit that her questions were thought-provoking. He never dreamed that a book could spark such curiosity in him.

On Friday, a quiz caught him by surprise. What the hell, he thought. He could give it a half-hearted effort.

Afterwards he went to the library and selected another book for them to read on the weekend. He knew Paulette would like that and he owed her.

The next book, Of Mice and Men by John Steinbach, drew Paulette's unmitigated enthusiasm.

On Monday, his quiz was returned with a grade of 100 per cent, despite his never studying for an exam, or for that matter, even showing up for one. His teacher couldn't quite figure out what had happened, but was, nevertheless, complimentary and full of praise for his effort. Of course, his classroom cohorts derided him for making any effort at all, and asked him what he was turning into -- was he too good now to go out stealing gas and breaking into cars? All of a sudden, he realized how stupid they were.

His friends were beginning to wonder where he was going every day after school and accused him of running home to Mommy, as if that were going to motivate him in some negative way to take up with them again.

The next day when he got to the hospital, Paulette had undergone her first physio treatment on her shoulder since her injury, and she looked very worn from it. He told her his good news about his English test, and she asked him what he had expected. She said she could tell that he was smart.

They talked about the power of choice in life. She challenged him to observe other people's behaviour and the result of it.

When he asked her why she had saved him, she said that it was her responsibility—her obligation. He was a person of worth. There was no possible way she could have chosen otherwise.

"How do you do in math, Keith?" she asked, and when he explained that it was his worst subject, she made a suggestion, "I'd like to do something for you, if you'll let me. I'd like to hire a math tutor for you, so that your math skills will improve and you'll be able to complete your year with the excellent marks I know you can achieve."

He didn't resist. He wondered if that was a choice. He never thought he could be friends with an old lady, but she was different. She spoke to him as if what he thought and said really mattered.

During her stay in the hospital, as a result of the books they were reading, they had some very interesting conversations.

* * *

Bruce made plans and researched the equipment necessary to move the granite blocks and timbers into place for the reconstruction of the carriage house, while Paulette researched bakery equipment: ovens, pans, display counters, cash registers. Paulette knew that she had the skills to take care of the money, marketing, budgeting, advertising, bookkeeping, and business development, but she was uncertain about the actual baking. She wondered about what kinds of products to make for sale. She approached Sarah about baking, and Sarah was elated with the idea.

Paulette planned everything. She wanted to start fairly small and have room to grow, extend their hours, and the number of days they would be open.

Bruce began construction of the carriage house in early March, and with his efforts and direction, the carriage house rose from the debris. Paulette ordered the ovens and materials required.

Between Paulette and Sarah, they made lists of supplies required, and tested the ovens to make sure they were operational and the recipes to make sure they were delicious.

Paulette decided to offer a variety of products and wanted them to be homemade, not factory produced. She distributed flyers offering a discount for first-time patrons, placed ads in the local papers, and had a banner and a sign painted. She was excited about the opening. There was no anxiety about failure. She knew the bakery would be a success. Instead of fretting about whether the business would succeed, she carefully planned every aspect.

On opening day of the Carriage House Bakery, vehicles started arriving before the doors were unlocked. People lingered in the bakery, tasting from the sample trays. Anne made sure the trays were filled, and by three in the afternoon, they had either sold or consumed everything they had baked for the opening.

Paulette scrutinized the guest book and the comments. She decided that if anyone ordered more than ten loaves of bread or pies or pastries, she could arrange for them to be delivered. She also thought that, because it had been so crowded in the tiny premises, on Saturdays she would have a pick-up window so that people could pre-order and pick up their orders without having to come inside.

The local newspaper ran an article on their opening with a lovely picture of all of them standing in front of the bakery, smiling and waving.

Business did not back off after the opening. Every Saturday was chaos, and by three o'clock, they were sold out no matter how much they baked. After two months, Paulette decided that they needed another baker to help, and contacted the local employment agency in Lossiemouth to see if there was anyone available. As summer unfolded, Bruce was building a sheltered patio area where Paulette could place some tables and serve tea, coffee, and desserts. Everybody was checking second-hand stores for interesting little tables and chairs for Liam to paint, and for teacups and teapots with personalities. Paulette bought a large bolt of floral cotton cloth and began sewing table linens.

Bruce decided that the majority of the patio should be covered, just in case of rain. Trellises and wind screens were constructed, and vines and roses planted to create a pleasant space.

Sarah always had a large garden and set about planting even more herbs to use in some of the specialty buns and breads. When the tea room opened, Paulette hired a couple of Anne's friends to serve and trained them herself. The Carriage House Bakery became known as the Carriage House Bakery and Tea Room.

CHAPTER SEVENTEEN

Ward's boat sat shining in the bright sun at the dock in San Megeulito, all ready for the trip through the Canal. A broker and a couple of men were walking up and down the wharves, scrutinizing various vessels, and their voices echoed over the water. Ward could tell the broker was trying very hard to find them the perfect boat. As they walked by, Ward said, "Excuse me. If you're interested, this boat may be for sale."

The men stopped, spoke in Spanish to each other, and then turned to Ward. "How much?"

As the men took a good look at the boat, Ward asked the broker, "What do you think a boat like this is worth in this part of the country?"

After a thorough inspection and a test run, Ward was no longer the owner of the Mystical Winds II. The new owners took possession the next day. When Ward had cash in his pocket, he tracked down his crew.

"Pack up boys. Party's over. I'll get you to the airport and put you on the next plane for Portland—all expenses paid, including your wages and a bonus. Thanks for the good work and fun times."

Apart from the fact that Ward loved sailing the Mystical Winds, he was happy not to have to worry about whether his plan to get her through the Canal was going to work, or how he was going to pay the boys if he did. This solved a lot of his problems. He could travel lighter without the boat, even though he had no idea what he was going to do. He would be long gone, if there were any problems with the boat's paperwork. He figured the two new owners, brothers who were flashing around a lot of cash, would work it out.

A few days later, the boat was no longer in the harbour. Ward was relieved that there wasn't going to be any confrontation about registration. That night at the yacht club, Ward met the broker again.

"I haven't seen you around here. Are you visiting or planning to stay here? You seem to know your way around boats. If you're looking for a job, I could use someone," the broker offered.

"Sure, why not."

"Come and see me tomorrow morning." The broker handed Ward his business card.

Ward rented a small room for a few nights while he muddled out what he was going to do. He thought about the job offer. How lucky can I get?

In the peace and quiet of his room, he unscrewed the cap from a bottle of decent scotch, and poured himself a glass to quash the nagging headache he had because he'd spent too much time in the sun.

CHAPTER EIGHTEEN

At the end of the next school year, Keith invited his parents, brother, sister, and Paulette to his upcoming high school graduation ceremony. He had changed over the year since his accident on the stairs, becoming a serious student. He'd let most of his old friends drift away. At first he, and his teachers, were surprised by his newly discovered academic abilities, but the more he achieved, the harder he worked. He and Paulette had long conversations about universities, where he might be able to go, and what he would do. Paulette suggested that he just take some general courses to see where his interests took him. His school counsellors encouraged him, but had their reservations. Paulette helped him complete the application forms. Keith had his heart set on a university in Glasgow.

One evening, before the ceremony, Paulette and Irma walked up the path to the house for a cup of tea with Bruce and Sarah.

"I came here for a reason," Paulette started, once everyone was settled. "Soon Keith will graduate and I think he'll do very well. I know he would like to go to university, and it would be my privilege if you would allow me to pay for his schooling." She saw that they were about to protest so quickly continued. "I have no children of my own. Keith is closer to me than any child I have ever known, and I really want to do this for him, but not without your consent, of course. It is no financial hardship for me to do this. I'll pay for as long as he wants to go, up to ten years. The same offer goes for Anne and Liam when the time comes. Please let me do this. It would make me very happy and grateful to you. Keith hasn't asked me to do this. I know he plans on working part time while attending school, and while this can help, it's also very difficult. Perhaps with my financial assistance he can achieve his dreams."

Bruce shook his head in amazement. "You've done so much for him, for us, already. With the tutoring in math and your encouragement, he's a changed boy. We weren't happy with the direction he was heading, but after the accident on the stairs, things changed."

Paulette smiled. "I'll pay for his tuition, books, accommodation, and an allowance for living expenses. He will have to make sure the money is used appropriately, and that he passes his courses. I'm hoping he won't need a vehicle, but that's not out of the question either. Anything else will be up to you. Please say yes. It is very important to me."

"God knows, Sarah and I can't afford to foot the whole bill for his education," Bruce said, "especially at some of the larger universities. Before we decide, we'd like to speak to Keith to see if his expectations are realistic. We know he's applied to some universities, but we don't know if he's been accepted."

On the night of the graduation ceremony, everyone was dressed for the occasion and Keith looked ready to take on the world. He was among the top ten graduates from his high school and the recipient of a substantial scholarship for his marks in English. His parents were proud and ecstatic. Keith was blasé with his schoolmates.

At the end of the evening, during the ride home, Sarah told Paulette, "We've considered your offer and we would, indeed, be honoured if you would pay for Keith's university education, provided he doesn't abuse the privilege."

By the end of July, Keith had received notice from his chosen university in Glasgow that he had been accepted. Bruce and Sarah held a celebration dinner and Paulette was invited.

Bruce and Keith took a trip to Glasgow to find accommodations for Keith and to expand the plan.

* * *

In September, the bakery and tea room had been busier than ever. Apart from local patrons, supermarkets, hotels, and restaurants were all ordering specialty breads and pastries. The two bakers could hardly keep up, and even though inclement weather was on the horizon, business was still brisk. Paulette put the word out for another baker. While Sarah lived just across the lane, the second baker lived in Lossiemouth and came every morning at 3:00 a.m. to start the ovens and prepare for the day. In the back of Paulette's mind, she toyed with the idea of building some apartments or duplexes so that employees could live on site. Paulette and Sarah were usually in the bakery by 6:00 a.m., but they were finding the pace too frantic.

"Bruce, do you think it would be possible to build some small cabins, or duplexes, on the property behind the carriage house, for rental accommodations? It may be convenient to let some of the bakers or servers live on the premises, to give Sarah and me a bit of relief."

Once Bruce got an idea in his head, there was no stopping him. Within a week, he had a plan for some cottages, similar to Paulette's in rustic appearance, but actually four-plexes that would run parallel to the property line, with staggered entrances.

Bruce thought that there would be room for three such structures, tucked behind the carriage house. They did not all have to be built at once, but could be developed over time. Of course, all hinged on the zoning regulations. Paulette took Bruce's drawings to the Town for some preliminary discussions. While at Town Hall, she met Scott MacFarlane, the historian she and Bruce had consulted when planning the carriage house.

"Hello, Miss McNeil," Scott greeted her. "Do you remember me?"

"Yes of course, Scott. So nice to see you again. Have you stopped by yet to see the finished product? The structure has been restored with some modifications. It's now a bakery and tea room. In fact, it's called the Carriage House Bakery and Tea Room. I couldn't be happier with the outcome!"

"Actually my wife and I stopped by during the chaos of opening day and were very pleased with what we saw. The bread and rolls we purchased were delicious!" Scott remarked.

"Well, you must come by again; we have even more items to choose from and we have a lovely outside patio now too for sunny days!"

Scott turned quiet. "To tell the truth, I haven't been getting out much lately. Shortly after the bakery opened, my wife took ill and passed away a couple of months ago. This is one of my first trips out since her passing."

"Oh Scott, I am so sorry. What a difficult time in a person's life. Please be gentle with yourself."

For the first time since she took the money, she thought of the many people who had passed through her life and how she missed some of them.

On the bus ride home, she was quiet and reflective. She saw things that reminded her of her former life and wondered what Victoria might be like now. Did anyone ever miss her?

Little Irma was skipping and dancing around when Paulette opened the door shortly after dusk. Irma's enthusiasm was hard to ignore, and Paulette filled Irma's dishes with her favourite food and some clean water. Paulette spread Bruce's drawings on the table, made a pot of tea, and clicked on the TV. She would ask Bruce to cost out the first four-plex and give her a time-line. The bakery was making so much money that she did not think she would even have to dip into her money, or rather, McDowell Hill's money.

* * *

Clark Walton, Eric McDonald and the team had finished the audit of McDowell Hill's accounting records and did not have any more answers than they did at the start, except for the fact that they could confirm two cheques had been written and cashed.

Ward, the number one suspect, had disappeared in his sailboat. His father, mother, wife, and children had no clue where he might be. He never told them that he was going and, according to them, had never contacted any of them since. Border alerts were in place across the United States, Mexico, and Central America.

Elisabeth Nielsen never returned to work at McDowell Hill and, for that matter, never returned to her apartment in Victoria. Despite viewing miles of surveillance footage of Toronto and Vancouver airports, no one could identify her. Inquiries had been made at hospitals all along her route of travel. A missing person's report was filed by Andrew McDowell, but he now doubted that she would ever be found alive. Eric thought that she was implicated in some way, and had, perhaps, been forced to do something against her will and later killed for it—her body disposed of in some remote part of Vancouver Island, or maybe even in the ocean.

Andrew paid the rent on Elisabeth's apartment for a couple of months after the missing person's report had been filed, and after discussions with Hilary, decided to let the apartment go. The landlord was pressing to have the apartment vacated for new tenants, rather than letting it sit empty. Hilary made arrangements for the furniture to go to auction, along with Elisabeth's vehicle. She donated her clothes and non-perishable food items to charity.

"If Elisabeth should ever return, I'll foot the bill for whatever she needs," Andrew told Hilary.

Hilary packed what she thought were Elisabeth's dearest and finest treasures—jewellery, photographs, and some trinkets—and stored them in rubber storage containers in her garage. As a goodbye to her friend, Hilary finished Elisabeth's last needlepoint project and hung it in her own dining room, just in case Elisabeth ever returned. Hilary could not imagine Elisabeth just abandoning her project because she was so good at the stitching and put so much love and energy into the creation.

Hilary had her mail redirected to the office.

* * *

Hilary came back to work to an enormous pile of mail and stacks of files balanced precariously on her desk. One particular piece of mail addressed to Elisabeth drew her immediate attention. She tore open a pink envelope with a return address from England. The card had pink flowers that matched the envelope and a note inside:

'Dear Elisabeth:

I just thought I would send you this quick note as I have not heard from you for months and I'm worried about you. I hope you are not ill, or that your shoulder is not bothering you and that things are going well.

I know our correspondence is sporadic from time to time, but we don't usually go for so long without a note or letter between us.

I myself have been busy helping my daughters with the grandchildren. Just around the end of winter, my husband and I went for a couple of weeks to the Isle of Capri. What a beautiful place! Not only was the scenery spectacular but the food was amazing. I bet I gained ten pounds.

Hope to hear from you soon.

All the best,
Isabella'

If Hilary had any suspicions that Elisabeth might have taken the money, they were dispelled by Isabella's note. She knew by the way Elisabeth spoke of Isabella that it would be very unlikely that she would have ever stopped communicating with her.

Poor Isabella, Hilary thought.

Hilary took the note down to Frank's office to show it to him and she faxed copies to Clark Walton and Eric McDonald to have in their files. In her covering note to Clark and Eric, she asked if it was appropriate for her to respond to Isabella's note, given the circumstances.

Both Clark and Eric replied that Hilary could send a note to Isabella just in case Isabella could ever lead them to Elisabeth.

Hilary puzzled over exactly how to word the letter to Isabella but eventually settled on:

'Dear Isabella:

I am Hilary Britt, a friend and co-worker of Elisabeth Nielsen. Elisabeth spoke regularly of her friendship and correspondence with you. It is with deep sadness that I have to tell you that Elisabeth mysteriously disappeared after attending a family wedding in Toronto.

The law firm we work for filed a missing person's report with the police and after months of investigation, Elisabeth's whereabouts could not be determined. Elisabeth's mail was redirected to the law firm, and that is how I received and opened your note to her.

I am so sorry to have to bring this bad news to you. I know it will cause you deep distress and sadness, as it has with all the staff of our firm, as well as her friends at church and in the community. The few relatives that she has are devastated by her disappearance.

If you have any idea where she might be, or if you ever receive any correspondence, or communicate with her in any way, please let us know immediately at the address and telephone number on this letter, or at my home address and number on the reverse side.

Condolences to you.

Sincerely,
Hilary Britt'

* * *

The bank did an internal investigation of every person who might have touched either cheque during the time period in question. Under the direction of the police, persons who might have left the employ of the bank shortly after the disappearance of the funds, or whose spending habits had changed shortly after that time, were particularly scrutinized, all to no avail.

If, during the bank's investigation, any of the customer service representatives at the local branch had been interviewed, none of them either remembered nor mentioned Elisabeth's last visit to the branch, but then, what appear to be routine or mundane matters rarely linger in anyone's memory.

Surveillance cameras were being installed in many banks, but not at the main Victoria branch of the bank. The bank premises were located in a heritage building and, while upgrades were scheduled, none had been performed. The only security in place was a yardstick by the front door to estimate the height of fleeing robbers and a silent alarm system to summons the security guard or alert security that a robbery was in progress. Not that security camera footage would necessarily have assisted in the investigation, as the investigators could only guess that the first cheque had been presented for clearing in Victoria and would have been sent on to Montreal for clearing through the national office. The bank practices were that copies of statements were kept by the bank but not cancelled cheques. They were returned to the customer.

Even Ward's wife and parents were investigated, along with Deborah Ruxton.

All leads twisted into dead ends. The tip line was still open and, as well, the Legal Services Bureau would investigate any leads or information reported to it. The office on Yates Street was closed, and the records packed up for storage in the Legal Services Bureau archives. Eventually, after liquidation of the assets of the firm and the money the firm held for future development, the Legal Services Bureau Insurance Fund paid out the shortfall.

CHAPTER NINETEEN

At first Ward liked his job, and familiarized himself with all the boats in the inventory, including the ones that may not have been actively listed, but were, nevertheless, for sale at the right price. He didn't know how much money he was going to make, but he kept the room he rented. What do I really need anyway? he thought. He didn't have many clothes or other personal possessions. Living alone was difficult. He had no idea how to do laundry or cook. Even in Panama City, eating at restaurants could get expensive, especially the ones he liked. Sometimes he would be invited to join a party at the yacht club, but not so much lately. He bought himself some good sunglasses after his first pay cheque, as he found the sun blinding. He thought they might help ease the headaches. He persuaded his landlady to provide him with laundry services, for an additional fee, but his wardrobe was not really first class enough for the yacht club. He resorted to shorts, Hawaiian shirts, and sandals. His once perfect appearance turned haggard as time went on, and his head of curly blond hair became a tangled mess in the humid and ever-present breeze from the ocean. Headaches, double vision, and vertigo plagued him. Sometimes the only relief was to drink too much in order to try to kill the pain. Then he would wake up with a different kind of pounding headache.

While Ward had once taken pride in having a certain *savoir faire* with women, his drinking and appearance were unattractive attributes to the elite women of Panama. Too often he would wake up in unfamiliar surroundings with someone he didn't recognize.

He didn't have many contacts, and as it turned out, didn't have the energy to develop them. As a result, his income was not what he had hoped.

As the headaches worsened, so did his temper. Of course, he did not want to go to a doctor. He thought it would cost him too much and he was afraid that he might be recognized. He wanted to stay under the radar, as he knew people were looking for him even after all this time. Sometimes when he drank too much, he would get melancholy and cry over his lost life of abundance. He did deeply regret leaving his children, especially Todd, and the thought that he might never see him again frightened him. When Todd and his sister were first born, he had wanted to be a good father—the kind of father that his father had been to him. He had seen himself in Todd, and despaired at how he had let him down. Ward had cut himself off so completely that, even if whoever stole the money from McDowell Hill had been found, he would never know. He thought about phoning his father.

One night, after he had made a surprisingly good sale, the new owner invited him to a party. Ward arrived slightly more than tipsy. The hostess was skeptical, but despite her serving him watered-down drinks, he got more obnoxious by the moment. After dinner, she asked her husband to ditch him before he embarrassed them any further. Ward became unruly when asked to leave, and started shouting at guests and insulting the hostess. In a fit of anger, he grabbed a bottle of rum from the liquor cart and staggered into the darkness, shouting and cursing all the way down the beach.

The next morning, he didn't have a job. Without an income, he couldn't pay for his room and was evicted. He fought loudly with the landlady too, but she was not about to back down.

After his eviction, with the few things he owned thrown into a pillow case, he set off for the beach to try to think things through. He was afraid to ask for help. He did not want to phone home. Morose, he thought that he would be arrested the minute he returned to Canada. He fell asleep between two beach logs, and very early in the morning, woke to the rising tide.

He mooched off acquaintances for a couple of months. He'd drop in for unannounced visits, usually around meal times, or would scavenge in restaurants off uneaten plates of food, if he could get to them before they were cleared from the tables. He would use recreation facilities or swimming pools in the city for showering. Once he liberated a busy mother's purse and went directly to the closest liquor store for a cheap bottle of scotch. The next morning, a man out walking on the beach found him passed out face down in the sand. An ambulance took him to the hospital.

A doctor—too old to be an intern—examined him, drew blood, took some x-rays of a large bruise above his right eye, and put him on an IV drip. The doctor at first thought Ward was just another alcoholic bum, until he saw the only possession Ward couldn't part with: his law school graduation ring that was a gift from his parents.

Instructions were given to the nursing staff to call the doctor when the patient regained consciousness.

CHAPTER TWENTY

Paulette was expecting the building inspector the next day. He was coming to inspect the first of three four-plex rental units that were under construction. Bruce had done an amazing job of designing them similar to her own cottage: built into the landscape and coordinated in appearance with the Carriage House. The plan was to have the baker from Lossiemouth live in one of the units. The other units would be advertised for rent and Paulette planned to give her employees first choice and a discounted rent.

More outside staff was needed, as Anne was now preparing to go to university studying to be a teacher. One of Anne's friends, Crystal, who Paulette employed, had been taking on more of Anne's duties with the bookkeeping and payroll, as Paulette and Sarah tried to free up some of their time.

That May, Keith was graduating from university and had invited his family and Paulette to his graduation ceremony and dinner in Glasgow. Paulette was so proud of him. He had done remarkably well and even got accepted to Edinburgh Law School.

What really pleased Paulette most of all, however, was that Keith, Anne, and Liam had taken to calling her 'Gee,' short for

Grandma. They didn't know either of their grandmothers, so one Christmas they told her they were going to adopt her as their grandmother. Paulette was thrilled. She realized that these children, now young adults, were as close as she was ever going to get to having children of her own.

This brought back a rush of heart-breaking memories. She thought about the time in her life when she'd desperately wanted to marry and have children, but the circumstances had eluded her. Whenever she thought about what she missed, she would try to put it out of her mind, but she would wake in the middle of the night with a tear-soaked pillow and a deep, deep sorrow. In the morning, she would purposefully have to count her blessings, be grateful for what she did have, and take Irma for a long, long walk.

CHAPTER TWENTY-ONE

Ward's return to full consciousness took nearly a week of close monitoring by Dr. Robinson.

"Hello Mr. Barton," I'm Dr. Greg Robinson. "You are at Panama City General Hospital. You've been here for eight days. You were found unconscious on the beach near the yacht club. Do you have any recollection of what happened to you?"

"No, not really," Ward responded, "Maybe just drinking a little too much."

"Are you ready to discuss your medical condition now?" Dr. Robinson asked Ward.

"Sure, but I don't think there's much you can do for me. I'm not from here originally. I was just passing through and ended up staying."

Ward looked past Dr. Robinson and out the tiny window of his hospital room.

"Well, let's see what we can do. I can see from your x-rays that you previously had a massive head injury, one that you probably never completely recovered from, and never will, for that matter. That head injury probably left you with concussion syndrome, headaches, maybe even dizziness and disorientation, fatigue, and weakness.

"You have complicated this with excessive alcohol consumption, so much so that your liver and kidneys are damaged and you're malnourished.

"My first piece of advice to you is that you stop drinking, right now. If you don't, your life will end well before your time, in a most unpleasant way. I suggest that, first of all, we put you in detox treatment. I know a treatment centre where I have sent patients before with good results. In the meantime, can you tell me about your physical symptoms from your head injury and what you're experiencing now?"

"Just to let you know, doc, I don't have any medical coverage or money to pay for treatment, so I don't think I'm a candidate. I don't have enough money for medication either and the job I had here has been done for a while." Ward trembled at the thought of how much his life had shrunk, and he sank limply into his pillow.

"Don't worry about money. Let's see what we can do to help you now. Just tell me about your symptoms."

Ward scrutinized Dr. Robinson's greying hair, strong tall build, and soft hands. His voice was compassionate and caring. *Can I trust him? He might ask me to tell more than I am willing to answer. But then again, if I'm going to die soon, what difference does it make?* He glanced toward the window again to see a soft ray of sun illuminate a patch on the old linoleum floor.

"Medical history," Ward began. "I think I was fairly healthy until I got mugged in an alley when I was 38 years old. I fell against a heavy metal garbage container and then onto the blacktop. My skull was fractured in several places. I was hospitalized, unconscious for several days, and my recovery was very slow. My speech was very garbled at first, and still is from time to time. I had to take speech therapy. Then the blinding headaches started and there was no respite from them. I never recovered my full coordination either. I probably drank more than was good for me before the mugging, and when I found myself here in Panama, my life sideways so to speak, I started drinking to get relief from the headaches, nightmares, and bad memories."

"How long ago was this, Ward?"

"About four years ago, I think."

"Where are you from?" Dr. Robinson asked thoughtfully. "And how did you get to Panama?"

"I don't really want to talk about that part. Is it necessary?"

"No, I suppose not. Do you have access to any of your medical records, or anyone I can contact to discuss your original injury?"

"No, not that I want to reveal."

"Do you want me to contact any relative or friend?"

"No. I can't. It's complicated."

"Okay then, let me contact the treatment centre, and in the meantime, I'll start you on a pain-management program. The therapist will come to see you before you go to treatment. You will stay here at the hospital until a space opens in the treatment centre, as I don't think you're ready to leave here yet. We'll get you up and walking, and that will help me better assess your condition."

Ward nodded, but was lost in thought, searching for the faces he would have desperately loved to see, but thought he never would again. He wondered if the agonies and the distinct possibility of failure were worth it; if he were worth it. Maybe he should just drink himself into oblivion.

His thoughts faded to black, as faces he had wanted to see floated through his mind. Now he pushed them out and sank into a dreamless sleep.

Dr. Robinson ordered small nutrient-rich meals for Ward. An occupational therapist arrived and did some tests, in order to develop a plan for appropriate therapy. Ward wanted to participate but wasn't sure he had the strength.

"Don't worry, Ward," Dr. Robinson assured him. "Give yourself some time. Work on one positive thing each day."

CHAPTER TWENTY-TWO

The first of the four-plexes was complete. There had been an almost frantic need for the units. Two more bakers were hired. One of them occupied one of the rental premises, as did the Lossiemouth baker. Crystal, who was Paulette's assistant, also occupied a unit and helped with serving, payroll, accounts payable, and anything else that was needed. The final unit was occupied by a young woman with a school-aged child.

Once Anne left for university, there had been an explosion of work. Paulette had sent out the word around the community that there was another job opening. Crystal was instructed to balance the workloads between all the employees, to try to alleviate the chaos.

As part of the bakery expansion, Paulette opened a warehouse and distribution centre in Lossiemouth, to accommodate the volume of business the bakery was doing for product that needed to be sorted, wrapped, labelled, stored, and distributed to the various businesses they supplied. Six bakers now worked two shifts in the early morning and evening, not to mention the bakers' assistants and serving staff who worked shifts throughout the day. The Carriage House Bakery and Tea Room was becoming quite an empire.

Paulette had also received a letter and proposal from a businesswoman in Glasgow, inquiring about a franchise for the bakery. While Paulette had never considered this before, the proposal sounded interesting. Maybe a franchise, or some other type of arrangement for locations in other cities, could be successful and another way to expand the business even more.

Irma and Paulette wandered up the driveway to talk to Bruce and Sarah about the possibilities.

Sarah was making soup. Bruce was in the basement building some shelving. Liam was their only child at home now, and in high school. Keith was doing very well in law school, much to Paulette's joy and encouragement, and Anne was nearly finished her teacher-training program. Liam seemed to follow in his father's footsteps and loved building things. Paulette encouraged him to take an engineering degree, so that he could open his own construction business, but Liam didn't seem overly enthused.

To Paulette, it just seemed like yesterday when she'd first met them all.

Over a cup of tea and a bowl of soup, Paulette, Bruce, and Sarah threw around the idea of a franchise.

"Paulette, why don't you talk to a lawyer about these ideas?" Bruce suggested. "You know Sarah and I don't know too much about this kind of thing. You could always ask Scott MacFarlane for a recommendation. He's worked on several business development projects as a consultant. He probably knows a good lawyer."

"You know, that's a good idea! He helped us so much with the carriage house. I suppose I could give him a call."

After enjoying another bowl of Sarah's soup for supper, at home with Irma, Paulette decided to give Scott a call. "Hello Scott, this is Paulette McNeil from the Carriage House Bakery and Tea Room. How are you?"

"I'm fine. I've been busy lately trying to tame my garden and get it back into some kind of order," Scott mused.

She smiled. "Well I won't keep you too long. Scott, I'm calling because Bruce suggested that you may know a lawyer that could help me with a business proposal I want to pursue. I've had an enquiry from a person interested in a Carriage House Bakery franchise. I don't know anything about this kind of thing in Scotland. Bruce said that you've advised on business proposals, and that perhaps you knew a lawyer versed in this area of law."

"Well, there are a couple of lawyers I could suggest. Did you want to go all the way to Glasgow or do you think a local lawyer could meet your needs, Ms. McNeil?"

"I would prefer the Glasgow lawyer, as I think a lawyer from a bigger centre would be more experienced. And by the way, please call me Paulette."

"Well, let me call you back. I'll get the name, address, and telephone number from my records. Thank you for thinking of me. I'll get back to you shortly."

"Thank you Scott. If you don't get back to me for a few days, that's fine. Don't worry. I'm in no rush."

Paulette pulled open the drapes to reveal turbulent clouds on the horizon. She watched the low clouds speed across the sky, while the dark heavy ones expanded exponentially. She sat down at her small circular oak table, with her pad of paper, and began to make some notes about the questions she would have about franchises.

Within ten minutes, Scott phoned and conveyed the information she needed, and he assured her that this lawyer, if he could not help her, could at least connect her to someone who could.

After filling pages of her pad, Paulette took Irma for a stroll around the gardens just as night was closing in. A stiff blustery breeze pushed through the foliage, and the first bits of rain began pelting down. No hint of spring yet. Irma looked back toward the cottage, anxious to be safe and warm.

* * *

Paulette soaked in a very soapy bubble bath and then crawled into bed with a stack of books she had borrowed from the library. Even though it was an hour past her usual bedtime, she didn't feel the least bit tired. She planned to phone the lawyer the next day and make an appointment. She thumbed through a travel book about Canada. She thought about how different her life was now as compared to the years she had spent as Elisabeth, working in the law office in Victoria. How hesitant and fearful she had been then. She couldn't do anything outside her comfort zone or even remotely take a risk of any kind. Now, here she was, contemplating the expansion of her business—the one she had only dreamed about, the one that had been more wildly successful than she could have ever imagined. She had learned her lessons well from the experience of some of those clients from the past and the lawyers she had worked for. Her business ventures were perfectly planned, including having a contingency plan in reserve. She managed the money of the business to the penny. And she found that her employees made all the difference. Training, supervision, and delegation were paramount to her success.

She had more money now than the total of what she'd had in her own savings combined with what she took from McDowell Hill when she left Victoria. She knew that whatever the outcome of staying in Victoria would have been, it would never have been as successful as what she had now. She doubted that anyone from her old life would recognize her.

* * *

The next morning, Paulette phoned William Kennie, Barrister and Solicitor, and made an appointment for Monday of the following week. That would give her time to get together her last set of financial statements and her notes.

Two days later Scott phoned.

"Hello Paulette, Scott speaking. I was just wondering if you had managed to make an appointment with Bill."

"Yes, I have an appointment for Monday at one o'clock. Thank you again for the referral. I appreciate it."

"I was thinking that maybe you would like a ride into Glasgow. I have some business I should attend to and I was thinking you might not be familiar with the area. Perhaps I can help you out."

"Well, you have caught me completely by surprise. I had thought I would take the bus, but you're correct, I have no idea where I am going. If it's not too much trouble, I would be very appreciative."

Plans were made. Sarah agreed to go to the cottage to walk Irma a couple of times while Paulette was away, and to cover for her at the bakery. She and Scott would leave early in the morning and come home the same evening, but probably quite late.

Scott arrived to pick her up punctually at 7:00 a.m. A red ribbon creased the eastern horizon. Paulette had made two travel mugs of tea, egg salad sandwiches, and Carriage House Bakery chocolate chip cookies for the trip and had her briefcase, purse, and camera. Irma danced about but reluctantly crept inside the cottage, where she seemed to sense she would be left alone for a while, when she was told she couldn't come.

Once on the road and outside the city limits, Scott was a font of interesting information about the countryside and Glasgow. He was better than a travel guide! Paulette found him to be an enigmatic man, very mannerly and eager to help. A good conversationalist, always engaging—and impeccably dressed—he smiled a lot. He was tall and his movements were economic but fluid. He was very knowledgeable about the history of the area, where to go and how to get things done.

The sun rose to reveal a fragile pale blue sky and finally a hint of spring. Scott found a turn-out parking area just past a bridge over a deep gorge, with a view of the countryside, where he pulled in for their tea and sandwiches.

"Only an hour more and we'll be there," he announced.

"I am really enjoying the scenery and all the information about each place we pass. It is all so interesting. I'm so glad you offered to take me. This is much better than the bus." Paulette smiled at him.

Back on the road, she thought to herself, I really must get out and see more of Scotland. Maybe I should buy a car or do some tours this summer.

Scott found a parking space near a quarried stone building with a bronze plaque mounted on an exquisite oak front door: 'William Kennie, Barrister and Solicitor'.

Inside, a welcoming voice from behind a high oak counter greeted them. "Hello Mr. MacFarlane. So nice to see you again."

"Thank you," Scott replied. "I've brought Paulette McNeil for her one o'clock appointment with Bill."

Paulette nodded and smiled at the receptionist, who lifted the phone receiver and announced her arrival to Bill. Within a few minutes, William Kennie came to the reception area with a wide smile, pumped Scott's hand, and slapped his shoulder with his free hand.

Scott introduced Paulette, and then nodded toward the door. "Just take your time. I'll meet you at the car when you're finished."

Paulette could count on one hand the number of times that she had received advice from a lawyer. It felt like an out-of-body experience. From up at the top of the high ceiling, she could look down and see herself take her file from her briefcase and talk with Bill. She could hear her own voice. Some things seemed so familiar and yet so alien. Bill patiently answered all her questions, and in the end, Paulette retained him, but before Bill was to do any work she was going to contact the woman who had inquired about the franchise directly. Bill gave her a blank copy of a franchise agreement, and she planned to take that to her accountant to get input from him as well.

At 4:30, Paulette appeared at the car, confident that if the woman who asked about the franchise was serious, there was a good chance that an arrangement could be made.

"Scott, I am famished. I have to eat before we start for home. May I take you to dinner in exchange for your driving me? Do you know a place that would be nice?"

"Yes, I know a place not far from here, but I insist, it is my treat."

After a couple of blocks, Scott turned down a winding little lane that led to a high stone fence with a wrought-iron gate. Inside the gate was a low but ornate, rambling stone block building. There were large green fields to the left, right and rear. Scott pulled to a stop at the front door, and suddenly their car doors were opened and a valet took Scott's keys. Scott and Paulette walked only a short distance to the entry.

"This is Scotland's National Soccer Club House. All the big matches are played here. The food is quite excellent. There are two restaurants; one is a dining lounge while the other is pub-style. I think we should go to the dining lounge," Scott suggested. Inside the very elegant lounge, Scott was greeted by name and taken to his table. Paulette was impressed but tried not to show it.

Scott, ever the gentleman, did not inquire about Paulette's meeting with Bill, and she did not volunteer any information, as there were too many ideas swirling around inside her head. Besides that, she was starving. As Scott had stated, the food was excellent. Surprisingly, one of the desserts on the menu was made at the Carriage House Bakery!

The drive home was equally pleasant as Scott entertained her with stories of his youth, his soccer playing days, and his university years.

Paulette said, "I actually have Scottish ancestry. Both my parents were from Scotland, but I was born and grew up in Canada, in particular the Pacific coast. My father died a few years after the Second World War, when I was quite young. When my mother became ill, I took care of her until her death. I never married; I didn't have any children either." She realized that she had been describing Elisabeth's history, and quickly refocused. "In any case, I came to Scotland on vacation after my mother died, and ended up staying. I had no other relatives to keep me in Canada and I fell in love with this place."

She steered clear of giving too many details, especially the real reason she left Victoria.

Damn it! One more thought oozed into her mind as the car sped down the road, its headlights two shafts of bright white illuminating the roadway ahead. How would she be punished? It had to be coming. She knew what she did was wrong, but she could always justify it.

So far, there was little evidence her God or the universe were punishing her. In fact, she thought to herself, it's painfully ironic that when I tried to lead a good and godly life, I suffered more. How is that possible?

Fortunately for Paulette, in the dark car, the tears that gathered in her eyes as she described her life and remembered the loneliness were hidden from Scott's sight, but he did hear the wistfulness in her voice.

"Would you like to stop for a cup of coffee at the next café?" Scott's voice broke the silence.

"Yes, that would be nice. It would be good to get out and stretch my legs after eating such a big meal."

Paulette was grateful that her dark thoughts were interrupted.

* * *

On Easter weekend, Keith and his girlfriend came home to celebrate the holiday. Anne was home too and the McAllister house was full of activity. Sarah had cooked a big ham dinner and everyone gathered around the dining-room table.

After dinner, Keith stood and held his glass high. "I have announcements. As you all know, this year I will graduate from law school. I have arranged articles in Glasgow, and Melody and I are engaged!"

Everyone toasted, laughing and crying all at the same time. The evening was one of the best Paulette could remember.

Keith and Melody were undecided about where to have the wedding, but Paulette offered: "If you go for a summer wedding, we can have it in the garden. I am sure we could make it lovely, and even if it rained, we could go inside, depending on the number of people you plan to invite."

The other option was to have the wedding in the St. Andrew's Cathedral at Aberdeen, Melody's home town—a suggestion that Paulette wasn't crazy about. She did not feel comfortable in church. She didn't think there was a place for her there as long as she had the money. She knew what she had done was a crime and a sin, and now she struggled to smother the conflict that raged within her. For the first time since she left Victoria, she was unsettled about what she had done.

CHAPTER TWENTY-THREE

After a few days of therapy and exercise, Ward's movement was better than he had expected. The pain medication was helping enormously. He walked with a walker, but he did feel himself getting stronger, and a hint of optimism motivated him.

"Ward, I have made arrangements for you at the Rosewood Treatment Centre," Dr. Robinson said. "You will be transferred there tomorrow. There will be testing to determine the type of treatment you will need. I hope you'll make every effort to maximize the treatment. I think that while you'll have a continuing problem with your old head injury, you can have a better life with proper treatment."

"Well, doc, it has been quite a while since I felt positive about anything. While I do, of course, want to get back on track, I don't know what's in store for me once I am." He picked nervously at one of his broken fingernails. "I don't see myself going back home, and I don't see myself having a career here in Panama. I guess I don't know where I fit anymore, or where I'm going."

"Small steps, Ward, one at a time. Let's get you healthy. You are on this journey for a reason you may not even know. I'm at

Rosewood every few days to monitor my other patients, and I can make any adjustments to medication that may be necessary. Your physical therapy will continue while you're there. The meals are nutritious, and after a couple of weeks, you will be asked to participate in meal preparation, cleaning, and the other chores required to keep the place operational. There are many different counselling options that will be offered, and I encourage you to participate. Here is a brochure from the Centre, in case you're interested."

The next day, the Rosewood passenger van took Ward to the treatment centre. Ward only had the clothes he was found in and his hospital gown, but when he got to the treatment centre, he found clothing in his drawers and some personal care items.

After another thorough examination, Ward learned that he did not need detoxification by intravenous treatment and was relieved by the news. He did, however, need proper glasses. He tried not to make judgements about the other patients who, like himself, volunteered little about their former lives.

Instead of brushing off the counsellors with bullshit and blather, Ward made an honest effort to answer questions and reveal insights without disclosing that he thought the police were looking for him. Everyone knew that each of them had a story, or they wouldn't be there. A few patients made connections with each other. Ward participated in all the programs offered, and after three months, definitely felt better than he had when he left Victoria.

"Ward, you've had the full treatment program; how do you feel now?" Dr. Robinson inquired. "Are you ready to go?"

"I don't think I'll ever be as physically strong as I once was. I just have to accept that I will never be playing soccer or hockey, or going downhill skiing again, but what can I really expect? I used to think I would recover completely, that it was just a matter of time. I now realize that I had a life-threatening injury and that my life will never be the same."

He looked at his now rough hands and unmanicured nails, and thought about how lucky he was to have survived the sailing trip from Victoria to Panama in his condition.

"I think that with self-discipline I can stay on a proper eating regimen and not medicate myself with alcohol and drugs. If I don't, I know I won't be so lucky the next time. What worries me is what I will do for work, as I do need to make a living. I don't really know if I can read for any length of time, or if I will be able to do any manual labour. I will need to work as soon as I get released though. Any suggestions?"

"I have a guest cottage on my property," Dr. Robinson said. "Why don't you take it until you get organized? I'm not expecting any visitors and it's just sitting there empty. You can have your meals at the house. My housekeeper is a great cook!"

"Doc, I appreciate everything you've done for me, but that's too much. I can't impose on you like that. You've done so much for me already." Ward was truly grateful.

"No imposition, Ward. I wouldn't offer if it was. Ever think you're the only person who has been in a difficult position? We all need help once in a while. Now, I think you're ready to leave here, and I will discharge you, if you think you're ready."

"I think I am ready, but honestly, I'm anxious about the future."

"Have faith. If you're ready to start the next phase of your journey, I'll pick you up just after six."

That afternoon, Ward folded his few clothes and packed his personal items into a plain plastic shopping bag that Rosewood had given him.

So this is part of my journey, he thought, as he stepped outside to wait for his ride.

Minutes later, Dr. Greg Robinson pulled up.

Inside the car, Dr. Robinson said to Ward, "From now on, I am not your doctor; hopefully, I will be your friend. Please call me Greg."

They drove past the white sandy beaches of Panama City, and down a little overgrown lane on the edge of the jungle, until finally Ward could see an estate appear between the trees, with manicured lawns, guest house, pool, and what looked like a croquet pitch.

Greg pulled into the driveway of the guest house, and passed Ward a key. "Supper is at eight in the main house. Make yourself at home. Feel free to use the pool. There are change rooms, showers, and swim trunks in the pool house. See you then."

Ward unpacked his shopping bag, snooped around, found a pen and notebook, which he tossed on the kitchen table, set the alarm clock for 7:45, and lay down for a nap.

Over the next couple of days, Ward had questions for Greg. Was there a library nearby? A gym? An English newspaper? Most importantly, was there an employment agency he could visit?

On Sunday evening they had dinner together at the house. Ward noticed that Greg did not drink any wine with dinner, or sit around the pool with a beer or drink of any kind, and wanting to make meaningful conversation, finally decided to ask him about it.

"I'm curious about that comment you made back at the centre. You asked me if I thought I was the only one who ever had problems. I notice you don't drink. What's your story, doc? Or do you have one?"

"We all have a story of some kind. I was a new doctor with a career, a wife, and a young family. The hours were exhausting, my employer demanding. There were too many patients, too many family obligations ... it all got to be too much. My coping skills got overloaded. I lost family, friends, job, money ... everything. I lived in the US then. Only by the grace of God, and kind people, was

I able to rebuild my life. Not all of it mind you, but enough that I feel good about what I do and where I am. Panama is a less stressful environment, and I try to keep my life simple now. I can tell by the ring on your finger that you had a former life. Looks like a university graduation ring to me. So ... what about you?"

Watching the red sun drop below the dark blue horizon, the glow of Panama City across the bay, and the stars that emerged from the darkness, Ward told his story about his life, the crime he didn't think he had committed, but thought he was going to be blamed for, his trip to Panama, and his dissent into madness in the bottom of a bottle. He shook his head. His story sounded like a made-for-TV movie. He wasn't sure if there was going to be a happy ending.

Greg listened thoughtfully, adding only small comments here and there, until there was nothing left to say. They sat quietly for a few minutes, enjoying the evening. Finally Greg yawned and stretched after being slouched in his chair for so long. "Time to call it quits for tonight. I have another early morning tomorrow. Do you want me to drop you in town on my way to work?"

"Yeah sure, that would be great," Ward nodded. "I got some information on the employment service, and I think it is time I got on with it. I did write to the University of Victoria for a copy of my graduation certificate. I don't think I can get my credentials from the Legal Services Bureau though without alerting them to where I am. What time do you leave in the morning?"

"About 7:30." Greg handed Ward a roll of bills. "You probably need this."

Ward hesitated for a moment and then accepted the money. "Thank you, truly; thank you for everything."

Ward felt a little air whish out of him when he thought about how far he had fallen to have to take charity just to live. He needed to find the determination and confidence he once owned.

CHAPTER TWENTY-FOUR

Paulette had two events that were dominating her mind: Keith's upcoming wedding, to be held the last weekend of August at the Tea Room, and the idea of the franchise of the bakery. Anne, Crystal, and Melody were handling all the arrangements for the wedding, including signs for the bakery announcing—well in advance—that the bakery and tea room would be closed for a private function the last weekend in August. Paulette was looking forward to just relaxing and enjoying herself.

Paulette read over the pro-forma franchise agreement that Bill had given her and added to her already lengthy list of questions that she wanted to ask the prospective franchisee.

The next day, Paulette made the call. "Hello, may I please speak to Stella Simms?"

"Yes, speaking."

"Stella, this is Paulette McNeil from the Carriage House Bakery calling. I received your letter of enquiry regarding a possible franchise for the bakery. I apologize for not calling sooner. When I received your letter, the bakery business had not been franchised but I thought that the idea may have merit. I had to do some research about franchises so that I would be able to speak to you more knowledgeably about the subject. Would you like to meet or would you prefer just to speak over the phone?"

"Thank you for calling. Of course, I have many, many questions, but since you're considering the idea, I think we should meet. I also have a particular location in mind that may help you make your decision. I think it's a perfect spot and that the business would do very well there. Shall we arrange a time?"

They agreed to meet at one o'clock on Tuesday, the last day of September, in Glasgow—at the proposed site of the new Carriage House Bakery and Tea Room—and that Paulette would send her a copy of the generic franchise agreement she had been given by her lawyer, so that Stella could review it before they met.

Once she was off the phone, Paulette and Irma walked up to the bakery and made two photocopies in the office: one for scribbling on and the other to mail to Stella.

After lunch, Paulette caught the bus to town to mail the envelope to Stella, see her accountant, and shop for a special outfit for Keith's wedding. Afterwards, she stopped for a quick snack before she headed home.

The sun was still bright, the air was warm, and there were a lot of people browsing about the seaside town of Lossiemouth, which had once been an industrial city. Now there were a lot of quaint little shops, curiosities, and historic areas, and in a small picture-framing gallery that she was drawn into, she quite literally bumped into Scott.

"Hello Paulette, a fine day!" Scott greeted her warmly.

"Oh, hello, what brings you here on this beautiful day?"

Scott held up his treasure. "I found this very old black and white photograph of Lossiemouth, taken not far from your place, from the top of the cliff overlooking the town. I had it enlarged and now I'm having it framed."

"That's very interesting. I wouldn't mind having a copy. I would love to take a picture from the same place. I could frame them both for the tea room ... a kind of then and now, before and after collage. If it is not too much trouble, I would pay for the copy."

"Yes, I could do that. No trouble," Scott replied.

"I'm going to the cafe across the street for a snack before I catch the bus home. Would you join me?" Paulette asked, and then immediately thought she was being too forward. Her invitation was just for the company. She didn't want Scott to read anything more into her invitation than that.

"Love to," he said with a smile.

They sat at a small round table, with a gold Egyptian tablecloth almost to the floor and a view of the street. They chatted easily about Scott's picture, the upcoming wedding, his latest project, and the possible franchise of the bakery. Seven-thirty came quickly, and Scott offered Paulette a ride home rather than letting her take the bus. She accepted, as she had amassed quite a few bags to carry home.

"Paulette, are you interested in attending a play at the theatre. All the actors are local talent. I assure you it will be very entertaining. It starts Wednesday, after the wedding, and runs to Saturday night. I have tickets for Saturday night."

She accepted, and then thought that perhaps she shouldn't have. She didn't want a 'date' in conventional terms, and a million thoughts started pumping through her head. Was he looking for a girlfriend or a wife? What did he expect from her? Was she too old?

Slow down, Paulette, she told herself. It's just a play!

As she let herself inside, Irma jumped and danced in circles, glad to see her home.

Dinner, on the following Friday night, was held at the fanciest restaurant in Lossiemouth. The bride and groom's parents, brothers and sisters, and grandparents were all invited. Paulette felt particularly happy to be included as one of the family.

The rehearsal was early Saturday morning.

Around three in the afternoon, cars started arriving and guests started gathering. A warm gentle breeze wafted the fragrance of the roses in bloom over the patio, and promptly at four o'clock, the wedding took place. The bride and groom made a perfect couple, each with so much to look forward to in the future.

Paulette sat silently, with her hands folded in her lap, and wondered why this had never happened for her. Maybe she had wanted it too much. Maybe she should have settled for less. Why, in the midst of such a happy occasion, did she feel so sad? Maybe this is just life, she thought.

She decided to put on her best smile and find the happy couple to congratulate them.

The Carriage House Bakery and Tea Room catered an absolutely spectacular affair. The grounds were perfectly manicured. The weather cooperated. A small orchestra played and there was dancing on the patio well past midnight. Anne, Melody, and Crystal had done a wonderful job of planning everything to the letter. If there had been any disaster of any magnitude, no one was aware.

The bride and groom were off to Paris for a few days, and then they would return to Edinburgh where Keith would begin his articles.

Sunday was a very subdued day. Anne wandered down to the cottage for a visit with Paulette and Irma. They sat on the porch and had tea, and some rhubarb muffins that one of the bakers was trying to perfect.

"Gee," Anne said, as she had taken to calling Paulette, "I'm starting my final year. I have a practicum in October, and if all goes well, and I am confident it will, I will receive my teaching degree and graduate at the end of April. I'm not sure what I will do after that. There are a lot of posters on campus about teaching abroad. Some of my friends want to try that, as it's a good way to travel and get experience at the same time."

"Anne, whatever you do, you will be successful," Paulette said. "Just look at what you did when you worked at the bakery and the way you organized the wedding. Travel is one of the greatest ways to learn. You can always count on me. If you find yourself somewhere you don't want to be, call me. I'll send money. You can always come home. When I was young, I would have given anything to have someone to rely on. My dad died when I was very young. My mom didn't work very much. She didn't earn a lot of money. I started working when I graduated from Grade ten, and I took care of most of the bills and groceries. When I turned 24, Mom became ill and I took care of her until she died when I was 28. At the time, I thought I was doing the right thing, but now, when I look back, I realize how much I missed. I don't want you to miss out on anything in life. You deserve it all. You have a good head on your shoulders, a loving family, and a good education. You can have your dreams."

"Thank you, Gee. I appreciate all that you have done for me, and my family too. You have been a wonderful friend and mentor to all of us."

* * *

Suddenly it was Saturday night. Paulette stormed through her closet looking for the perfect outfit to wear to the play. Should she wear pants? No. Maybe a dress? No. Pants? Is red too bright? Or pink? Is pink too childish? What about black? No. She discarded that colour too. I don't want to look like I'm in mourning, she thought.

Finally she settled on a simple royal blue sweater and pants, with a matching scarf.

What about her hair? Was it too white? Did she look too old? Why was she so nervous and second guessing herself? She hadn't behaved that way since her days in Victoria.

The play was, as Scott had predicted, very entertaining—hilarious in fact. At some parts, she laughed until she cried. Afterwards a group gathered for drinks at the pub across the street from the theatre. Paulette knew many of the people in attendance from serving them at the Carriage House and she felt quite comfortable in Scott's company. He was a genuinely nice man.

CHAPTER TWENTY-FIVE

Ward arrived at the employment service full of expectations. He read the posters on the wall and nodded at others seated in the waiting area. Finally his name was called, and he followed a middle-aged man into a cubicle for his interview.

"Tell me about yourself, Mr. Barton."

"I have a degree in English and a law degree. I did practise law for eleven years; however, I had an accident and did not fully recover before I moved to Panama City. I have not been employed since. Because of my accident, I don't think I can do heavy manual labour. Again, because of my accident, I don't seem to be able to read or concentrate for long periods of time without getting a headache. I think my success would all depend on the type of job and the hours I would have to work. Also, I don't speak Spanish or any other foreign languages fluently."

The man nodded slowly and regarded Ward with an expression that seemed to acknowledge the challenges he was facing without seeming daunted by them. "Maybe we should do some testing to see where your capabilities and interest lie before we think about any placements. As a matter of fact, we have the initial tests starting this afternoon. Does that fit in your schedule?"

Ward nodded. "I'm anxious to get going. I can stay in town and take the tests this afternoon."

By the time Ward arrived home, his head was in a vice. His eyes were slits and his ears were ringing. He pulled the curtains closed, grabbed a cold pop from the fridge, and slumped into a chair, holding the cool bottle against his temple. He knew he had done too much walking, talking, and thinking. After he drained the last few drops of soda from the bottle, he lay across the bed and immediately fell into a paralysing sleep.

Greg came to check on him around ten o'clock. When Greg's polite knocks became loud pounding, Ward stumbled to the door.

"How are you, Ward? How did it go today?"

"I don't think I did very well," Ward replied. "I got a wicked headache on my way home. I had trouble reading and understanding the questions. Also I found it really confusing switching topics from one question to another. I don't know. Maybe it was too soon."

"Why don't you come up to the house and float around in the pool. That may relax you and tame down the headache," Greg suggested. "Don't get discouraged."

After a swim in the pool, and some sandwiches that the housekeeper brought to them on the patio, Ward felt much better.

"Do we need to review your medication or do you think it really was from doing too much? Be honest. We don't want the pain to get out of hand," Greg said.

"No. I think I just did too much walking, too much sun, and too much concentrating. I really did feel anxious and nervous. I think I just got very stressed. Let's just leave it the way it is. I'll monitor myself over the next little while, and if I find I am not coping, I'll let you know."

Ward received a call from the employment agency a week after the testing, with a request to come in to review some part-time jobs that were available. He made an appointment for the following day.

He was greeted by the receptionist. A few moments later his counsellor called his name, and he followed him into the office.

"Good morning, Mr. Barton. We have three part-time jobs that might suit you, and I thought we should review them.

"The first is a job at a private English-speaking school working in the library; the second is working in an American department store, handling customer complaints, and the third is working at a golf club, renting out carts and helping in the sales area. Do any of those sound like you might be interested?"

"I think I will pass on the customer complaints job, but either of the other two sound just fine."

"Well, let's go with the golf club. The school job doesn't start until next month, so if you don't like the golf club, you could still try the school."

Arrangements were made for Ward to meet the manager of the golf club. Thanks to Greg, he had proper clothing and Greg arranged for the housekeeper to drive him to work and pick him up when he was finished.

The first few days were a bit tense as Ward tried to learn the cash register. He was fine if the purchase was American cash or credit card, but if the transaction was complicated, and he had to do a currency exchange, he would get flustered and short tempered with everyone around him. He still had a bit of golf savvy left, even though he had not played since before the assault. The manager alerted the other employees to keep Ward off cash duties. Even so, if he worked more than three hours, he would get one of those buzz-saw headaches. By the end of two weeks, Ward was exhausted and spent the next two days sleeping. He decided to try the school job instead.

As it turned out, the school job was not that far from where he lived. The job was receiving new books, unpacking and reconciling them with the order, placing identification on the covers, and shelving them. Also there was a huge stack of books, which had been borrowed by students, to be re-shelved at the end of each day. While it was a job, the books were children's books and the reading material not the least bit stimulating. He worked every day from two until five, and this was ample time to complete his tasks. If the students were too noisy, he did find them aggravating, but the really devastating matter to deal with was how much the children reminded him of his own, and how much he was missing.

He kept at it for longer than he would have thought possible, but eventually, he fell into funk of depression.

One Sunday night after dinner on the veranda at Greg's house, Ward shared his thoughts, "Greg ... I can't ever repay you for your kindness and help ever since we met, but now I feel like I'm imposing. Health-wise, I feel the best I've felt since the assault, but now I have this incredible desire to go home. I can't figure out how to make it happen without perhaps ending up in jail though. I'd give anything to go back home to see my kids, and try to mend the damage I've done. I don't have a clue what's happened to my wife and children, or my parents, since I left but I think I have the strength and courage to face the situation now."

Greg understood. "Well, you know, when I think about it, I have a friend who might be able to help you. He's a lawyer here in Panama City. We go way back. He and I went to school together. He used to practise law in San Diego, but married a woman from Panama and lives here now. I can set something up for you. Maybe he has some ideas."

Ward shrugged his shoulders. "I guess there's no harm speaking to him."

***

A few days later, Ward found himself in the office of Samuel Rinnard on the tenth floor of Panama City's newest and most unique high-rise.

Ward poured out his whole story and his wish to return home. "I don't know, maybe I am guilty and just can't remember. If there's new conclusive evidence that could convict me, maybe I could make a deal, but I still don't think I took the money. I just can't remember."

Sam took detailed, meticulous notes, with dates, names, and addresses.

"At this point, one thing I don't want to do is let my family know that I'm trying to get home. I don't want to get their hopes up in case it doesn't work out," he breathed sadly.

"Yes, I understand," said Sam. "I want to check some things out and get back to you. If you want an update, call my office and speak to my assistant, but I will get back to you when I have a plan to review with you."

Sam shook Ward's hand and walked him to the door. The cool breeze of the air conditioner ruffled Ward's long thin hair and stirred the papers on the assistant's desk.

Once he was alone, Sam kicked back in his chair and thought about the details of Ward's story.

What a nightmare for everybody! he thought.

After a couple of days of mulling over Ward's situation, Sam asked his assistant to find out if Clark Walton was still at the Legal Services Bureau of British Columbia, and if he was, to schedule a call with him.

"Hello Mr. Walton, I am calling with some questions about the law firm of McDowell Hill, Barristers and Solicitors in Victoria, British Columbia. Perhaps you remember that the firm suffered a loss of trust funds, an investigation ensued, and the firm collapsed. I don't believe any criminal charges resulted from the investigation, but I wondered if you could provide me with an update. Has any new information or evidence come to light? Has anyone been charged or convicted?" Sam inquired.

"Who is calling, please?

"I am a lawyer and represent an interested party. My name is Samuel Rinnard."

"I don't believe I am able to comment on the case, as to the best of my knowledge, the investigation is still active. Perhaps you could call the City of Victoria Detachment of the police and speak to the investigating officer, Eric McDonald. He may be able to provide more information."

"Thank you," Sam muttered, as he slowly hung up the receiver, deep in thought.

Sam's next call was to Eric McDonald. He was no longer in Victoria, but worked out of Vancouver. The call went straight to voice mail.

Before the end of the day, Eric retrieved the call and listened to the message several times. He asked his assistant to check the telephone number and see if she could ascertain where the call originated from, and, if she could, to confirm that Sam Rinnard was indeed a lawyer in that jurisdiction. After he was assured that Sam Rinnard was a practising lawyer in Panama City, he wondered if this could be a break in the case. He was reasonably certain that Sam Rinnard represented Ward Barton, but didn't want Sam to know this.

At precisely 4:45, Sam's assistant announced that a call was waiting for him from Eric McDonald. Sam reached hesitantly for the phone.

"Sam Rinnard here."

"Mr. Rinnard, this is Eric McDonald from the police department in Vancouver, British Columbia. I am returning your call about the law firm of McDowell Hill. I should advise you that this is still an active investigation. At the time of the investigation, I worked from Victoria. Since then I have been relocated to Vancouver, British Columbia. I do not have the file on my desk as we speak, but I recall many of the details of this case. How may I help you?"

"Yes, thanks for returning my call. I represent an interested party who is wondering if any charges have been laid, or if any new evidence or information has come to light about the disappearance of trust funds from that firm in 1984."

Eric answered carefully. "I can tell you what has been reported in the newspapers and is public record. The last article was published shortly after the disappearance of one of the suspects in the case.

"Prior to the suspect's disappearance, a large sum of money went missing from the firm of McDowell Hill. Ward Barton, the lawyer who had conduct of the file involving the money, disappeared. He left on his sailboat and never returned. We believe that he picked up a couple of young men in Oregon, who crewed for an unidentified person, presumed to be the missing lawyer, until the boat arrived in Panama bound for a trip through the Panama Canal. On the advice of the young men's counsel in the US, no further statements were provided for fear that the young men would be implicated. However, I personally don't believe they were complicit in the crime; they just wanted the summer adventure of crewing on a sailboat bound for some exotic place. The skipper of the vessel did pay them for crewing, provided accommodation, meals, and return passage to their port of origin. To my knowledge, they have never been in contact again. Despite alerting authorities in the surrounding countries, and the embassy in Panama, no trace of the missing lawyer has arisen to date.

"Coincidentally, a staff member, Elisabeth Nielsen, who left on vacation near the time of the theft, never returned to work or to her home in Victoria. A missing person's report was filed by the law firm, in the absence of any relative or friend filing a report, and an investigation as to her whereabouts ensued. She was never located. We do not know if she took the money or was complicit in the crime. It was also speculated that she herself might have been the victim of a crime when she attended a wedding in Toronto.

"Further, a young woman who worked for the bank, and quit a couple of months after the disappearance of the money, was watched for some time. She claimed that she inherited money from her great-grandmother's estate and decided to go travelling. She was later cleared when she returned to Canada with an Irish husband and a baby on the way.

"Of course, we have never completely ruled out Herb Myers or Joe Piquette, the principals of the vendor company, Wilderness Holdings Ltd."

"Is there sufficient evidence to charge any one of the suspects?" Sam inquired.

"After the disappearance of funds, we could not place the money in any one person's care or control. We just couldn't find the money. All evidence is circumstantial. The fact that Ward Barton fled could indicate his guilt. Not only did he leave Victoria, he left behind a wife and four children, an expensive home, a lucrative law practise, and whole lot of questions.

"There has been a lot of speculation about what might have happened to the employee who disappeared, and whether the two were in cahoots, but we could never substantiate anything.

"The lawyer, unfortunately, suffered a violent assault shortly after the disappearance of the funds. He sustained a severely fractured skull, perhaps brain damage, and some amnesia about what happened immediately before the disappearance of the funds. We did however find a link between the funds and the lawyer, but never the actual funds themselves.

"May I ask who you represent and why you are calling?"

"I am not at liberty to say, and would have to seek further instructions from my client to disclose that information," Sam replied.

"I am going out on a limb here, and let's say, for speculation's sake, that you represent one of the missing parties. Why don't you send me a letter outlining your client's circumstances, the nature of your enquiry, and the ultimate goal of your enquiry? Again, I am speculating that, if you represent one of the missing persons, you want some sort of guarantee that since no further evidence has come to light, no charges will be laid without further evidence being discovered?"

"Yes, that's pretty close," Sam acknowledged. "Also, I would request that you do not discuss this enquiry with anyone until you receive my letter, or try to search for my client at this time."

"I would agree to that, provided that I receive your letter within two weeks." Eric spoke tersely. He did not want to be jerked around. If this was the break in the case he needed, he didn't want red tape hanging him up. "If I do not hear from you by that date, then I will be at liberty to commence further investigation in your jurisdiction."

"I do not have instructions to agree to that stipulation, but let me consult my client, lay out your conditions, and get instructions. I will call you back as soon as I have spoken to my client."

* * *

Sam locked the door of his office and sprinted to his car. He drove straight to Ward's cottage.

"Ward, I have lots to tell you, but first of all, I want you to come and stay at my place for the next little while. I will explain everything on our way there."

"Sure," Ward agreed. "What's going on?" He grabbed his bag and stuffed a few things inside. "Do I need to tell Gregg where I'm going?"

"No, we can call him later. First of all, you're not in danger, but I did contact the person who investigated the disappearance of funds from McDowell Hill, and spoke to him today. His name is Eric McDonald. Does that name ring any bells with you?"

Ward nodded yes.

"What I don't want to happen is for the police in Victoria to contact the police here in Panama City, and for them to come looking for you and apprehend you before we have a deal in place. We have a tentative agreement that this will not happen, but I don't trust anyone."

"What did the police say?" Ward asked.

"Well, the good news is that there is no new evidence, but your disappearance certainly drew the investigator's attention and made him look harder at you. In any event, Eric McDonald requested that I send a letter to him, outlining the circumstances and asking for an assurance that you will not be charged with this crime, unless other mitigating evidence comes to light in the future. If we put this request in writing, he will review the file, and ask the principals of the law firm, and the Legal Services Bureau, if they will agree. He will confirm by letter if there is agreement or specify any other stipulations. He also asked me to identify you, as I have only described you as an interested party and my client."

Sam went on to explain to Ward about the female employee who had disappeared and what the police speculated her role might have been.

"Ward, I want you to stay with me. Imagine, worst-case scenario, the Panama City Police are alerted that you are in Panama City. They commence a search for you, find and question you. I don't want you to say anything that might lead them to believe you're implicated in this crime. If you're with me, I am your counsel and they must deal with me. It would be very easy, either by accident or coercion, for you to say something—especially if I am not present—that might be construed as a statement of fact detrimental to your case."

"Okay, I understand," Ward said. "What now?"

"Well, I am going to compose the letter to the police with the proposal that, since no new evidence has come to light, you be allowed to return to Victoria without consequence. If evidence ever comes to light at some future date after your return, you will be able to retain counsel in Victoria to defend yourself. Also, I will request that your family not be alerted to your return home and that this matter be treated as confidential by all parties. If the partners of your former firm and the Legal Services Bureau do not agree to your return home, then they will not pursue you in Panama, unless they have more evidence than they have now. The agreement hinges on any further evidence being discovered. If it is, it won't matter if you are in Panama City or in Victoria, or any other place for that matter; the police will come looking for you, and in all likelihood, you will be charged and tried."

"Well, I am willing to take that chance," Ward said. "Even though my situation looks bleak, I still don't think I took the money. Go ahead and send the letter on the terms you propose, and let's see what happens."

CHAPTER TWENTY-SIX

Paulette was letting the younger employees take on more duties, and was focusing on finalizing the franchise agreement with Stella, who hoped her bakery would be opening in Glasgow on Thanksgiving weekend. Paulette had put together a recipe book, and basically, the product was the franchise. The premises were up to the franchisee, subject to Paulette's approval. Paulette wholeheartedly approved Stella's choice of premises: a beautiful old-character house in a very charming part of Glasgow.

* * *

One of Paulette's passions had always been reading almost anything she could lay her hands on and, in September, she decided to join the library's reading club. The format for the club was that its members would be given a couple of weeks to read a book, chosen by the members; then a discussion of the book followed, as well as plot and character analyses, with different people in the club taking on different characters. It always led to stimulating and sometimes hilarious conversations. She thoroughly enjoyed the first book and was anxious to attend and find out the next assignment.

As she hurried up the front stairs of the library, in the dimming evening light, she met Scott on his way to the book club too. He had been late starting, as he had been away visiting one of his children for a couple of weeks. They found seats just as the meeting was getting under way. At the end of the meeting, coffee and treats were served and people bantered back and forth.

Scott offered her a ride home, as well as a couple of other attendees. He dropped Paulette off last.

Before she got out of the car, he asked her. "Paulette, I wonder if I could ask a favour of you. As you know, I belong to the soccer club, and this year I'm the president. We have a very formal Christmas party in December, and I was wondering if you would accompany me. There is a very elegant dinner, speeches, awards, and dancing. It's a formal affair. I didn't go after my wife died, but since I am the president this year, I feel I really should attend. I don't want to go alone. Would you go with me? There would be no expense for you. I will take care of everything," he said charitably, as if the expense would have made a difference in her decision.

"I, I don't know," she stammered. "Just to warn you, Scott, I haven't danced for years. I don't know if I even know how to dance anymore."

"Well, really, I don't think I'm that good a dancer either, but it's not so much for the dancing as for the company. Everyone will be with someone."

She thought for a few moments and decided. "Why not, I can't remember the last time I went to a formal event. Let's plan on it. We can work out the details later."

Scott was ecstatic, and to her surprise, so was she.

After her evening walk with Irma, Paulette soaked in her warm bath longer than usual. Afterwards, she got out her bank statements and added up the total in her accounts. Even though she was generous with her favourite charities and the bonuses for her employees, she still couldn't spend all the money she made with the bakery and tea room.

Paulette lifted Irma onto the bed and crawled in between the warm sheets. She lay awake in the dark and wondered what her life would be like if she were still in Victoria as if nothing had happened. She wondered what the lives of her former workmates had become. Were Frank and Andrew still working? What about Hilary and Joan? Did Joan get fired? Who did they blame for letting the theft happen? It was the first time she had ever let her mind wander down that path.

Her mind drifted back to those nights that she used to spend alone and lonely. There was no comparison to what she had now. Sure, she still didn't have a husband and might never have one, and she never had children of her own, but she loved Keith, Anne, and Liam as if they were hers. She had the respect of her employees, associates, and even her community. She rarely had the panic attacks she used to get when she thought of how she would live if she lost her job, or if anyone would take care of her in her old age, or—after she took the money—if she was being watched by anyone who was suspicious of the crime she had committed.

She was secretive about her past and rarely spoke of it. Now, instead of worrying about getting caught by the police for the theft, she worried that someone she loved might find out that she was a thief and a liar.

Finally, with Irma curled and snoring at her feet, just before she dozed off, a thought whisked through her mind: Stella was ready to open the first franchise of the Carriage House Bakery and Tea Room and had asked Paulette to come and see the place and be there for the ribbon-cutting ceremony.

Perhaps she would call Scott in the morning to see if he wanted to go with her.

* * *

Eric McDonald received a faxed copy of Sam's letter indicating that Ward Barton was his client and requesting that Ward be allowed to return to Victoria without any charges being laid against him on the basis of the present evidence, and specifying that Ward's request remain confidential. Eric read and re-read the letter. He requested his file from Victoria, so that he could review the evidence and notes.

Sam's letter also contained detailed information about Ward's health and prognosis.

The next day, Eric called Clark Walton and went to see him. Clark was astounded that Ward had surfaced and shocked at the medical evidence disclosed in his lawyer's letter.

After the sale of assets, liquidation of the accounts receivable and investments held by McDowell Hill for future development, and funds from the insurance claim, no client of the law firm of McDowell Hill had suffered any loss, despite the fact that the whole fiasco had caused horrendous anxiety for everyone involved for quite some time. Clark and Eric felt compelled to disclose Ward's request to the partners of McDowell Hill, and to allow them to have input on the final decision.

Clark telephoned Andrew McDowell, but Andrew was away. Next he tried Frank Hill.

"Hello Frank, this is Clark Walton from the Legal Services Bureau of British Columbia. I have received some sensitive information that I would like to discuss with you and the other partners of McDowell Hill. I would prefer to meet with you. What might work for you?"

"Clark, you've instantly sparked my curiosity. Andrew is in Hawaii and spends quite a bit of time there now. Because many of us have gone our separate ways, all the other partners have given either me or Andrew authority to act on their behalf. Is there new information? Have you found Ward or Elisabeth?"

"I'd prefer to leave discussions until our meeting. Please treat this call confidentially."

"All right. I'll get in touch with Andrew and call you back. Did you want us to come to Vancouver or do you want to meet us in Victoria?"

"Why don't you come to Vancouver? Eric McDonald will be at the meeting too."

"I'll get back to you as soon as I can," Frank advised.

Frank took a couple of hectic hours to track Andrew down.

"Andrew, I just had a call from Clark Walton. He wants to meet with us as soon as possible. He said that he didn't want to tell me anything before the meeting. Eric McDonald's going to be at the meeting too. Can you come? What's your schedule like?"

"Well, that news is very interesting," Andrew said. "I wouldn't miss it. I'll try to get there tomorrow, if I can. Give me a few minutes and I'll call you back as soon as I can arrange something."

"If you can make it to Vancouver by one o'clock in the afternoon, I could pick you up from the Vancouver Airport," Frank replied. "Bring Lenore. Melissa wants to go to the new exhibit at the art gallery. They can go together, and after the meeting, the four of us can have dinner and catch up."

"I'll call you with flight particulars as soon as I've made a reservation."

* * *

The next morning, Frank and Melissa were on the first ferry to Vancouver. At the meeting, both Andrew and Frank were anxious to be briefed. Clark gave a copy of Sam Rinnard's letter and enclosures to each of them, and waited patiently for them to read and digest the information.

Tears welled in Andrew's eyes as he read Ward's medical reports.

"Jesus Christ! Poor Ward!" Andrew exclaimed as he thought back on how everyone had wanted to lynch Ward—himself included—when Ward disappeared in his sailboat.

"His injuries from the assault really were much more serious than I had thought. What now Frank? What do you think?"

Eric injected, "On the evidence we have now, the chance of a conviction would be very slim. We still can't place the money in Ward's care or control. With or without your consent, he can come back to Canada any time he wants. I think his lawyer probably advised him to send this letter to let you know that Ward wanted to return home, rather than him just showing up here years later. Can you imagine the kerfuffle that would have caused, if he'd just shown up out of the blue one day?"

"I know how much Ward's parents have suffered over this whole matter," Andrew said. "Ward's wife divorced him and has now remarried. Ward's own children don't even know him. I don't even know if Todd remembers him. I keep in touch with Todd at his birthday, Christmas, and some special occasions, and I know he's struggled with this whole thing. When he was young, he didn't understand what happened, and as he's gotten older, he's never wanted to believe his dad stole the money."

"While I want someone to be accountable for what happened to McDowell Hill, I can't, with a clear conscious, deny Ward's request to come home and fix what he can," Frank said. "If we find out later on that he's guilty, then the full force of the law will be on him, but until then, for all concerned, I think a little mercy is in order."

"I guess we are all agreed. Who will answer Sam's letter?" Andrew asked

"The letter was addressed to me as the investigating officer. I think I should," Eric concluded.

CHAPTER TWENTY-SEVEN

Ward wanted to phone Sam Rinnard's office every day to see if Sam had any news. The anticipation was almost more than he could bear, and he struggled to contain himself. He tried to make an alternate plan, in case his return to Victoria didn't work out, but he couldn't come up with anything reasonable. He was singularly focused on returning. Nothing else would work.

Sam was non-committal.

Exactly two weeks after Sam had sent the letter to Eric McDonald, just as he was about to switch off the lights for the day, Sam's fax machine lit up and produced Eric's reply:

'… upon review of the evidence of the above-noted matter, and with the agreement of Clark Walton, on behalf of the Legal Services Bureau of British Columbia, and the principals of the former firm of McDowall Hill, charges will not be laid against your client, Ward Barton, with regard to the disappearance of trust funds … unless further evidence is discovered … as a result, Ward Barton is at liberty to return to Canada.'

Sam tore the fax off the role and headed home.

* * *

The reply was bittersweet for Ward, as now the reality of getting home was daunting. He needed his birth certificate and a passport before he could travel. Thanks to Greg's generosity, he had managed to save a little money from his job, and he wondered if he would be able to manage the long flight directly from Panama to Victoria, with at least two stop overs for plane changes, or if he should do it in stages. A jumble of thoughts pressed on his mind.

Ward phoned Greg to share the news.

That night Ward couldn't sleep. He was back to making lists of the things he had to do, and turned over and over in his mind all the things he wanted to say. He tried to imagine what his children looked like six years later, and if he could make up for lost time or if it was lost forever.

CHAPTER TWENTY-EIGHT

The first franchise of the Carriage House Bakery and Tea Room opened on schedule. The premises were perfect and everyone was confident that Stella's operation would be very successful. A steady stream of customers lasted until 4:00 p.m., when the final loaf of bread was sold, along with absolutely everything else.

In conversation with Stella, Paulette had mentioned an upcoming visit: "I'll be coming to Glasgow again later in the month, as I want to do some shopping. I need a formal dress for the annual soccer club Christmas celebration, so I'll pop by again to check on you."

"Where are you staying when you come? Why don't you stay with me?" Stella offered. "I have lots of room."

The arrangement worked perfectly. Stella even made a list of exclusive stores for her where she could shop for her dress. Scott stayed at his club.

Paulette found an exquisite dress for the occasion, and ended up with three pairs of shoes as well. She also bought an evening coat, in case she needed it, as December could be bitterly cold and damp.

Scott picked her up early from Stella's for some sightseeing on the way home, since they had the entire day. They stopped along the way to see some ancient ruins, an old-fashioned farm, where they had lunch, and finally a stop at a Robbie Burns monument.

Paulette was tired when she got home, but before she could unpack, Sarah was at the door requesting her help at the bakery. Apparently one of the bakers was sick and they were expecting a busy day the next day with many catering orders. The bakery was busy over the next few weeks, and it was time to start the Christmas cakes. No sooner had the Christmas cakes been distributed than the decorations were ready to put up. There were a lot of weddings, receptions, and office parties scheduled over the holidays.

Scott stopped by to make arrangements and a plan for the soccer club Christmas party.

"We need to be there by 6:00 p.m., Saturday, December 12th, for the dinner, entertainment, and dancing afterwards. I've arranged with some friends to meet for brunch on Sunday around eleven. We'll probably take a couple of hours for brunch. I thought we could wait until Monday to come home, as that would give me a good night's sleep before we drive back. I can arrange for a room at the club for each of us.

"We can leave early Saturday morning and be there in time to dress leisurely and be ready by 6:00 pm. If you think that Saturday would be too long a day, we could go on Friday. I'm sure we could find something to do on Saturday in Glasgow, as there will be lots going on in town."

Paulette thought about everything Scott suggested. "I think travelling on Friday would be better. It would be a very long day if we left early Saturday morning and then stayed up late on Saturday night. I have always wanted to go to the Museum in Glasgow, so maybe we could do that on Saturday."

"Perfect. I will make all the arrangements," Scott said confidently.

Paulette invited Sarah to come and see her in the new dress she had bought, to confirm that her outfit was appropriate for the occasion. Sarah assured Paulette the dress was lovely and she would look perfect. Paulette couldn't remember the last time she wore a formal gown. She studied her image in the mirror. Her frame was slight now, compared to how chubby she used to be. Her hair was snow white, but her eyes were still vivid blue.

Sarah agreed to take Irma to her house for the four days Paulette would be away.

Paulette wore her three pairs of shoes around the cottage for days, trying to break them in before she needed to wear them.

Scott arrived exactly on time as usual. That evening they had dinner at the club and said good night around 10:30 after a leisurely drink in the lounge and some piano jazz. When Paulette opened the door to her room, a dozen red roses were waiting for her along with a box of Swiss chocolates. The next morning, Paulette and Scott decided to go to the Carriage House Bakery for a light breakfast and a visit with Stella, and then to the museum. They were back by three for a short rest before the festivities.

Scott knocked on Paulette's door at 5:45. Paulette was ready. In fact she had been ready for nearly an hour.

Paulette looked radiant in her very simple but exquisite sapphire blue silk gown, pearl necklace and earrings, and a midnight black Spanish lace shawl delicately draped over her arms. Scott tried his hardest to be nonchalant, suave, and sophisticated, but he was overwhelmed. But then, he was quite used to seeing her in jeans and gumboots, rooting around in the gardens, or in a flour-dusted bakery apron.

Scott was quite a handsome figure himself, in his formal dress kilt, with his clipped moustache and wavy silver hair.

They were escorted to their seats at the head table, and once seated, formalities were underway.

The evening was a mixture of entertaining speeches, toasts, presentations, and dining on the most delicious meal Paulette had ever eaten, each course paired with the appropriate wine. After the meal was over, the guests were entertained by some of Scotland's most noted singers, the recital of Robbie Burn's most famous poem, and an absolutely hysterical comedian.

When Scott said that he wasn't a good dancer, he lied. He was an excellent dancer, so good that Paulette hardly stumbled. Scott was a very gracious companion, and while he knew everyone there, he included Paulette in every conversation and was very attentive to her. The evening ended at 3:30 a.m., when he walked her to her door, held her gently in his arms, kissed her cheek, and said, "I had the most wonderful time tonight. Thank you for coming with me. You look absolutely beautiful. I could not have wished for a better companion."

Once inside her room, she kicked off her shoes, gently wiped the makeup off her eyes, slipped into her nightgown, and attacked the box of chocolates. She devoured five, they were so delicious. No one had ever bought her red roses. She touched the petals very delicately, then she crawled into bed, but her eyes just would not close. She was too wired. Of course, the chocolate didn't help.

CHAPTER TWENTY-NINE

Ward waited impatiently for his birth certificate and then his passport. He and Greg mulled over travel plans and decided that Ward should make the trip in stages. This way, the trip wouldn't be too stressful or tiring. Ward contacted the airline to make his reservations. While he was not sentimental about Christmas, or had any particular religious convictions, the thought that he would be home in time for Christmas calmed his soul.

After an evening meal with Greg, a lot of speculation about how Ward would fare on his trip to Victoria, and discussions about medication prescriptions and the doctor's letter Greg had composed, Greg promised that, if he could, he would come to Victoria for a visit in the summer.

At six the next morning, Greg collected Ward and his luggage from the guest house. Ward was nervous, but he wanted to go home more than anything. The trip went according to plan and Ward landed in Victoria tired and relieved. He didn't recognize the airport at all. It was much bigger than he remembered. He did recognize the pale blue, misty sky fringed by the jagged Cascade Mountain peaks that were shrouded with ominous clouds foretelling rain, and the smell of the ocean in the air. A brisk breeze made the Canadian flag flap loudly overhead when the next taxi pulled into position to collect him. He sat in the back seat like a sightseer visiting for the first time.

The cab ride to his parents' house took nearly an hour. Victoria had grown and the traffic was busier. The gate was closed, so the cabbie dropped him at the edge of the road. He stood for a few minutes on the sidewalk, surveying the yard and what he could see of the beach below lost in a swirl of warm memories.

He wondered how he should begin his conversation, and whether his parents expected him or if the confidentiality of his return remained intact.

The place looked empty. He couldn't see inside and the garage doors were closed. He rang the bell at the front door. He waited. He rang again. Finally, a thin frail man clad in a plaid dressing gown, with hair much like his own, squeaked open the door and peered at him over his reading glasses.

"Dad?" Ward's voice quavered.

"Oh my God! Ward!" his father cried, as he dropped his newspaper, pulled open the heavy oak door, and wound his arms around his son's neck. "You're home!" Phillip shouted.

Ward put his arm around his dad's back and helped him into the foyer, then hugged him tightly. Both had tears of joy at being together again and tears of sorrow for having been apart.

They were interrupted by Ward's mother, who shuffled in to see what the commotion was about. She stood motionless in the hallway trying to comprehend who had arrived.

Ward went over to her, gently lifted her hand in his, and looked into her dazed eyes. "Mom, it's me, Ward."

"Ward?" she said half questioningly, still trying to comprehend.

She reached out her arms to hug him, as the tears began to flow, and whispered, "Thank you for finally coming home where you belong. I missed you. We all missed you."

She relaxed her grip, her gaze turned vacant, and she shuffled away to her bedroom, which had been moved from the top floor to the former maid's room, as she could no longer manage the stairs.

His father looked after her in amazement. "Those are the first words she has said in months. And yes, thank you for coming home! Are you here for long? Will you stay here? Are the police looking for you? I know, so many questions, but so much time to make up!"

"No, the police are not looking for me. I'm here to stay. I don't have a plan yet, but I thought we could talk and you could help me make a plan. I do need a place to stay though, if that's okay?"

"Of course, stay as long as you want! Would you like some breakfast, some coffee?"

"I'm off caffeine, and I had a sandwich on the plane. I would have a cup of herbal tea though, if you have it."

Before Ward could follow his dad to the kitchen, the front door opened unexpectedly and Jackie stood in the doorway with Ward's suitcase in her hand. "I found this by the front—" Her eyes met Ward's and for a few seconds she was speechless. She didn't know if she should be happy or angry ... or if she should hug him or slap him.

"Jackie, I, I am so, so sorry!" Ward managed to stammer out the words.

She wasn't sure what to say. "I ... I usually drop by in the morning before I go to work ... to check on your parents. When did you get here?"

"Just now. Dad's making some tea. Do you have time for a cup? There's so much to say. I'm here to stay, and I want desperately to see the kids. How are they?"

She fumbled with the suitcase and then blurted out, "You know I divorced you. I didn't think you were ever coming back. I had no idea where you were. I had to make a life ..." She spoke quietly and quickly, as if trying to say everything she had to say in ten seconds or less. A mascara-stained tear trickled down her cheek, and she instinctively wiped it away.

Ward took the suitcase from her hand.

"It's okay. I understand. I was wrong. It was me, not you. You had no choice. Come and have some tea with us. I didn't want to tell anyone that I was coming home, in case the plan didn't work. I know it comes as a shock to everyone, but I am here to stay now, and I hope to be able to re-establish relationships and keep my life on track."

Over tea, Ward showed his father and Jackie the medical reports and told them how his life would be restricted as a result of his injuries. "I was not myself when I made the decision to run, and in hindsight, I wish I never had, but I can't change that now. I still don't know if I was responsible for the money disappearing from McDowell Hill, but I don't think I was. The police have told me that I will not be charged unless further evidence comes to light that would incriminate me, and I think it is unlikely that will ever happen given the time that has elapsed."

Jackie glanced at the wall clock and jumped up from the table. "I have to go. When would you like to see the kids? I think you should see them before word gets out that you're here."

"What about tonight? Can you bring them over here?"

"Yes, after supper."

"Perfect," Ward agreed.

All the way to work in the car, Jackie was in disbelief. She was astonished at how Ward had changed in appearance and demeanour. Her day at work was very unproductive, because she kept mulling over what she was going to say to the kids when she got home. 'Incredulous' was the only word she could find to describe her morning.

When Jackie picked up Todd from soccer practise, her other children were already in the van. "Tonight, I am taking you out for supper," she announced. "Then we have an important meeting. Where do you want to go to eat?"

The kids knew this must be important, as their mother rarely treated them to a restaurant meal during the week unless it was an absolute necessity. Usually it was because they had too many conflicting activities for her to coordinate, and ended up being a quick drive through a fast-food restaurant.

This night was different; Todd could sense it.

"What's going on, Mom?"

"I don't want to explain now," she told him. "I wouldn't know where to start. You'll just have to wait."

After a good meal and a strawberry sundae for dessert, she pulled the van into their grandparents' driveway and the motherly lecture began.

"Listen carefully. This is important. I don't want any whining, anger, rough-housing, or excuses," she warned them. "Please make sure you use your best manners, and be polite and respectful during your visit."

They piled out of the van and Carla rang the doorbell. Her grandfather answered the door, and they all swarmed inside with a kiss on the cheek for Grandpa. "I have someone here to see you," he said, as he led the way to the living room.

The children hung back in the doorway, not recognizing the stranger who was waiting for them.

"This is your father," Jackie said. "He's come home and he wants to see you."

The younger twins looked at him and then at their mother.

Carla, who always led the way, said, "Our real dad?"

"Yes," Ward answered for her. "I am your real dad, and I am so sorry I had to leave you."

"Why did you leave?" Todd asked belligerently, and received a barely noticeable squeeze of his arm from his mother, for using that tone of voice.

"That is a very long story, Todd, and maybe someday soon we can talk about that. Right now, I just wanted to see you all and tell you that I'm home. I have some health issues that will keep me from doing certain things for the rest of my life. I get headaches, dizziness, and I lose my coordination at times, but I want to get to know you again. I made a big mistake when I left, but I never stopped loving you."

Grandpa served some milk and cookies, and Erica and Carla jabbered non-stop. They told Ward about their ballet lessons and their school. Todd and Janet were more distant, and Ward knew it would take time and patience to re-establish any kind of relationship with the teenagers.

Ward took an upstairs bedroom and settled in.

His mother was very frail and more than forgetful. She hardly spoke. His father made breakfast and lunch. Before Ward's return, Jackie would very often bring dinner over for them, and while she was there, she would do some of the laundry. They coped as best they could. Every week, a cleaning lady came to scour the bathroom and kitchen. They lived on the main floor of the house and rarely ventured up or down the stairs. Their lives had shrunk considerably. They only went out to doctors' appointments and had very few visitors, if any. Very occasionally, old friends would phone, but most of those friends were in the same condition as they were.

Ward tried to take over some of the cooking and cleaning. The situation saddened Ward, but he resigned himself to it. They were very elderly.

The house had been neglected over the last few years. There was dust on dust. Some of the tiles in the kitchen and main bathroom were cracked and discoloured, something his parents never would have allowed in the past. The yard was overgrown, and only by the kindness of the neighbours, who had children that needed chores, were leaves raked and the driveway swept from time to time.

Ward applied for a disability pension and contacted the Legal Services Bureau to find out if he was eligible for any other benefits or assistance. He stuck faithfully to his regimen of diet, exercise and medication. Every Sunday he invited his children over for supper, and he was working on his cooking skills.

One day, a week before Easter, he got a call. "Hi this is Todd. I have a hockey tournament this weekend. Do you want to come to one of my games?"

"I'd love to; just tell me when and where," Ward replied.

"Esquimalt Arena. Six tonight."

"I'll be there. What position do you play and what's your jersey number."

"Centre. Number eleven. Bye."

Ward hung up the phone and almost cried. This was the first time since his return that Todd had reached out to him. He hoped this was real progress and not just Todd's mother putting him up to making the call and the invitation, but when he thought on it, really, he didn't care. He would take anything.

He felt uncomfortable being the only parent not known in the group, but thoughtfully, Jackie eased his way. He met her new husband too.

There was still so much to say and do to re-establish relationships. He had to remind himself this was a work in progress—maybe his life's work.

CHAPTER THIRTY

Paulette was very tired after four days of travelling to Glasgow, attending the party, and trying to squeeze too many activities into too short a time. Even after a good night's sleep in her own bed, with a happy little Irma curled at her feet, every day thereafter until the New Year was a whirl of work. Sarah felt pressured too, and on Christmas Eve at 5:30, when the doors of the bakery and tea room were finally locked, they all relaxed with a glass of sherry and a plate of shortbread.

On Christmas Day, Bruce cooked a big turkey dinner for his family and Paulette. He invited the bakers too. Keith and Melody were at Melody's parents. Anne had returned to Africa. Liam came home for a few days, and brought some single friends with him who didn't have a place to go for Christmas. They were busy making the rounds, appeared for supper, devoured almost everything Bruce cooked, and after supper, the cards came out and anyone interested in being fleeced by the boys played a few rounds of poker.

* * *

On Boxing Day, Scott phoned to see if he could drop by.

Paulette was curled on the couch reading the book club's assignment, snuggled in her favourite lamb's wool blanket. Irma was at her feet curled in a ball, snoring and occasionally twitching.

When Paulette saw Scott's car coming down the driveway, she got up and put on the kettle. While she managed to decorate the business premises quite elaborately, her home didn't get the same attention. Her only decoration was a plastic poinsettia in the middle of the kitchen table. The only gift left under it was Scott's.

Paulette opened the door for him and Irma did her welcome dance.

Over a cup of hot tea and some pastries from the bakery, they talked about what a wonderful time they'd had at the Christmas party, the next book club book, and their respective plans for the coming year.

Paulette bribed Scott to stay for supper with the promise of a pot of stew and a bottle of Guinness.

After supper, when the dishes were cleared away, Scott presented Paulette with the gift he had bought for her. She opened it hastily. After the wrapping was torn off, she could tell from the box that it was jewellery, and indeed, it was a beautiful gold bracelet, which he'd had engraved: 'Christmas 1999. All my love, Scott.'

Paulette became very quiet and looked like she was almost going to cry. "It's very beautiful Scott."

He touched her cheek tenderly. "You know I love you, don't you?"

"Don't say that. Please. My relationships with men end badly. They all leave me. I don't want you to go too," she exclaimed, through quivering lips.

"It doesn't have to be like that," Scott comforted her.

"Just wait and see," she said bitterly.

Scott didn't know what to think, and he picked at the corner of the wrapping on his gift.

"Open it, please. I hope you like it," Paulette encouraged him a little more lightly.

In Paulette's usual fashion, she had boxed the gift and wrapped it twice. Scott fumbled with the box, and the meter of tape Paulette used to keep it secure. Then he tore through the paper and the box as well, to discover a framed photograph of Lossiemouth taken from exactly the same spot on the cliff as where the old photo, which he had discovered in the antique shop, was taken. The dimensions and framing were identical so that they would match.

"Oh Paulette, this is a magnificent photo! It matches the old one exactly. You said at the time we should take a new one to compare the two. What a brilliant idea! Thank you so much!"

He stood up and held her tenderly in his arms. Feelings were different now. This was no longer the hug of two friends. He wanted to feel close to her. He raised her face to his and kissed her delicately. He could have sworn he felt a tear on his cheek.

"Scott, it's late ... and I have to open up tomorrow morning. Thank you for the beautiful gift. I will treasure it forever," Paulette said sincerely.

He realized it was time for him to head home and added, "One more thing before I go, my children are coming for New Year's Day. Well, I mean they aren't children anymore. They are adults themselves now. You know what I mean," he fumbled. "In any event, would you like to meet them? I know they'd love to meet you."

He wasn't sure she would accept the invitation, since his revelation seemed to rest uneasily with her, but she replied, "Yes. I'd love to meet them."

Early the next morning, the sound of hurricane-force winds woke Paulette before dawn. A wicked storm lashed the coast. Sleet pelted down so heavily that it was nearly impossible to see. Paulette thought the roof was going to blow off! From her bedroom window, she could faintly see lights in the bakery, so she knew the bakers were busy getting ready for the morning opening. Since she was awake, she decided that she may as well get up and pitch in.

She was looking forward to a lull in the business of the bakery and tea room, so she could recoup her energy after such a frantic December.

* * *

The second week in January, she had an appointment with her accountant, and in the normal course of conversation, her accountant asked, "Just out of curiosity, do you have any plans for retirement?" He carefully avoided asking her about her age.

Amused by his chivalrous caution, she smiled, knowing that her white hair often led people to believe that she was older than she was.

"I haven't really thought about it, but maybe I should," Paulette acknowledged, wondering how long she wanted to keep working as hard as she was when she certainly no longer needed the money.

Over the next few weeks, instead of reading her club book, Paulette tried to make a plan to please her accountant.

Thoughts of Scott kept creeping into her head, but she shunned them, only to have them surface later as 'what ifs'.

Sooner or later, she knew she would sell the bakery and tea room.

She decided she wanted to do something special for Bruce and Sarah. They were such wonderful friends—family really. She wouldn't have had the success she did without their incredibly hard work. The thought struck her that she should give them the house. Who else would she give it to?

In the evening, before her favourite TV show came on, she phoned Scott.

"Hi, Scott, you know I've been mulling over this retirement planning, and the thought occurred to me that I should give Bruce and Sarah the house that they rent from me. What would I have to do to make that happen?"

"I think you would need a surveyor. I'll come over in the morning. I'll need to see your deed with a description of the property and we can talk about your plan then."

The next morning, Scott drew out a rough sketch of the property and divided it into sections for the bakery and tea house, Bruce and Sarah's house, the rental units, and lastly the cottage. Of course, Scott knew a firm of surveyors and engineers, and after a quick phone call, they set off for an appointment with them.

Paulette engaged the firm to do a full survey of the property and draft up a subdivision plan. After Paulette had approved the plan, she took it to Bill Kinnie, who dealt with the municipal authorities and registered the subdivision plan to create the lots.

Paulette asked Bill to give her the deed to the portion that was to be transferred to Bruce and Sarah when the transfer was finalized, so that she could deliver it to them.

The whole process took several months, and was coordinated with her accountant, who recommended that Paulette also form a company to own the bakery and tea room business, both its land and chattels, in case she ever wanted to sell.

* * *

Paulette spent hours in the stationery store, searching for the perfect card to send to Bruce and Sarah, along with the title to the property she was gifting to them. Once she had made her selection, she sent the deed and card to them by registered mail.

A few days later, the mailman knocked at the McAllisters' door and announced that they had a registered letter. Bruce accepted the envelope, saw it was from Paulette, and signed for it. In the kitchen, while Sarah was preparing their lunch, he slit the envelop open and extracted the deed; at first he wondered why Paulette had sent a registered letter when she could just walk up the driveway and give it to them.

He read the enclosed document twice. "Holy Christ, Sarah! Look at this!" He held it up for her to see.

Sarah stopped what she was doing and peered inquisitively over his shoulder.

"What is it? What does it mean?" She could see their names and address on the deed, but could not relate it to any action she or Bruce had taken.

"Look Sarah. Paulette gave us the house. Look. Here's her card. She sent a copy of the plan of the property that's included around the house too!"

"No. It can't be," Sarah murmured. "There must be some mistake."

"I don't think so." Bruce shook his head.

"Why don't you call her and invite her up for tea. Don't say anything about what we got in the mail today. Just tell her the kettle's on."

A few minutes later, they could see Paulette and Irma coming up the driveway.

Paulette's cup of tea and scone were waiting on the table when she came in. She had only taken her first few sips of tea, when Bruce could no longer contain himself. "Paulette, we received something in the mail today that completely baffles us. It looks like a property deed in our names, for this house, from you."

"Exactly," Paulette replied.

"We don't understand. You can't just give things away like that, and you know we can't pay you for the house."

PUZZLE OF PIECES

"I don't expect you to pay anything. The house is a gift to you both, from me. No payment required. Oh, and by the way, don't send me any more rent cheques. The tenancy is over. I don't want to get into any emotional explanations. I have had so many wonderful, happy times with you here in this very house; you deserve this place. You've lived here for a long time and paid for it over and over in rent. What else am I going to do with it? What's the point of waiting until I'm dead to give it to you?"

"We can't express our gratitude at your generosity. It's unbelievable. God sent us an angel when he delivered you into our lives."

"Don't get all mushy. It's just part of my retirement plan. You know eventually we will have to sell the bakery and tea room or close it. I think it has too much value just to close. Sarah, have you thought anything about it? You have worked so hard over the years, but we can't go on forever."

"Maybe we should offer it for sale and see who makes an offer. Do you know how much the business would be worth?"

"No, not really, but I could ask my accountant to put a value on it. I thought maybe one of the franchisees might be interested, now that another location has opened in Aberdeen. They really don't know that much about the business that we do here, all the baking and distribution, but at least they know the products and the operation of a retail bakery and tea room. Maybe some of the staff would be interested in taking it over. We don't really need to ask for cash up front. I think enough income is generated that a purchaser could pay us instalments for our retirement and still make a living."

"Maybe we should have a meeting and let everyone know," Sarah proposed.

"Let me think about it a little more, and in the meantime, I'll ask the accountant for a valuation," Paulette said.

Late in the afternoon, after she finished cleaning up the herb garden, she phoned Scott. "Hi, I haven't heard from you for a couple of days. Are things okay?"

"Yes everything's okay. I do have a bit of a cold though, and I didn't want to spread it around. How are you?"

Paulette described her plan for working toward retirement.

"What will you do when you retire?" he asked, and then he realized she might think that was a baited question, so he added adroitly, "I have never seen you still for more than a moment unless you're reading."

"Irma and I will probably grow old together, wrapped in our lamb's wool blanket, cuddled on the cottage porch, watching the ever-changing North Sea and reading more books."

"I'll probably be dead by then," he replied sarcastically, and immediately regretted it.

"Oh you're in a fine mood today, aren't you?" she teased him.

She knew in that moment, if she had to face the stark-white honest truth, that he meant everything to her, although she had never said anything to him and maybe never would. Could she risk telling him what she'd done and hope he'd accept it? She didn't think that was possible. He was far too honest to ever be able to do that.

On the off chance that he would accept what she had done, how long would their relationship last before she would lose respect for him for settling for her? She knew what she had done was wrong, and for him to overlook it would be wrong too. Would it be better to reject him outright or just hold him off until he went away on his own? It was like she drew him to her with one hand and then pushed him away with the other. How long could that go on before he would disappear? Maybe she should just walk away. Maybe that would be best. Maybe she should go back to Victoria and face her punishment. So many maybes.

She was boxed.

Without thinking, she whispered into the phone, "Scott, don't give up on me."

"Do you want to come over?" he asked quietly.

"When you're feeling better. I'll talk to you later," Paulette whispered, and hung up.

Scott stood by the window, staring blindly into his garden.

He wished more than anything that he could find a way to connect with her the way he wanted to—the way he hoped she wanted. What stood in her way? She said all her relationships with men ended badly. What exactly did she mean? Why would a relationship with him end badly when he worshipped her?

He thought she was the most generous person he ever knew. She always tried to help everybody. If anyone was in need, she was first in line to help. She gave money to the families of sick children and victims of house fires. She was a patron of any worthy cause. He admired her business acumen. He acknowledged that she rarely spoke about her past, and when she did, she always sounded sad. Was there something else? He could only imagine.

* * *

Paulette awoke in the dark early hours of the morning. She gathered up her lamb's wool blanket and warm pillow, scooped Irma under her arm, and headed for the porch. The air was surprisingly warm. Light from the sliver of a crescent moon twinkled off small patches of rippled North Sea waters.

Did she have remorse or regret for what she had done? It was hard to have remorse when her life had turned out to be so much more than she thought it would be.

Regret? Yes, she had to admit that she had regret, but she had never anticipated this. She thought she was beyond finding anyone who would love her or that she would love in return.

Maybe this was her punishment. Maybe this was God's way of getting even or karma catching up with her. Maybe she would never click the last piece of the puzzle of her life into place. Maybe she was doomed. An unhappy memory washed over her.

Just before her mother's death, and when she thought she had no prospect of ever having a husband and all that meant to her, a man at St. Andrews Church, quite a few years older than she, told her, "I don't really know how to say this, but you know my wife died. I've been very lonely. I've watched you so often here at church; I've seen how kind and friendly you are. If you would like, maybe we could get to know each other. I really miss being married. I'd be a good husband. I have a job. I'm neat and tidy."

She remembered perfectly what she said to him: "Ken that is very kind of you, but the timing is awful. You know my mother is very ill. She's very near death and probably won't last more than a month or two. I can't leave her now. After she passes away, and I've had a little time to adjust, I'd like to get to know you too."

"I understand. I admire your commitment to her; that's what makes you such a special person. We can talk again soon. Let me know. Take care of yourself."

Over the next two months, she missed most of the church services and the women's group meetings. Her life during that time was working and caring for her mother. Some ladies from the women's group would stay with her mother when she was at work, but at the end, she took some time off work to be with her.

After her mother's funeral, and a couple of weeks to begin to adjust, she dressed in her best outfit and attended the first morning service at St. Andrews. There, seated a couple of rows in front of her, was Ken in the company of another woman.

She snuck out the side door in a blur of tears.

* * *

On Sunday morning Scott phoned. "Would you like to go out for lunch and a drive this afternoon? It looks like it is going to be a beautiful day."

She was torn. Should she say no right then and there and end it? Maybe, but she just couldn't and before she could stop herself, she heard herself say, "That sounds like a wonderful idea."

"I'll pick you up at 12:30."

They drove up the coast to a seafood café Scott knew about, overlooking the water. The North Sea was calm, blue, and the tide on the swell.

"It seems like this is the first time we've been out and free after having such a horrible winter. The fresh air and sunshine feel good," Paulette remarked.

"Yes they do. Have you thought any more about your retirement plan?"

"I've asked my accountant for a valuation for the bakery and tea room. I'll definitely go with his advice, as I know nothing about how these things are handled in Scotland. Eventually I will sell it, but I don't think I can part with the cottage."

"Do you have any other plans for the summer?" he asked, trying to make more conversation.

"Yes, I was thinking about going to visit my friend Melanie in Maidstone, you know, Fiona's sister. I haven't seen her for a while. I do have some business to take care of, and it would be a good opportunity to do both. I'll probably be gone about a week. I want to go soon. Before July. You know how busy we get in July and August. What about you?" Paulette watched him carefully to gauge his reply.

"I haven't been on a vacation since my late wife died. I was tossing around that idea, but I'm not really sure where to go."

* * *

A couple of days later, Scott put Paulette on the train for London. She was excited, but she thought he seemed a little sad.

When she got to Maidstone, she silently reminisced about her first visit there. She must have been in shock or denial or some other altered dimension. Her memories of that time seemed more like a dream than a reality, although the flowers and gardens were just as beautiful as she remembered them.

Her friend Melanie had aged. She had taken Robert's death hard, as they had been constant companions and best friends. She still ran the sweater shop, but she wasn't as active or adventurous as she used to be. Once the shop was closed for the evening, they ventured only a couple of blocks down the street for a fish and chip supper.

The next morning, Paulette caught the train through the Chunnel, changed trains in Paris, and took a train direct to Lucerne. She had travelled there before and felt comfortable enough travelling on her own. Once in her hotel room, she telephoned the bank and made an appointment for the next morning, precisely at 9:00 a.m. The Swiss banking system was so efficient that by 10:00 a.m. her business was concluded. She caught a cab back to her hotel room.

As she was checking out, Paulette asked the hotel clerk, "Can you recommend a hotel in Paris?"

"Of course, would you like me to telephone to see if I can make a reservation for you?"

"Yes, I'd appreciate that. I've always wanted to spend some time in Paris and do some sightseeing."

"A moment please," the clerk said, as she made the call.

After a few moments, she had an answer. "Yes, Miss McNeil, they do have a room for you for tonight, and I have reserved it under your name. Is there anything else?" the clerk asked, as she handed Paulette a pamphlet with a map for the hotel.

"No. Thank you. Oh, wait, yes. Do you have a phone where I could make a long distance call?"

The clerk pointed to a pay phone on the wall across the foyer.

"Thank you." Paulette searched her purse for the correct change and dialled the operator to place the call.

"Scott, this is Paulette."

"Hello, I didn't expect to hear from you so soon. Are you home already?"

"No. Not yet. But, I was wondering," she hesitated, took a deep breath, and then continued. "You know how you once offered to show me Paris? Could you meet me there? You said you wanted a vacation but didn't know where to go. I'll understand if you can't or if you say no ..." she added to let him off the hook, but she truly hoped he would come.

"Well ... well I could. I'm sure I could. Are you there now?" he spluttered. Recovering his composure, he asked, "Where should we meet?"

"I'll be there this evening. I've made a reservation under my name at Hotel de Notre Dame. I'll wait for you there. Do you think you will make it tonight? Or tomorrow some time? Oh, I'll give you the address and phone number," Paulette added, pulling the brochure for the hotel from her purse and trying to subdue her excitement.

"I'll be there as soon as I can."

Scott hung up the phone and immediately called the airline. He booked the next flight from Glasgow to Paris.

He arrived just as Paulette was sitting down to breakfast. She saw him and waved excitedly for him to join her. She picked up a bright red and blue pamphlet from the table and unfolded it to show him.

"Look what I found! A bus tour of all the sights of Paris," she said enthusiastically when he arrived at the table. "Can we do this first?"

She looked different. She was different. Her eyes sparkled even in the broad light of day. There was something else that Scott could not precisely identify. He brushed his lips against her cheek. "Whatever you want."

After a light flaky croissant, a deliciously juicy orange, and a couple of cups of strong dark coffee, they crossed the bridge over the Seine to the magnificent Notre Dame Cathedral. They lit a candle in the chapel, put a donation in the box, and inspected and photographed every corner of the Cathedral. When they were satisfied that they had seen all there was to see, without any tension or cares in the world and lost in the exquisite beauty of Paris, they caught Le Bus Rouge for the next stop.

EPILOGUE

Back in Canada, time ticked inexorably onward. Clark Walton finally became eligible to retire from the Legal Services Bureau. He had been slowly packing up some of the memoirs he had collected over his long career, when he came across his personal file from the most perplexing case he had ever worked on: the disappearance of funds from the law firm of McDowell Hill. He began to thumb through his notes, even though he didn't need to refresh his memory about the events. They were carved in his mind forever.

Clark hoped that since he hadn't solved the puzzle, perhaps someone else would before he died. He was actually torn between retiring and giving up completely, or staying, and trying to find the answer, even if it took his last dying breath.

Clark's wife had told him to let it go—that she didn't want him dragging the beast into his retirement. He'd had a good career. He did good work. It was time to let go.

Over the years, he knew and kept in touch with all the lawyers involved with McDowell Hill at the time. Some of the younger lawyers still practised in British Columbia. Andrew McDowell, now nearly 90 years old, had retired to Hawaii and would, on special occasions, return to Victoria. Frank Hill, in his mid-80s, was retired now too. His wife had passed away a few months before, but Frank lived in the same house and pursued the same interests he'd always had.

For several years, Clark, through his connection with Eric McDonald, watched Herb Myers and Joe Piquette, unobtrusively. Herb died about three years ago, and Herb's wife moved to Calgary to live with her oldest child. Joe Piquette and his wife retired to Salt Spring Island, where they lived quietly.

There was still the possibility that Ward had taken the money. Ward wrote the second cheque on Sunday and was mugged on Monday—Easter Monday at that, a banking holiday. Was that Ward's real plan—to issue two cheques to confuse the matter? Maybe that is why he went to Panama. Maybe he thought he could hide the money there. But the time frame just never did fit; and then there was the complication of Ward's mugging. Surely he would not have been foolish enough to arrange his own mugging, especially the way it turned out for him.

There was also the problem of the first cheque. The bank statement said that it was paid to S & H. No one knew who or what that was, and no one could produce the cancelled cheque.

The only person who lived high-on-the-hog was Deborah Ruxton; but she had lived that way before the money disappeared, and so Clark had, with some reservation, dismissed her as a suspect.

No one ever wanted to admit that Elisabeth Nielsen could have taken the money. Despite the fact that a Canada-wide bulletin had been issued for all public and government offices, which stayed in effect for nearly ten years, she never did appear alive or dead.

There was speculation that Elisabeth's punk cousin, who drove the Camaro, might have coerced her into stealing the money, taken it from her, and then killed her. He died in a car accident, in that very Camaro, racing on the Pat Bay Highway a few years after Elisabeth disappeared. If he had the money, it was never evident. He was constantly in and out of trouble. Anyone would think that, if he had taken the money, he would have disappeared with it to some place more promising for him than Victoria.

An unthinkable thought had passed through Clark's mind at one point, years after the investigation had formally ended, that perhaps Andrew and Frank had misdirected the money somewhere in some sort of twisted attempt to get Ward to smarten up, and then the plan had gone horribly awry. But that thought was just too bizarre and Clark always put it at the bottom of his list.

One notch above that idea was that, despite the bank launching its own very thorough investigation, the money had been taken by a bank employee, or employees, who had managed to evade scrutiny during the investigation. He thought this unlikely, but nevertheless, possible.

Ranking ahead of that idea was that the bank had just fouled up the posting of the cheques, wouldn't admit to the error, and refused to account for the money.

One more idea that had just recently occurred to Clark was that, if the money were placed in a Canadian bank account and never touched by the owner, after several years of account inactivity, the balance would be turned over to the Bank of Canada. He would have to alert his predecessor to check the Bank of Canada for large unclaimed balances, with the remote possibility that the money languished in just such an account. If not in Canada, perhaps the money might be traceable in some other country with similar laws.

Of course, there was always the conspiracy theory, but no one could put that together in any sort of cohesive or believable scenario.

Some unscrupulous person could have gotten control of the money and used it as a payoff, or for some illegal purpose, or just hidden it off shore.

The possibilities were still almost endless.

None of the individuals involved, while some of them lived very good lives, ever developed the behaviour or spending patterns of multi-millionaires.

* * *

Eric McDonald was the first to give up trying to find the answer. He retired shortly after Ward returned to Victoria and now lived in Phoenix in the winters and Kelowna in the summers. When he could, he taught bridge on cruise ships around the world.

* * *

On the first day of his last week with the Bureau, an unusually hot day in early July, Clark's mail folder arrived in his 'IN' tray with half a dozen pieces of mail. He slowly went through the mail, piece by piece, wondering who would be opening these letters once he was gone and would they ever solve the McDowell Hill puzzle. When he slit open the last plain unmarked envelope inside was a cashier's cheque payable to the Legal Services Bureau of British Columbia for $14,400,750 with a simple notation: 'McDowell Hill'.

Clark's hands shook as he cautiously placed the cheque in the centre of his desk and stared at it in disbelief.

Was it a fake? Could it possibly be real?

At first he thought it was a practical joke being played on him by his colleagues who knew his obsession with the case. He half expected to see them pop up from behind the credenza, laughing and jeering.

But what if it's real? He snatched the empty envelope out of the garbage, in case it had fingerprints on it that could be traced.

He punched the phone extension for the Chief Executive Officer. "Can you come to my office," he asked nonchalantly. "I have something I want to show you."

The Chief Executive Officer joined Clark in staring doubtfully and suspiciously at the cheque.

Finally, the Chief Executive Officer phoned the manager of the bank across the street, where he had his own personal accounts, and asked him to come over.

The manager verified the cheque.

The money had been returned!

This was a huge piece of the puzzle, but Clark still couldn't see the whole picture. He wanted a name and a face.

"Clark, realistically, how much more money and manpower do you think the Legal Services Bureau will spend trying to solve a twenty-year-old crime, especially when they find out that the money has been recovered?" the Chief Executive Officer asked him.

"If it's any consolation," he continued, "think of all the changes that have been made to the rules for lawyers, some of those changes initiated by *you*, because of this case, not to mention the banking procedures that have been developed over the last few years. No one would ever be able to get away with something like this now—not in the age of computers, and not with all the safeguards, checks, and balances in place today."

Clark continued to stare at the cheque. He wasn't sure what to do next.

Printed in Canada